Nicole
TROPE

Hush, Little Bird

ALLEN&UNWIN
SYDNEY · MELBOURNE · AUCKLAND · LONDON

Grateful acknowledgement is given for permission to reproduce extracts from 'The Adventures of Isabel' by Ogden Nash.
Copyright © 1936 by Ogden Nash, renewed.
Reprinted by permission of Curtis Brown, Ltd.
All rights reserved.

First published in 2015

Allen & Unwin
83 Alexander Street
Crows Nest NSW 2065
Australia
Phone: (61 2) 8425 0100
Email: info@allenandunwin.com
Web: www.allenandunwin.com

Cataloguing-in-Publication details are available
from the National Library of Australia
www.trove.nla.gov.au

ISBN 978 1 76011 372 8

Internal design by Lisa White
Set in 13.5/18 pt Minion LT by Midland Typesetters, Australia
Printed and bound in Australia by Griffin Press

10 9 8 7 6 5 4 3 2 1

MIX
Paper from
responsible sources
FSC® C009448
www.fsc.org

The paper in this book is FSC® certified. FSC® promotes environmentally responsible, socially beneficial and economically viable management of the world's forests.

For all the women in my life past and present:

the grandmothers,
the mothers,
the daughters,
the sisters,
the aunts,
the nieces,
the cousins,
and the friends

Chapter One

She's coming today. She's coming here. Right here to where I am.

I thought I would have to wait until I was free to see her. I thought I would have to wait two years to see her. Two whole, long years. I haven't seen her for a lot longer than that. I haven't seen her since I was eight years old and now I am thirty-three years old. That's twenty-five years.

When I was eight, all I wanted was to get away from her, from him. From them. I wanted to go far away and forget them, but even after I moved away they stayed in my head. They stayed in a corner of my brain, not doing anything, just there, but one day something happened, something horrible and awful and bad and then they were almost all I could think about. And I knew I had to see them again.

I had a plan. I was going to catch a bus to her house. First I was going to catch a bus to *their* house, but now there is only her left. So it's only her house.

I know about catching buses and trains. I know how to use my phone to 'get directions'. I can go anywhere I want to, but I can't go right now because right now I have to stay here. I know that. I can learn and I can remember things if I'm told over and over again. I just need to hear things more than once. Sometimes I need to hear something lots and lots of times. The door to my brain is always open. Stuff comes in but before I know it, it goes out again. I can't seem to close the door fast enough.

I know things now. More things than people think I know. I'm not that stupid. I can read and write and add and subtract. I know who I am and what I am. I know I am not clever. All through school none of my teachers ever said, 'She needs to work harder.' All of them said, 'She's doing her best. She's really trying.'

Sometimes on her report card Lila's teacher wrote, *Lila is not working to her full potential*. Potential means what you can do. Lila is clever, very clever, but Mum said she is also lazy. They never wrote that about me. I always worked to my full potential even though that was not very much potential at all.

I'm smart enough to know I'm a little bit stupid, or 'slow' as Mum likes to say. I'm smart enough to know I'm slow. That's how smart I am. I used to get angry about being slow, about not understanding things and about having to learn them over and over again, but now I just accept it. 'Not everyone can be the top of the class,' Mum said to me every time I brought home my report card. But I didn't want to be the top of the class. I just didn't want to be right at the bottom. But right at the bottom is where I stayed. I never had very much potential at all.

Mum said she was fine with me being at the bottom of the class, but she wasn't. Not really. Just because she told me she was fine doesn't mean that was the truth. I knew how she really felt. When I was little I heard her. I heard her tell the truth all the time.

'How am I supposed to deal with something like this? I don't have a husband to help me. How can I cope? I'll have to watch over her for the rest of my life. When do *I* get taken care of, Violet? When?'

I wasn't supposed to be listening. I was supposed to be playing next door, but I was hiding and I was listening to Mum talk to Aunty Vi who lived in London. I used to be good at hiding. I could stay quiet for a long time. When I was quiet I would hear lots of things I wasn't supposed to hear. That's how I knew that Mum wasn't fine with me being at the bottom of the class.

'I know, Violet, I'm not saying I've given up on her, but she's always going to be a little different, isn't she? I mean, she's nearly eight now and the other children are already starting to notice it . . . I know that there's nothing you can do. You live in another country. I'm not asking you to do anything. I just need someone to talk to. You have no idea how difficult it is to be alone in this world, no idea at all.'

I was in the cupboard under the stairs where the winter coats were stored. I was touching the fur coat that belonged to Mum. She never wore it because she didn't like it, so it lived under the stairs like a lonely pet. It was soft and warm.

'I don't know what will happen to her. I'm just not coping right now. I've had to sell the house. Did I tell you? We're moving to a dreadful little shitbox out in some horrible suburb. It was all I could afford Violet . . . I'm not asking you for anything, I'm just trying to talk to you. I am so . . . so humiliated by all this. What have I done to deserve such a life? What?'

Mum's voice was all wobbly. I knew she was crying. She was crying about the house, because she had to sell it so the bloody bank wouldn't come and get it. Back then I thought the bloody bank was a giant who could lift up our whole house with one hand and take it away. At night I had dreams about being crushed in the bloody bank's giant fingers. I had hidden my most special toys behind my chest of drawers. When the bloody bank took the house I was going to grab them and jump out of the front door. Under the stairs I patted Mum's lonely pet fur coat and thought about hiding it as well. Now I know that a bank is just a building where you keep your money.

I was afraid the bloody bank would take everything away, but I wasn't sad to be moving. I wanted to leave the big house more than anything in the world. I hated it. We were moving far, far away. Our shitbox was very small. I would still have my own room, but the carpet was grey with sticky patches on it, not like my carpet in my bedroom in the big house. That carpet was peach-coloured and soft. I liked to put my cheek on it and feel it tickle me. I knew that the sticky grey carpet wouldn't feel nice on my cheek, but I still liked the shitbox better than the big house.

'Stop talking to me about new beginnings, Violet,' said Mum. 'Your husband hasn't left you for someone else. Your husband is probably sitting in his armchair right now reading the newspaper. This is not a new beginning for me. It's the end of my life as I've known it. He could have had the decency to allow me to live here for another few years, but the bitch he married wants her own house.' Mum was finished crying and she was shouting at Aunty Vi. She shouted at Aunty Vi a lot after Dad left to live with the bitch. Lila and I never got to meet the bitch. Mum wouldn't let us. 'Your father doesn't give two hoots about either of you,' said Mum.

I have not seen my dad for almost my whole life. He had blue eyes and he would shave the hair off his face and cut himself and say 'bugger'.

When I hid under the stairs I was scared of Mum shouting at Aunty Vi and crying. Some days Mum shouted at Aunty Vi and then when she was finished shouting at her she shouted at me. I didn't like shouting days.

That was so many years ago. Some things stay in my brain even when I don't want them to. Sad things and bad things won't go out even when I leave the door open.

They stayed in my brain. They stayed and stayed. I think about him and I think about her. They are both stuck in my brain, but now he is gone and she is coming here.

She is coming here today.

I thought I'd have more time to plan before I saw her. I didn't expect them to bring her here to where I am. I needed time to plan what I wanted to say and what I wanted to do, but now that I know she's coming I don't know what's going to happen.

No, that's not true. I know what's going to happen; I just don't know *how* it's going to happen.

I don't know who first found out she was coming here, but now everyone knows and everyone is jumpy and excited. The news about her coming was whispered from person to person and ear to ear until everyone knew. No one whispered to me, but Jess told me. She tells me everything I need to know. 'A real celebrity here, imagine that,' said Jess, but she didn't smile so I don't think she was happy.

For weeks and weeks all the women in my unit have watched her on television and tried to decide: did she do it?

I live in unit seven with Maya and Mina and Jess. They shout and argue and laugh when they talk about the 'did she or didn't she'. They shout and laugh and talk about lots of things. They all know about so many things. They know about celebrities and sport and history and the weather. They know about cooking and sewing and people you can't trust. Jess says, 'I think . . .', and Mina says, 'Well, in my opinion . . .', and Maya says, 'I know.'

I don't talk with them. I am quiet. I am good at listening.

I don't care if she did or she didn't. I'm just glad that he is dead and buried under the ground with the worms. I hope they are crawling all over his skin. I have to rub my arms when I think about the worms crawling on his skin. I have to make sure there are no worms on me.

When I think about her coming here I have to swallow and swallow so I don't throw up.

Last night I lay in bed and I wondered if she would know me or not. I chewed my nails as I lay in the dark and thought and thought. I made my fingers bleed. In the dark I could feel the sting on my skin that means I have torn off a big piece of nail, and now when Jess sees it she'll say, 'Oh, Birdy, you were doing so well.' I hate disappointing Jess. She was going to give me a proper manicure at the end of the week. I had already chosen the colour. It's a pretty pink colour and it's called 'No Baggage Please'. That's a funny name for nail polish but I like it anyway.

I got some blood on the sheets because even when it hurts I can't stop myself from tearing off pieces of nail, and I know when Allison comes around to do her inspection she'll shake her head and sigh but she won't let me change the sheets. I'll have to sleep in them until laundry day.

This morning when I woke up I looked in the small mirror over the basin in the bathroom and I knew that it was silly to worry about her knowing me. The me she knew is not the same me now. I dye my hair black and I'm an adult. I take up a lot more space as well. A *lot* more space.

'You don't need all that starch,' Jess says to me when we make dinner, but I like the potatoes and rice. I like being bigger. Besides, rice and potatoes are cheap. They fill you up nicely. We have to buy all our own food and there is never enough money. I am good at counting out my money. I keep it safe until canteen day.

On canteen day we get to spend our money on things that we want, not just things that we need. You need bread but you don't need chocolate. Maggie runs the canteen and when she sees me she smiles and says, 'and what can I get for you today, young Birdy?' I like Maggie. Once she gave me a free bar of chocolate. It was all squashed but it still tasted the same. Jess doesn't like to see me eating chocolate. She shakes her head and says, 'If you would just cut back a bit you could lose some weight.'

'But I don't want to lose weight,' I always tell her. 'I like being big and strong.' 'There's no one to be afraid of in here, Birdy,' says Jess. 'You don't have to be big and strong.'

I would like to tell Jess that she has no idea what I have to be afraid of, but she knows some things about me and she also knows about being afraid. Everyone here knows about being afraid. We are all locked up in here because of the things we've done when we've been afraid.

Anyway, I'm not scared of anything here. I'm just making sure that I can be seen. When I was small I couldn't be seen. Even after I had grown up and I was as tall as Mum, some people couldn't see me. Mum never really saw me. I wanted to be seen but I also wanted to be light and free to fly away. You can see things that are light and free if you look carefully, but as quickly as you see them, they're gone. Now I am big and I cannot fly away, but at least I can be seen.

'Move out of the way, you big lump,' said Jess when she wanted to get to the kettle, and then she said, 'Sorry, Birdy.' I don't mind being called a big lump. You know a big lump is there. You can't pretend that it isn't. When I was light and small there were a lot of things to be afraid of. Now I'm a big lump and sometimes people are afraid of me.

I wonder what she was afraid of. I wonder if she was afraid of him. I wonder if she is afraid of coming here.

It doesn't matter anyway. I don't care about her thoughts and feelings. I don't care about what she did or didn't do.

Mostly, mostly, I care about what I'm going to do to her.

Chapter Two

This place is really not as dreadful as I feared it would be. It is almost a relief to be here now, to have the waiting over and done with. There were some surreal moments in the last few weeks where I became convinced that I would be locked forever in the limbo of waiting to know my fate. Some nights, as I waited for my sentencing hearing to finally begin, I found myself drawn to those lamentable television prison dramas. I watched them with growing horror and I decided that there was a fair chance I wouldn't make it through the first week of my incarceration without being stabbed in the shower by some woman sporting a giant tattoo of a skull and crossbones. The thought of having to get into a communal shower was beyond humiliating, although I had no idea if the showers were communal or not.

One night I stood in front of my full-length bedroom mirror for nearly an hour, looking at myself from every angle, identifying flaws. I knew as I was doing it how ridiculous it was to worry about such a thing, but I still kept looking. I imagined the eyes of hundreds of strange women on my body, and I wanted to curl into a ball and stay under the bedcovers forever.

'It's not going to be like that at all, Mother,' said Portia when I told her what I was dreading.

'Then what's it going to be like?' I asked, and I had to struggle to keep myself from dissolving into tears. Portia does not tolerate self-pity. She spends too much time with underprivileged children and teenagers and doesn't think that anyone else has a right to complain. 'If you had seen what I've seen' is one of her favourite mantras. It ends every conversation very quickly. It is of little value to remind her of my own childhood in a suburb populated by immigrants trying desperately to make a new home for themselves. Perhaps I have glossed over what it was like when I reminisce about those days to my children. I am sure I have never told her of the nights when Lena, our next door neighbour, would knock on the door, waking us from sleep. Her face would always be sporting a fresh bruise. Her three-year-old twins would be by her side, tearful and exhausted, and hasty beds would be made for them all on our living room floor. 'Sleep it off, Rolf,' I would hear my father shout through the locked front door when the banging began. 'Sleep it off.'

Sometimes Portia is insufferable, but lately she is the rock I have come to rely on. Logic rather than sympathy is what I need right now

'I don't think you're going to be sent to prison. And if the worst happens, Eric will appeal. If that doesn't work, he'll appeal again and again until we get you out. You are not without resources, Mother.'

'Money can't solve every problem, Portia,' I said.

'It can solve a fair few of them,' she replied. 'I'm sure in the end money will get you out.'

'Out of where?' I shouted.

'Calm down. Just calm down! Look, whatever happens you have to know that we will do our best to ensure that we keep you out of prison. If by some chance you do get sent to prison, I'm sure it will only be a minimum-security facility. After all, you're hardly a threat to anyone.'

I don't know why Portia thought she knew what was going to happen. It may be that she found it inconceivable that I would be locked up like a common criminal, just like she might once have found it inconceivable that I would be charged with such a crime. Life can be filled with nasty surprises. I've spent most of the last eighteen months in a state of shock.

Although I wanted to believe her, I couldn't put aside my fear that the absolute worst would happen. I had been right about the trial. I had known that, despite everything I had been told, the jury would find against me. I knew that there was no reason why I should not be sent to prison for manslaughter.

'Prison is a last resort,' said Portia.

'Then that is where I will be going' I said, making Portia shake her head at my apparent stubbornness.

The trial seems very long ago now, although little more than a month has passed. If I close my eyes I can still summon up the stale smell of the courtroom. I can still feel the acid in my stomach as I listened to the prosecutor demolish my entire life.

I knew that the jury were going to find against me. I'd been watching their faces throughout the trial, and there was a point when they just stopped looking at me. Of the twelve jury members, seven were women. I had thought that would be a good thing, but it didn't seem to help at all. There was one woman who looked to be about my age, but she was missing a couple of teeth and had that worn look of someone who has had to struggle for everything. I've seen that kind of face before. My mother had that face. I could see her hating me from day one. Perhaps I shouldn't have worn the Chanel suit, but it's not like they didn't know who I was. His face was all over the news for months before it happened. And then afterwards, so was mine.

If I had been allowed to speak to them I would have explained that I was wearing the pale pink suit to mourn him, to celebrate him. On our first trip to Paris he'd pulled me into the Chanel store and insisted I try it on. I'd only indulged him because I thought we were simply amusing ourselves, but then he bought it for me, signing the credit card slip with a flourish and a smile. 'It's too much,' I'd said. 'Nothing is too much for you,' he'd replied.

Of course the prosecutor brought money into it. When the huge sum was mentioned, I watched the eyes of most of the jurors glaze over. Talk of millions of dollars belongs in magazines, not real life.

'They will discuss his life insurance,' Eric had told me.

'I didn't even know about that,' I said.

He nodded. 'We'll make sure the jury knows that.'

From knowing nothing about the Australian legal system, I now feel as though I could write a book about it. *Is this me?* I often thought during the trial. *Am I really sitting here listening to this? Could I possibly be the person they are talking about?*

'What has happened to our lives?' wailed Rosalind after she read the first of many articles about the trial. Rosalind has not dealt well with everything that has happened. The trial was merely the horrible culmination of an appalling year and a half. Eric assured me that I wouldn't even be charged with anything, especially after what we had all been going through; but when I was charged and the whole system shunted into top gear all I could do, all the girls could do, was just hang on.

I could have spoken to Rosalind about my fears regarding prison life, but she would have simply dissolved into tears with me and that would have achieved nothing. Rosalind, even more so than me, seemed to be coming apart at the edges. I wanted to help her but I couldn't seem to concentrate on anyone but myself. It was not the kind of mother I had always imagined myself to be. I was supposed to be selfless, not selfish.

I knew once all the jurors stopped looking at me that I was doomed. I knew what they were doing. It must be very difficult to know that someone's fate hinges on a single decision you have to make. It would be hard to look into the eyes of someone whose life you are about to destroy. It must be easier to make that decision if you dehumanise that person. At some point I must have gone from being Rose Winslow, mother, grandmother and the well-dressed lady sitting quietly next to her lawyer, to Rose Winslow, the accused. Rose Winslow, murderer. Murderess? I don't know what you call someone charged with manslaughter.

The press referred to me as a mother and grandmother, but in some articles I was also described as beautiful. I would never tell anyone I had picked up that particular detail as I read about my alleged crime, but it stood out when I saw it. I quite liked being called beautiful even though I am not beautiful, merely well put together. In court I wore my long brown hair in a low bun and my face was only lightly made up, just enough to cover the small age spots on my face and the dark circles under my eyes. The only jewellery I had on was my plain gold wedding band. I suppose that on a good day with the right makeup I can look fifty, maybe even late forties.

Life is supposed to begin at fifty now—or is it forty? I can't remember which. Not that it matters. My life is, I think, essentially over.

After the sentence was handed down, Eric immediately stated his intention to file for an appeal. He was more in control of himself at the sentencing hearing. At the trial he was as shocked by the verdict as everyone else. You wouldn't have known it to look at him. The only thing that changed about his usual upright demeanour and impassive face was a slight thinning of the lips. I'm sure no one in the courtroom noticed but me. But then I was the only one there who'd known him for thirty years.

'A good family always has a good lawyer, my dear,' Simon had said after I'd been introduced to him for the first time. Eric was just starting out then. Now his name is on the front of his own building. 'Look how far we've come, old friend,' Simon would say to Eric in his later years, and then they would toast each other with cigars and whisky. 'Eric will always be here for you Rose and he will help you when I am gone,' Simon told me whenever we talked about our old age.

'What if I go first?' I asked Simon when he lectured me on what to do after he was gone, because the idea of a life without him was unthinkable to me. I was sure that without him I would be reduced to sitting on the couch waiting to die.

'Oh, my darling girl,' laughed Simon. 'My darling, darling girl.'

He had taken care of me for so long that at first I couldn't even begin to think about how to take care of myself. I know that frustrated Portia. 'What do you mean you don't know the password for online banking?' she said when we were discussing money to pay for the funeral. 'Your father must have written it down somewhere,' I said. 'I just never needed it before now.'

'Give her a break, Portia,' said Rosalind.

'Stop mollycoddling her, Rosalind, these are important things to know. You're going to have to step up to the plate on this, Mother. I have a job and Roz has kids. You have to grow up and take care of yourself.'

Had it been a different time I'm sure I would have squared my shoulders and said, 'Don't you dare presume to patronise me, Portia.' As it was I did feel somewhat like a child who had lost a parent. I felt adrift. Adrift and bereft.

'Please don't lecture me,' I said instead. 'It's hardly the time.'

'I'll make some tea,' said Rosalind, hoping as usual to distract Portia before she worked herself up into a frenzy.

'Oh God, spare me another cup of tea,' said Portia. 'What is it with everyone and tea? It's not like it brings back the dead.'

'Please, have some respect for Mum,' said Rosalind.

'Girls, I think I might have a little lie-down,' I said. I have had a lot of lie-downs in the last year. During the trial and in the weeks awaiting sentencing I spent quite a few hours hiding in my bedroom from my girls. They meant well, but together they were a little too much to handle.

After the guilty verdict, the whole courtroom erupted. Portia and Rosalind, who had both been outward models of composure throughout the trial, let me down by losing control. Portia started shouting and Rosalind wept into her hands. Simon would have been very disapproving. He had been raised by an English mother who had taught him the importance of a stiff upper lip. (In fact, he seemed, at times, more English than Australian. It was an affectation of his that he held onto tightly. Most people on meeting him for the first time assumed that he had not lived in Australia for most of his life. Simon was always delighted when that happened. 'I could have been in the House of Lords,' he liked to say. I never contradicted him. His fantasy life as an Englishman was something I got used to.)

'She always impressed upon me the need to keep my emotions in check, especially when my father behaved badly,' he used to say about his mother.

'What do you mean by behaved badly?' I asked, but he never had a clear answer for me. Simon's true past was a secret he sheltered. Occasionally he would speak of a home filled with violence and humiliation, but just as quickly he would retreat from his words and refuse to say any more. 'But what do you mean he was violent, Simon?' I would ask. 'What did he do?'

'There are some things, Rose, that are too terrible to say, just too terrible to even think about. I would not want to burden you with the knowledge.'

I don't know if it was the truth. I never got to meet anyone from his family. During interviews he would sometimes smile mysteriously when asked about his family, 'Oh, I don't think they would want their private affairs discussed,' he would say, leaving the journalist to make his or her own assumptions about his past. I remember one article where it was speculated that he was descended from royalty. How he loved that. 'Where did they get that idea?' I asked him, but his only reply was an odd little laugh. I'm sure that one or two reporters went looking for his family, but they never looked very hard. It was a different time, I suppose, and there were fewer resources to track down the truth, and more respect for the aura of untouchability that surrounded celebrities.

When we first met I thought his inscrutability was part of his charm. Now I regard myself as remarkably gullible to have let him get away with saying such things. If I had questioned him more I might have known more. Or perhaps not. Knowing now how carefully constructed his persona was, how much he was concealing, I cannot believe he would have given up his secrets so easily.

At the judge's reading of the verdict, the members of the press who had been granted access were also unable to restrain themselves. There was a lot of noise. They wanted me to turn around and so kept calling my name. They wanted to see the look on my face.

I sank into my chair and then I sat very still with my hands in my lap. I heard the raised voices calling out, but distantly, as though they were coming from another room. My heartbeat was louder than the sounds being made by my daughters, who were sitting right behind me. I twisted my wedding ring around and around and concentrated on my breathing. *What?* I thought. *What?* When I looked at my daughters and Eric, for a moment I had no idea who they were.

I had both expected the guilty verdict and not expected it. Now I realise I would have been better off to just assume that everything would be fine. I could have used the time to simply enjoy being in my home rather than spending every waking moment worrying about whether or not I would be found guilty. I heard Eric ask for bail while I awaited sentencing and I heard it granted.

Even though I knew that worrying cannot change anything I still did just as much fretting as I awaited my sentencing. There really is no rest for the wicked.

Eric's lips thinned a little more at the chaos after the verdict. I have often wondered what Eric looks like at the point of orgasm. I have never wanted to sleep with him or anything, but I would like to know if his face changes. I would ask his wife, Patricia, but we are not so close that I could say something like that to her. Over thirty years of dinners and lunches and brunches I have never seen Eric look any different. Even when he smiles and laughs, the top of his face stays still and only his mouth moves. It must be disconcerting for Patricia and their children.

The barrister we had hired was also a little rattled at the result. His wig slipped to one side and I would have laughed at him but I'm a little awed by him. He has a tattoo of a snake all the way up his muscular arm. The first time I went to meet him in his very imposing wood-panelled office in the city, I thought he was a builder who had come to fix something. The man was actually holding a hammer and chewing on some nails.

'Sorry,' he said when he saw that Eric and I were already seated in his office. 'If you want something done, it seems easiest to do it yourself.'

He was wearing black pants and a shirt with no tie, and when he leaned forward to take some papers from Eric his sleeve slipped up and I saw the tail end of something tattooed on his wrist.

'It's a snake,' he said, catching me looking.

'Oh, I didn't . . .' I said. I felt my cheeks flush.

'Don't worry,' he laughed. 'If I'd known I'd have to spend my whole life explaining it I would never have done it. What can you do? The folly of youth.'

I nodded my head to let him know I understood, but the tattoo wasn't the reason I blushed. Robert has wide strong wrists and broad shoulders. He is entirely too good looking to be a barrister. However past it society thinks I am, I am still very capable of being attracted to a good-looking man.

'He's the best in the business,' Eric said to me as we left Robert's office.

'He better be for that amount of money,' I said.

'Rose, we will keep you out of jail. I know that's what Simon would want, and I will not let him down,' said Eric, and then we were both quite sad for a few minutes.

Those little bouts of sadness are the hardest to handle. Strange though it may seem, great waves of grief are easier, because you know that all you can do is sit tight and allow them to pass over you. They are so overwhelming that you can do nothing except give into them. You may be tumbled about a bit, but eventually you will be able to stand up and breathe again. The little waves that just lap at your feet come with no warning and somehow manage to be more devastating. They tend to arrive right in the middle of an ordinary moment, rushing in when they're least expected.

I didn't think Simon would have liked Robert—he was always suspicious of a man who didn't wear a tie. Simon loved silk ties. For years they were a standard birthday and Christmas gift from the girls. The night before closing arguments and the verdict, I found myself sitting on the floor of his closet rubbing my face with his favourite paisley tie. It smelled vaguely of cigar smoke and the aftershave he loved. *I cannot live without him*, I thought. *I simply cannot go on.* I don't know what would have happened if Rosalind hadn't knocked on my bedroom door.

'You believe me, Eric, don't you?' I'd asked Eric as we waited for a cab after that first meeting with Robert.

'About what happened, I mean?' I have probably asked Eric that question at least a hundred times since it happened. His answer is always in the same vein. He never actually answers yes or no, so I am always left wondering. Mostly I'm left wondering because I'm not sure if I believe me.

'Rose, I've known you for thirty years,' he said on this occasion. 'You've never even had a parking ticket, and I know how much you loved him. You would never have wanted to hurt him.'

A cab pulled up next to us, and Eric opened the door for me. I would have preferred to catch the train home from the city, but Eric would never have allowed that. I stared out of the window at all the people going about their ordinary days—perhaps wondering what they would have for lunch—and mulled over Eric's words: *You would never have wanted to hurt him.*

Those closest to me had seemingly accepted my version of events. There was no one who could challenge me on them, after all. I was and am grateful for their support, but I have spent many nights questioning what they actually believe. I know Rosalind would like to question me further, but she has never been one to press the point. Portia's stance on things has become her stance as well—or it had before I was convicted. I am sure if my mother or father were still alive I could count on them for the truth of what they believed, but I have lived without them for years.

I play out the events of that night in my head again and again, trying to come up with a different outcome, trying to bend reality. I know what I did and I thought I knew why I did it. *But what if I was wrong?* I keep thinking. *What if I was wrong?*

'I am very confident of a not-guilty verdict,' Robert had said to me, Eric and the girls as we waited for the jury to return after they had been sequestered. We hadn't bothered to go home, because Robert thought the verdict would come back quickly, so we were sitting in a cafe eating a rather poor lunch. I had a piece of salmon quiche and salad. The quiche was bland and the salad was limp and sad. Portia had ordered a glass of wine and a pasta dish. I'm not sure you can trust wine served in a cafe, but she drank it quickly enough. It probably made the pasta more palatable. Rosalind ordered a piece of cake and then didn't eat it because she was worried about the children.

'I'm sure Jack can manage just fine,' I said to her after she had checked her phone for the tenth time in five minutes.

'Oh, of course he can,' she said, but then she checked it again.

'They're still at school, what are you getting so hysterical about?' said Portia.

'Portia, why don't you concentrate on your lunch?' said Rosalind.

'Now, girls,' I said, without meaning to. I sometimes forget they are grown women. They still argue like children. Eric looked uncomfortable, but Robert was happily making his way through a steak sandwich. He ate neatly and carefully, only pausing to look at Portia or say something reassuring to me. Portia had tied up her hair, but it's curly and has a habit of escaping. One blonde lock had curled itself under her chin and I wanted to lean forward and brush it away from her face. I think Robert wanted to do the same thing, raising his hand a couple of times only to run it through his own hair.

Portia is bewitchingly beautiful. She is the type of woman men fight over. Rosalind and I look alike, but Portia looks like Simon. Lips that were just a little too full on a man are perfect on Portia.

The cafe was opposite the courthouse so it was very busy with people coming in and out, and just about everyone looked over at us. I can't stand being recognised. As I salted my quiche I daydreamed a little about taking a long trip once my case was over; although I knew that I probably wouldn't get the chance. I didn't know then that you get to go home after the verdict and return a few weeks later for sentencing. Neither Robert nor Eric had discussed this part of the trial process. The assumption was that I would return home, vindicated and free to get on with my life.

I knew I would be found guilty and I didn't know. I thought that if I prepared for the worst it wouldn't eventuate. That is, I now see, entirely the wrong way to think. Just because you prepare for the worst doesn't mean you won't be completely blindsided when it occurs.

'We've made the case that you didn't mean for it to happen. It was more his choice than yours, and we've explained about your state of mind and his state of mind.

They have to take your state of mind at the time into consideration,' said Robert to me as he sipped his Diet Coke and stared at my daughter.

I really didn't mean for it to happen, or maybe I did. I have no idea anymore. Robert's summation made a great deal of sense, and once he was done I knew that he had explained the situation perfectly, but then the longer we waited and waited for the jury to come back, the less sure I was of what had really happened. It seemed to me that the twelve people on the jury had not only seen into my very soul but had also seen past any lies I may have been telling myself. I knew it was silly to accord them such omniscience, but they were, after all, holding my life in their hands.

I had been in a state of uncertainty ever since that dreadful night. I would wake up from a fitful sleep convinced that I had been a victim of circumstance, and then a couple of hours later I would be berating myself and declaring that I was a murderer. Murderess? Back and forth I went and round and round. I was exhausted.

Finally we gave up on lunch and walked back to Robert's offices. 'They're going to convict me,' I said to Eric.

'Rose, you're fifty-five years old. No one is going to convict you of this crime. Robert has explained the extenuating circumstances to the jury. I'm confident they will vote the way they should.'

Well, that wasn't how it turned out.

Unless Eric and Robert manage to get their appeal through I have to stay here for a non-parole period of three years. A journalist from some tabloid paper wrote a long article on the unfairness of my short sentence. Portia told me about it when I was allowed to call her. The journalist blamed the 'cult of celebrity'. I would like to invite her to live here for even one day and then we could discuss how short three years is.

I thought it would be vile, but as Portia predicted, it is only minimum security. Apparently, many strings have been pulled to get me in here.

Sentencing took place one month after my conviction. It was too soon and not soon enough at the same time. I just wanted it over with, but I was also terrified of the sentencing decision as I tormented myself with all the possibilities of prison life. Portia simply moved into the house to be with me while I waited.

Robert had the girls speak on my behalf at the sentencing hearing. Patricia came as well and some other old friends, although I hadn't heard from many of them for months and months. I was grateful for their appearance, but I couldn't help feeling that what they were really doing was collecting fodder for dinner conversation. I tried to appear composed. I even smiled at Joan whom I had not heard from for twelve months.

The judge was not swayed by the glowing testimonies on my behalf. He still sent me to prison. It emerged that Robert and Eric had already thought through this eventuality. 'We'll lodge the appeal as soon as we can,' Eric said.

Once the trial was over the press backed off a little, but only a little. Portia and I spent a lot of time drinking wine and watching old movies. We didn't discuss Simon. At night, alone in my bed, I fretted and worried. I did not sleep very much at all.

'I feel I've let you down,' said Eric just before I was led away to wait for transport to my 'home' for the next three years.

'Robert was in charge, and he did his best,' I said. 'Neither of you could have predicted this outcome.' Even to my own ears my voice was flat and devoid of emotion. I seemed to have run out of energy.

'We'll get you out of prison as soon as possible, Rose. I will not sleep until you are free.'

'You have to sleep,' I said. 'Patricia will be angry with me if you don't.'

'It will be bearable. The place where you're going will be bearable.'

'How do you know?'

Eric gave me a small smile and patted my hand reassuringly and then I felt the hand of the policeman on my back as he pushed me forward towards a door at the back of the courtroom—away from Robert and Eric, away from my daughters.

And now I am here. I think that Eric and Robert had this place in mind for me even before the trial began. I suppose they are paid to think about every eventuality.

It looks like a very basic health retreat, but it is

definitely a prison. It's a collection of small buildings dotted across a large property. There is a fence but it's only made of wire and the gate stands wide open day and night, as if to indicate that no one would ever want to escape from here. Perhaps that's because the surrounding bush stretches all the way to the mountains without another building in sight. 'Where would you go?' the open gate seems to be asking. The air feels cleaner and colder as though it comes straight down from the ring of mountains. It only took a couple of hours to get here from the city, so Portia and Rosalind will be able to come and see me whenever they can.

When I arrived they took away all my clothes and I had to select something to wear from a room filled with cast-offs. The choice was limited to tracksuit pants and flannel shirts. Once I was dressed I resembled a bag lady. Everything was far too big on me. In my weeks waiting to learn my eventual fate I had found it difficult to eat.

'We don't like clothes to be anything except functional,' Sergeant Rossini told me.

'These are certainly functional,' I said, and then I had to bite down on my lip. I didn't want to burst into tears in front of her. I had been appalled at the thought of getting undressed in front of hundreds of women, but undressing in front of one was strangely even more humiliating. I had to be searched. I don't think I will be able to forget that experience for a long time.

'You can call me Natalie,' said Sergeant Rossini. 'We

like to keep things a little casual here.' Natalie was dressed in a uniform but her dark hair hung halfway down her back. While she was talking to me she twisted it into a knot, exposing her long neck. She is rather pretty with olive skin and dark eyes. She took away my clothes and my jewellery and carefully logged everything in a book and stored it away. 'It will be given back to you when you leave.'

'Can't I keep my wedding ring? It's just a gold band.'

'I'm afraid not. We like to make sure that all the women here have more or less the same things. We don't want anyone bullied because they have nice things, or shamed because they don't. We don't like to worry about things getting stolen either. If you all look the same and you all have the same, it makes things less complicated.'

It was becoming harder and harder not to cry. I have worn my wedding ring for nearly forty years. I have never taken it off. Even when my fingers swelled during my pregnancies I kept it on.

'Now,' said Natalie, 'I'll take you over to your unit. You're in unit four. You'll share with three other women. People come and go quite quickly here, so the makeup of units changes all the time. If you don't get along with someone it's not worth making a fuss.'

'I won't be gone soon,' I said.

'Mmm,' said Natalie—not allowing me to draw her into conversation. 'You'll have to cook and clean for yourself. Everyone gets ten dollars a day and from that you need to buy food and anything else you may need. Once you've been here for a few months and earned some trust you'll also be able to work at the aged care facility we have an agreement with, or at some of the other outside jobs that are available, and you can earn money from that.'

I must have looked utterly shocked, because she smiled at me and patted my shoulder. 'Don't worry, Mrs Winslow. You'll get used to it soon enough, and it's really not such a terrible place.' For a fleeting moment I thought about giving into my despair. Despite where I was I felt that I would be in safe hands with Natalie if I just sank onto the floor and gave up trying to appear strong. Instead I took a deep breath and swallowed.

Natalie turned and I followed her out of the main building into the prison grounds. 'This doesn't really look like a prison,' I said.

'No, it doesn't. We don't want it to, but it is and there are rules and ways of doing things. It will make your time easier here if you learn them quickly.'

'Yes,' I said because I had no idea what else to say.

I stumbled along behind her with my thin prison-issue towel, sheets and blanket, forcing myself not to try to work out how many hours in this place three years equated to.

'We count everyone about five times a day,' Natalie explained. 'An announcement will come over the speaker system or a siren will sound, and whatever you're doing you need to stop and move to a meeting point until you're checked off.'

'Oh dear,' I said, and I knew I sounded ridiculous. I hadn't run out of milk for my tea.

'Don't worry, Mrs Winslow, you'll get used to it. I promise,' said Natalie again. I suppose I should have told her to call me Rose, but right now I'm happier with Mrs Winslow. I don't have my wedding ring on. How else will they know I am . . . I was . . . I'm still married? 'Now, I'll give you some time to settle in, and then I'll come and get you so you can meet Allison. She's the governor of the prison.'

Small fibro cottages are dotted all over the place. These are the units. Each one can house up to five women, but mostly there are only four. The bathroom is shared, but I have my own bedroom. It's very small, as though one regular-sized bedroom has been divided into two, but there is a desk that I have decorated with a few precious reminders of home which Natalie allowed me to keep. I brought all the wrong things with me.

Most of the things I brought are now locked away. They should give you a list of things you can and cannot bring, but I suppose this is not a school camp.

I have been allowed to hold onto pictures of Portia and Rosalind, of Lottie and Sam and Jack, and of course there is a picture of Simon. I have a collection of my favourite books and my face cream, although I wasn't allowed to bring in my perfume. 'Too expensive,' said Sergeant Rossini—Natalie.

The three women I am sharing with were out at work when I first arrived. I was pleased to be able to unpack and cry in privacy. I can see that I will have precious little of that. I thought I was through with tears after the last months, but apparently not.

After half an hour Natalie came to get me. I waited in the office for Allison and tried to get myself under control. It wasn't as though I had never had to live in a poky little flat or had to make do with virtually no money. I had done it before and I told myself that I would be able to do it again.

I closed my eyes and tried to remember the first flat Simon and I ever rented. I was so young I didn't feel at all like a married woman. I felt like I was playing house. The landlord lived downstairs in his own two-bedroom unit. 'A rose for a Rose,' he would say to me every Friday when I walked past his door to go out and do my shopping. Then he would hand me a single red rose. He waited for me, I'm sure of it. I thought he was very sweet.

'I don't like him leering at you,' Simon said when I told him about it.

'Simon, he's about a hundred years old. He's only being nice.' Looking back I realise the poor man couldn't have been much more than sixty.

I was trying to remember the colour of the carpet in our old living room—it was either yellow or green—when a woman walked in, holding a phone to her ear. 'That's fine, yes, yes,' she said impatiently. She put the phone on the desk in front of me and I felt compelled to stand up. 'I'm Allison,' she said stretching out her hand and I shook it, feeling absurdly like we were both at a business meeting.

'Sit, sit,' she said dropping into a chair on the other side of the desk. I sat.

'So, Mrs Winslow,' she said, 'settled in?'

'As much as I can be, I suppose.'

'It will be difficult for the first few weeks, but I know you'll be fine.'

'I wish I could say the same thing,' I said.

Allison, sensibly, ignored my petulance. 'Where would you like to spend your days? You might have realised this already, but we are a working farm with gardens and animals.'

I had realised it. The smell of manure choked the air. I could hear the cows off in the distance even as I sat in Allison's office. Lowing, I think it's called. Simon and I once took the girls to a farm stay for the weekend where they delighted in being able to milk cows and collect eggs. Rosalind tried to get us to bring home a newborn lamb for a pet. Simon hated the place. 'The smell is just too much for me, my dear.' He spent most of the weekend in our cottage, reading. The cottages had been described as luxury farm accommodation, but 'luxury' turned out to be code for 'clean'. They did not look unlike the units here.

'Well, I think I might be most useful in the garden,' I said, surprised. 'I never really imagined that I'd be given a choice.'

'This particular prison is one of very few of its kind in Australia. The aim here is to help to prepare women who are unlikely to reoffend to go back out into the world. To that end, we offer a number of classes to help them work on things like computer skills or getting their HSC, but we also have a large vegetable garden and run a cooking school. You're welcome to take a class of your choice in the afternoons.' Allison slid a thin brochure across her desk to me. It contained a list of classes I could choose from.

'I'm a bit old to be taking classes,' I said.

'No one's too old to take a class.'

'How do you know if someone is unlikely to reoffend?' I said.

'Most of the women here have come from other prisons. This is sort of a halfway house between that and the real world. Everyone has a measure of independence and has to take care of themselves. We hope that once you leave here you have some skills to take with you so that you won't go back to old ways.'

'Old ways?' I said.

'Drugs, alcohol, dangerous friends … anything that could cause a former prisoner to be put back in the system.'

'I've never … I mean I haven't ever done anything like that.'

'No, and that might be why you've landed up here. Or some strings were pulled because of your … well, your relative level of fame.'

I'm sure my face gave me away. I had no idea how Eric and Robert had managed to get me into the place. I was silently grateful to them.

'I wasn't famous, my husband was,' I said. I wanted to make sure that she knew I would be free of any airs and graces. There are two kinds of people I've run into as the wife of someone famous. One kind adores you without even knowing you, believing that you have somehow found the secret to everything. They want to be your friend, so they fawn over and compliment you. The other kind hates you because they think you feel yourself to be above them. Allison, I saw, existed somewhere in the middle. She was more irritated with my fame than anything else, perhaps fearing that it would be a disruption to the smooth running of her domain.

'I know, and I know that an appeal has been lodged already, so you might not be with us for very long. Hopefully while you're here you can make the best of it.'

'I will do my best,' I said, and Allison smiled at me. She is a sturdy-looking woman in her forties or maybe late thirties. Her hair was pulled back into a no-nonsense ponytail and she was dressed in jeans and brown work boots. She does not look like anyone's idea of a warden, and yet it was clear to me that she would not tolerate any misbehaviour from her inmates. When she stood up to show me out I caught sight of the gun on her hip. However nice this place may seem, the doors are still locked at night and it is still a prison.

'Oh, and Mrs Winslow . . .'

'Yes,' I said, turning back to her.

'It's best not to ask anyone what they've done to get in here—prison etiquette, you know.'

'Oh, I understand about that,' I said. 'Believe me, I do.'

After all the months of talking and explaining and defending myself, I'm only too happy to be able to shut my mouth and get on with something else. I would prefer to get on with a trip to Greece, but I'm sure that the need to be away from this place is probably a feeling shared by all the inmates. I closed my eyes for a moment and tried to summon up a memory of the afternoon Simon and I had spent at a restaurant in Santorini overlooking the Mediterranean, but it was difficult to conjure up the salty sweet smell of the sea over the tang of manure. We were there to celebrate my fiftieth birthday. How long ago that seems.

Natalie gave me a tour of the place and listed all the rules and regulations that I would find in the handbook. 'Obviously no alcohol and no drugs,' she said. 'You can't miss any of the counts during the day. You need to help keep your cottage clean . . .' There were a lot of rules but I wasn't really concentrating. I was glad to have the handbook to read over.

'Breaking any of these rules may lead to removal of privileges,' said Natalie.

'Privileges?' I said, paying attention again.

'Being able to work outside the prison is a privilege, having visitors is a privilege. There's a list at the back.'

Like school, I thought.

I received a few sly looks from the inmates who were working in front of the cottages, planting and cleaning, but for the most part no one seemed to care who I was. I felt my shoulders relax a little and I took a deep breath. *I can do this*, I thought. *I can do it.*

'If you're afraid of something, my dear,' Simon used to say, 'hold your head up high and pretend until you're no longer afraid. People will think you're in control and confident and they will treat you that way and soon enough you will begin to believe it yourself.'

I tilted my head back a little and lifted my face to the sun. I only knew I was crying when I tasted salt on my lips. *Oh, Simon*, I thought as I followed Natalie to see the canteen, *I am trying, but I'm so terribly afraid.*

'Rose, darling girl,' I heard him say. 'Oh, my darling girl.'

Chapter Three

Before I came here I was in the other place. I wasn't Birdy before I came here. When I lived at home I was Fliss, which is short for Felicity. I hate being Fliss. Fliss is a hiss of air, a sound you make through your teeth. Lila calls me Fliss and Mum calls me Fliss but I hate being Fliss.

In the other place they didn't call me Fliss or Felicity. They called me 'retard' and 'idiot' and 'cunt'. They spat words at me like I was dirty. Everyone there was angry and sad. The sadness was in the grey walls. No one talks about where they were before they came here, and if they do they all call it 'the other place', even though there are lots of different 'other places'.

The other place is real prison. The other place is ugly and creepy. The other place is small cells with no space to breathe. It's being scared the whole time. It's hell on earth. That's what Jess calls it—'hell on earth'.

The other place wasn't a good place for me to be. I didn't look at anyone. My stomach went round and round and my fingers were always bloody because I had to tear off big pieces of nail.

'She doesn't belong in a conventional prison,' said my lawyer to the judge. A lawyer helps you when you're in trouble. My lawyer was Lucy. Lucy has dark shiny hair and brown eyes. 'Don't worry, I'll take care of you,' said Lucy, but the judge didn't like her. He shook his head when she talked. 'There is nowhere else,' said the judge and he patted his white hair that wasn't real. It was a stupid wig. It made him look like an ugly old dog. 'Woof, woof,' I wanted to say to the judge but I kept quiet, just like Lucy told me to do.

'She is a danger to herself and society and her tests show she understands what she did. Her IQ is within the normal range.'

I tried to be far away from everyone at the other place but everything was so small and close. I didn't want anyone to hurt me. Lots of people got hurt. It's the angry sadness that makes people hurt each other. I did get hit once. I got hit and kicked over and over again, but I curled myself into a ball and lay there until it was over, and when the guard asked me who had done it I really didn't know. I didn't look at their faces. I shouldn't have bumped into the big woman with the orange hair. No one liked to be bumped into at the other place.

Almost everyone here has been somewhere else before they came here. I didn't think I would be allowed to come here, but I only have three months left of a two-year sentence for assault. That's what they call what I did—assault. A salt. Assault is when you hurt someone. I hurt someone.

The therapist I saw once a week and the governor at the other place said that I was a model prisoner and just right for here. Also Lucy kept calling and calling and saying that I wasn't coping.

I am not a model anything. I am angry and filled with hate. I told the therapist that I wasn't angry anymore. She wanted me to forgive everyone. Forgive your mum, forgive your dad, forgive yourself. I don't forgive anyone, but I didn't tell her that. I'm smart enough to keep a secret and I have lots of secrets. I even have secrets from Jess, who knows most things about me.

The first night I spent at the other place I lay awake and counted the people I hated. There are only four, but it takes a lot to hate four people. Sometimes I feel tired of all the hating. One, him; two, her; three, Lester; four, Mum. One, two, three, four. In my hard bed at the other place I held up my thumb for him and my first finger for her and the next one for Lester and the next one for Mum.

Then I pushed down the finger that was for Mum. I pushed it down hard.

'I won't press charges,' Mum told the policeman who came when she called on the phone.

'I'm sorry, ma'am. We cannot let this go,' he said.

'She's my daughter,' said Mum. 'She's not normal. She didn't mean it.'

I hate it when she tells people I'm 'not normal'.

The policeman took off his hat and scratched his head. 'Nothing we can do now, I'm afraid. I'm sure you can explain it all in court. Now, let's get you into an ambulance.'

I had to go in the police car and Lila had to come to take care of Isabel.

'I'm scared,' said Isabel while we waited for Lila.

'Don't be scared,' I said. 'Be Isabel.'

'Isabel, Isabel didn't worry,' she said.

'Isabel didn't scream or scurry,' I said.

'What happened?' said Lila, coming through the open front door.

After that it didn't matter what Mum wanted, I was in the system anyway, and once you're in the system there's no way out except the back door at the courthouse. You learn stuff like that once you've been through it all. The system doesn't care if you're a good person or an evil one. It doesn't care about why you did what you did. It just pushes you through and gets you out of the way. Next case, please. Everyone here and everyone at the other place hates the system.

I never wanted to hurt other people until I stood in front of a judge in a stupid white wig who talked and talked. I know the only reason I went to court was because I had already hurt someone, but that happened so quickly

I couldn't believe I'd done it. My hand moved by itself. 'It wasn't me,' I wanted to tell the judge with the white wig, 'it was my hand.' But Lucy told me to be very quiet, so I didn't say anything.

Everyone talked but I had to keep quiet. Lucy talked and the judge in the white wig talked and then I was sent to the other place. I had to ride in a bus with five other women. One of them had a spider on her cheek. It looked real but it was only a picture. At the other place the governor talked. Her name was Mrs Wotton. It rhymed with cotton. Mrs Wotton told me to behave and do as I was told. By the time I got to my small grey room called a cell I had nodded my head so much it felt like it was going to fall off.

I was cold in bed in the dark because I only had one blanket. I couldn't sleep and I couldn't cry because I didn't want anyone to hear me. I didn't think you were allowed to cry in prison. That was when I counted all the people I hated. I thought there would just be Mum but there was also Lester and then there was him and her. They had been waiting in my brain and when I was cold and sad in my grey cell they came out of hiding and I remembered. I had hated him for a long, long time but I had stuffed my hate deep down inside. They had been in my brain all along, just waiting for me to remember them. I didn't know anger and hate could come bubbling up and burn your throat. But up they came on that first night, burning and bubbling. Once Mum took me to see a movie and there was a girl in it who could turn herself into flames. I felt like that girl, like I was on fire.

I have spent most of my life pretending that the things that happened didn't really happen. You can't do that. Stuff follows you and sneaks up on you when you're not paying attention.

'You need to face your demons,' said Emily, the therapist at the other place.

I looked behind me because I thought there was a demon standing right there, but Emily didn't mean it like that. Demons are like bad thoughts and feelings. Better to face your demons. Better to fight your demons. Better to find a way to murder the bastards. That's what I think anyway. Jess calls everyone she doesn't like 'bastard'.

I was tiny and skinny when I spent my first night in the other place, but as I listened to the other women through the walls snoring and farting I knew that I needed to be bigger and stronger. I had been tiny and skinny for my whole life. My boobs were only ever proper boobs when I was pregnant; otherwise they were just little bumps on my chest. In the other place some of the women lifted weights and built up their muscles so they looked like men. I ate. I ate white bread and rice and potatoes and all the sugar I could get. By the time I got here I was big, but no one starts with you here.

There is no angry sadness here. There is just worry and a little bit of hope. Everyone worries that they might muck up and get sent back to the other place, but they also hope that they get to go home soon. We're all nearly at the end of our sentences. No one wants to mess that up. We can see the mountains and the fields outside the gates and we know that we're close enough to touch them. There's lots of space here, and in the morning no one says, 'Get out of the way, retard.' They say, 'Morning, it's a great day, isn't it?' I say 'Morning' as well.

I'm doing a good job of fooling everyone here that all I feel is worry and a little bit of hope just like them. I do my work and I listen when I'm spoken to. I turn up to be counted, and if they say 'jump' I jump until they tell me to stop.

That's because I have an agenda.

I learned that word from Jess. She told me an agenda is a plan that you have that you keep secret. Sometimes your agenda can make you do things that no one else understands. Whenever anyone is cranky with her Jess says, 'Tell me, love, what's your agenda?'

What's your a-gen-da?

Jess is my friend, so I don't get cranky with her, and she knows most things about me except my agenda. My a-gen-da. That's just for me.

I'd never done anything wrong before I was in the system because Mum called the police on the phone. I worked hard to finish school. I didn't get my HSC because I couldn't write exams, but I can read and write and I worked in the fruit shop. I remember all the codes. The code for crimson seedless grapes is 4701 and the code for grapefruit is 2314.

I put the codes into the till and Frank said I was his best cashier.

I worked hard and I was happy and Mum was happy and Frank was happy. I was his best cashier, and then late one night, after stocktake, he said I was his best girl. But Frank already has a wife and she was very angry and Mum shouted at me but I didn't mind. I liked being Frank's best girl, and I like having Isabel.

Frank and I didn't talk much but he made me feel nice. I don't talk to many people. Mum doesn't ask me what I think. She asks Lila what she thinks. Lila went to university, and even though she's my little sister she's like a big sister because she told me to 'just ignore the crap they tell you and do what you want with your life. You're as smart as anyone else.'

Emily the therapist wanted to know everything about me. 'Tell me about your childhood, tell me about your friends, tell me about your mum, tell me about your dad.' She made me think too much. I wanted to stop seeing her. Sometimes at night I added her to my list of people that I hated. But then she told me about this place. So I stopped hating her, because she was trying to help. 'You're a really good candidate for the Farm. I know that you've found your time here difficult. If you can just hang in there and work with me I'll do my best to help you.'

I hung in there. I know how to say the right words. I forgive Mum, I forgive Dad, I forgive myself. I want to do better.

I can say, 'Yes, I love you,' even though what I really want is for your body to be underground in the cold and the dark. With the worms. Under the ground with the worms. Just like he is now.

I said the right words and now I'm at the Farm and I will be going home soon.

I thought I would have to wait to go home to see them. To see him, to see her, but now he is gone and she is here and all the bubbling anger is just for her and a little left over for Mum and Lester. I want to get rid of the bubbling anger, so I have to get rid of her. Some nights it makes me feel sick and I have to sneak into the kitchen and stuff some bread down on top of it. I don't want to feel this way anymore. I'm going to face my demons. That's my a-gen-da. But I don't tell Jess that. I don't tell anyone that.

I am here because I did the wrong thing. Assault is wrong. Hurting people is wrong. People cannot get away with doing the wrong thing. But assault isn't the only way to hurt someone. Assault breaks bones, but there are other parts that can break. Mum says Dad broke her heart, but you don't go to jail for that. You should, but you don't.

I'm going to be smart about it. I'm not going to do something stupid. I'm going to be quiet and I'm going to be smart but I have to get it done.

I saw her being given the tour by Natalie. She is much smaller than me. She used to be bigger but that was when I was a child. She was an adult and I was a child and she was bigger and she could have helped. She even said it to me once. She said, 'You can come over whenever you want and if you need anything, any help at all, you only have to ask.' But she didn't mean that. What she meant was—words, words, words, bullshit smile.

I would like to see her try that on me now.

Chapter Four

The other women in unit four alarm me a little at first. Their faces speak of lives lived on the edge. The lines at the corners of their mouths drag down their smiles and even when they laugh they still look unhappy. When they sit on the couch I'm conscious that their bodies are tense and coiled as though waiting for attack. I don't want to judge anyone but it's hard not to think about what kind of a person goes to prison. I'm aware of the irony of that. I'm hardly here to run the cooking school.

Heather, who looks about forty, has large hands and pale freckled skin and I am immediately struck by her height. She gives me a brief smile upon meeting me, but then seems to be looking at something else in the room. Sal—'short for Salvation, don't ask me about it, my idiot parents were hippies'—is about my height and is probably younger than me but looks older. She sweeps her dark eyes up and down my body, appraising me inch by inch. Then there is Linda, who is a recovering drug addict. Her cheeks have caved in and her teeth have fallen out and her hands shake so hard she spends a lot of time sitting on them. I have never seen another human being like her except on television. Some situations are so overwhelming that instead of panicking about them you actually find yourself quite calm. I look at the women I am to share a unit with and instead of falling apart I simply accept it. There is nothing else to be done.

'Here are the rules,' says Heather after we have introduced ourselves. They have them written on a large white sheet of cardboard and taped to the fridge.

No eating anyone else's food.

No using anyone else's shampoo or conditioner or soap.

Clean up after yourself.

The majority decide on what to watch on TV.

Don't touch other people's stuff.

Don't whinge.

Do your job.

'Are these the rules for everyone here?' I say.

'Nah, just us in this unit,' says Sal. 'You can add your own if you like, but first we have to have a discussion. This is a . . . what's that word, Heather?'

'A democracy?' I say.

'Yeah.'

'Except it's not really a democracy,' says Sal. 'The screws can come in any time they want and check for drugs and stuff. They also do inspection once a day to make sure everything is clean, so we've got to keep it clean. Do you know how to clean?' Sal speaks fast, getting everything said before I can add anything to the conversation. She is nervous in my presence. I want to laugh but don't.

'I certainly do,' I say. Heather and Sal and Linda were obviously expecting a certain kind of person when they heard I was going to be sharing a unit with them. I can see that I will have to work fairly hard to dispel any ideas they have about me. The unit smells of cooked food and pine-scented spray. I don't bother thinking about how much I miss my home that smells of jasmine in the summer and wood fire in the winter. I know that would be unproductive.

'Good,' says Heather, holding my gaze just long enough so that I look away first, and then she goes outside to smoke a cigarette. Everyone here smokes. I noticed that when Natalie was showing me around. The smell of manure is almost but not quite overpowered by the smell of cigarette smoke. Even in the open air I find myself taking shallow breaths. I'm sure I will hardly notice it in a few days.

'Don't worry about Heather,' says Sal quietly. 'She's a bit of a bitch but you'll get used to her. It's not so bad being here. I mean it could be worse. You'll be fine. I'm sure you'll be fine.'

'Thanks,' I say. I feel a rush of warmth towards Sal. I lace my fingers together so that I won't be tempted to hug her. Kindness always makes me more emotional than it should.

A siren screams through the air.

'What's that?'

'Muster,' says Sal. 'Come out onto the veranda.'

I go outside and stand next to her. Every veranda is filled with women and we all stand there as Natalie walks past with a clipboard in her hand, nodding and presumably putting a mark next to our names. We obediently wait until we are checked off and then herd ourselves back inside.

Heather cooks dinner tonight. We have spaghetti. The sauce is weak and watery and the meat tastes like a cheap cut. There's no parmesan but there is a giant block of bright yellow cheddar.

'We have to make this last,' says Sal, cutting me a small piece. In my fridge at home I have left brie and gruyere and a crumbly aged gouda. I hope Rosalind takes it all before Portia throws it out. She isn't fond of cheese. Portia has volunteered to stay in the house for a couple of nights a week just to keep an eye on things.

I nod at Sal and obediently cut my cheese into tiny squares to throw on my spaghetti. There isn't much conversation while we eat. I can't think of anything to say. I'm afraid I'll ask a question that they don't want to answer. I'm sure they have no idea what to say to me either.

After dinner we all clean up together. 'From tomorrow, we'll roster you on for different days for cooking and stuff,' says Sal.

'Okay,' I say, because she seems to want a reply.

Heather turns on the television and we watch the news together until my face flashes up on the screen. I'm heartily sick of my own image. When pictures of me first began appearing on television and the internet I would scrutinise each one, trying to place where it was from and when it had been snapped, noting the sag of my chin and the wrinkles around my eyes. But eventually I grew bored with that and I simply stopped caring. The aim of every photographer has been to capture my face at the height of emotion—anger and grief are favourites. I don't look good in any of them.

Heather and Sal stare straight ahead at the television, deliberately refusing to acknowledge what we're looking at.

'Isn't that . . .?' says Linda.

'Shut it,' says Sal.

I have to swallow a lump in my throat at her compassion.

'Goodnight,' I say quietly, and I leave to go and lie on my bed. It's only seven o'clock and I know we're counted again at nine so I can't even go to sleep.

On this first night I'm not sure how I will even make it through the next day or week or month. When I'm finally in bed for the night I pray that Eric will get the appeal through, and then I close my eyes and try to feel Simon lying next to me.

My body feels his absence more than my mind does. I know he's gone but I find myself reaching for him in my sleep. When I was at home alone I used to turn my head to look at something and see him walking past the room. Or the wind would rattle a window and I would look up and he would be standing there. At first these sightings shocked me deeply. I thought his ghost was back to punish me for what I had done, but then I found out that both Portia and Rosalind had experienced the same thing. It is, apparently, perfectly natural to see someone you loved everywhere once they are gone.

Before I came here I spoke to him all the time. When I was alone his presence was palpable. For months I laid the table for two. I apologised, of course. I apologised over and over again. Some nights I would yell at him. I would scream abuse at his spectre, ranting about the horror of what he had hidden from me, yelling questions about his true nature. My house is big enough that I could get away with that. One night I went down into the wine cellar where the walls are thick and the air is always cool and yelled for so long that I lost my voice. That night I felt him sit down on the edge of the bed. When I felt the dip of the mattress I struggled up from sleep and switched on the bedside lamp, hoping to catch him there, but he was already gone.

I was angry with him; it made a change from being angry at myself. I was furious about the lies and the deceit, but I also despaired at what had been lost.

We had been planning for this time in our lives for years. We were in the process of booking an extravagant five-week cruise around Europe; we were going to buy a small cottage in the mountains—far enough away so we would feel we had left the city behind but close enough to have Lottie and Sam come and visit. I wanted to spend as much time with them as I could while they were still young. Simon was going to devote one room in the house to model trains so he and Sam could build sets and learn together. And now everything he worked for, everything we dreamed of, is simply gone. Portia, Rosalind and I, in fact everyone in our family and I'm sure our friends as well, have been fundamentally changed by what has happened. Even food tastes different now.

He had been keeping such dreadful things from me.

I want to hate him. I understand that I should hate him, but no matter how hard I try I don't seem to be able to.

For years I sat beside my husband on the couch watching the news and shaking my head at women who stand next to their men supporting the unsupportable. I comfortably assured myself that I would fling the adulterer or the rapist or the fraudster to the kerb without a second thought. It is easy to sit on the couch in smug judgement of the choices made by others.

But when it did happen to me, when the allegations about him began, I could not see him off so easily. He was my husband, my lover, my friend. I knew everything about him, except for the one thing that made him into a completely different person.

How could he have kept that from me? How could I have missed it?

And now because he is gone only I know the truth about him. The allegations have gone with him, and his obituary in the newspaper chose not to mention anything but his achievements. It was all only rumours and speculation, after all. He had not been charged with anything. Lucky him.

I stood beside him and I supported him, and even though I now know what he did I have still allowed him to leave the world a cherished man, famous throughout the country. He is tarnished by how he died, of course he is, but in a few years all anyone will remember is the fact that he was an icon of Australian television. 'What was it he was supposed to have done?' they will say when his name comes up. 'How did he die again?'

His daughters can choose to forget the things they have heard about him and instead mourn a wonderful father, and the world will believe it has lost a star.

I have been, I suppose, the perfect wife all the way to the very end. And now, rather than speak the truth I have allowed myself to be locked up. Perhaps the truth would have made no difference anyway. But it might have helped. If the jury knew what I know, if they could have seen what I have seen, they might have gone a different way. And yet I have kept it to myself, hiding the man he was, if only to avoid confronting the woman I was.

When Robert explained to the jury the circumstances surrounding his death, he droned on and on about how stressful it had all been, how depressed Simon was, how hard it was for both of us to cope with the press and the vile things being said about him. But he didn't say if any of it was true or not.

He didn't say that, because despite everything I told my lawyer and my barrister I did not tell them that, and I was clever enough to hide the evidence that would have gone a long way towards proving his guilt. There is a drawer in my closet that comes out and underneath it there is a space where I used to occasionally hide jewellery when I went away. Now it holds ... them, I suppose. It holds them. All of them.

I don't know why I did that. I don't know why, after I understood exactly what he had done; I didn't want to expose him to the world for condemnation and disgust. We had been together too long, perhaps. It was difficult for me to see where he ended and I began. So perhaps I was only protecting myself.

What kind of a woman stays married to a man like this? asked one journalist in a scathing article on the internet. *What kind of a woman?*

I don't know. What kind of a woman am I?

Chapter Five

'So tell me how this week has been, Birdy,' says Henrietta.

Henrietta is tall and has smooth chocolate-coloured skin. She doesn't just walk into a room, she glides into it. She is like a swan moving on a lake. Today she is wearing a tight grey skirt and a white blouse. Even in flat shoes she is much taller than me. I hold my back straight when I walk into the office to see her.

'Did you used to be a model?' I asked her when I saw her for the first time. She looks like the models in the magazines Mum and Lila read. I never liked magazines because the words are too small and the sentences are too long, but sometimes I liked to look at the pictures.

'I did model to help pay my way through university,' she said.

'Why wouldn't you have just stayed a model? It must be much easier than doing this.'

'I wanted to help people, I guess. But we aren't here to discuss me. We're here to talk about you. Now, from your file I can see that your real name is—'

'Don't say it,' I said. 'Don't say it at all. I don't like it.'

'Okay, I'm happy to call you Birdy. Why Birdy?'

'It's silly,' I said.

'That's okay, I'd like to know.'

'Jess gave me the nickname. I take care of the finches in the aviary. I have done ever since I got here. They like me.'

'Does Jess know your real name?'

'Jess knows everything about me, well, most things, and I guess I know the same about her.'

'So she's a good friend.'

'Yes, she's a good friend.'

I have to see Henrietta every week. It's part of the deal. I don't think therapy helps me at all. Therapy is talking about your feelings and then being told how to feel another way. 'Forgive your mum, forgive your dad, forgive yourself, forgive everyone,' said Emily at the other place. When I told her, 'My dad went away and never came back and never called and I don't even know what he looks like,' she said, 'You need to forgive him for not being a perfect parent. You need to forgive him so you can move on with your life.'

I told Emily that I forgive everyone, but I don't. I'm still bubbling with anger and hate. 'Henrietta doesn't talk about forgiveness. She talks about feelings. 'How did you feel when your father left? How do you feel today? How did you feel yesterday?'

Sometimes when I leave, my stomach is twisting and I have a headache. Not because Henrietta has found out my secrets, but because I'm afraid that she will. I think Henrietta is smarter than Emily. I think her brown eyes can look inside me, and when I see her I sit on the couch with my arms over my chest just in case she sees into the bubbling anger inside me.

'Birdy?' says Henrietta, and I realise that I've been staring out of the window at the aviary. I like that I can see it from the room where we meet. I like to be able to keep an eye on the little birds. They're so small, so . . . so . . . vulnerable. That's a word Lila taught me—vulnerable. After I was Frank's best girl she said to me, 'You have to keep yourself safe. Because some things are harder for you it makes you vulnerable to creeps like him.'

'What does vulnerable mean?'

'It means that you're in danger of someone making you do something you don't want to do. You can get hurt.'

I wanted to explain to Lila that I wasn't vulnerable. Not anymore. Frank only did things I wanted him to do. He would ask nicely. He would say, 'Is it okay if I touch here?', and I could say yes or no. Not everyone asks nicely.

I'm glad I'm here to protect the birds. Finches are vulnerable. They shouldn't get cold and they get sick easily. If you frighten them too much their hearts can stop working. They are always in danger of dying.

If it hadn't been for Jess I would have landed up working in the toolshed making badges that say 'Smile' or in the cooking school or with the stinking cows. When I first got here I was sent to work in the gardens and I was very bad at it. I didn't know Jess well then and all she did was shout at me that I was digging up the wrong things or overwatering or underwatering or planting too close or too far away. I wasn't really paying attention. I was too busy looking at the aviary filled with finches. It is a very big cage. I can get inside it and stand up and turn around. I love finches. I love Gouldian finches the most. The ones here are beautiful colours. Red and green and blue and purple and yellow.

I know a lot about finches. The aviary here has a mixture of zebra and Gouldian finches. Zebra finches can be pushy but Gouldian finches are sweet and polite. I know more about finches than anything else. Finches don't like to be friends with humans and they don't make much noise. They need to have shell grit in the cage so they can digest their seeds. They eat the grit with the seeds. They like to eat fruit—and if you mix some of their seed with a little bit of honey, they love that. I have heard all about finches over and over again. Over and over again. Everything about finches is stuck in my head.

On my first two days I kept wandering over to the cages and Jess had to keep calling me back. At the end of the second day she came to get me again. 'Hey, you,' she said, but I didn't answer. I was watching them search for fresh seed. They were not very well taken care of. I could see that they had to look very hard to find seeds that hadn't been eaten yet. Also their water was dirty and there was just a little bit of shell grit in a bowl on the floor. They don't like things to be on the floor.

'Hey, you,' said Jess again. 'You, bird woman, bird woman, birdy, birdy . . .'

I turned around then. I wanted to hit her but I knew better than that. I'd only hit one person in my whole life and that had landed me in prison. 'They're not being cared for,' I said.

'Yeah, I'm doing my best, but they freak me out, especially the way they flap like crazy things every time I go near them. I don't know much about them. The woman who used to take care of them left last month. It was stupid for them to even start an aviary if you ask me, but some guy who owns a pet shop in town built it. He thought it would do the prisoners good to have to take care of the birds. Everyone's always got to be a bloody hero.'

'I could do it.'

'Know about them, do you?'

'I know everything about them,' I said. 'I used to help someone take care of theirs.'

Jess nodded and I knew she wanted to ask me who I was talking about, but in prison you don't ask questions. You wait until someone wants to give you the answers. 'Okay, I guess that can be your job then. I'll clear it with Allison, but I'm sure she won't mind. They wanted to be able to sell them but I can't get the little buggers to breed.'

'I could get them to breed,' I said. 'And I'll clean up the cage and keep them in good condition.'

'Well then, Birdy, they're all yours.'

This time I didn't mind being called Birdy. I was happy to leave my real name behind. Jess is a leader in here. She's been in prison for two years already, and she's been here for six months. Once she started calling me Birdy, everyone else did as well.

I stand at the window in the office Henrietta uses when she comes here and I watch the finches in their cage, trapped like me but happy because they have just enough space and freedom that they don't go mad. I didn't have enough space at the other place.

'This week's been okay,' I say to Henrietta when I finally sit down.

Henrietta is very patient. Her full name is Henrietta Whine. Jess thinks that's funny but I don't know why.

'Have you heard from Lila?'

'Lila emails me every Wednesday night. She never forgets.'

'That must make Wednesday nights quite special.'

I nod. 'She sent me some pictures of Isabel. She's grown again. Lila had to buy her new shoes. She chose pink ones that have butterflies on them.' Lila makes sure that her emails are filled with things Isabel is doing. She even scans in pictures she has drawn so I can see them.

'I'm sure Wednesday nights must be a little bittersweet.'

'Bittersweet?' I say.

'Like happy and sad at the same time.'

'That's a good word,' I say, because that's exactly how I feel when I read Lila's email. I'm happy that Lila is so nice to Isabel, that she loves her so much, but I'm Isabel's mum. I want to buy her pink butterfly shoes.

Still, I love Lila for keeping me up to date with everything that Isabel is doing. If she hadn't agreed to take her when I was sent to prison she would have landed up in the foster system. Some other women here have children in the foster system. Heather has two children living with 'a complete bitch'. I wouldn't have wanted that to happen to Isabel.

'When you're in the system, your kids are in the system too,' said Jess when she told me about her daughters. 'You're bloody lucky your sister can take care of Isabel. I haven't got a soul in the world that my kids could have gone to, especially not their piece-of-crap father.'

There was no way I was letting my mother take care of Isabel, and I don't think she wanted to do it either. Lila has had to stop working so hard so that she can be there for Isabel, but she hasn't complained about that at all. She loves Isabel. Isabel is smart like Lila. They have the same blonde hair and blue eyes even though Isabel is my baby.

I don't think Lila will ever have kids. She's too important to her company. They fly her all over the world to open new shopping centres and they pay her lots and lots of money. She lives in a unit but it has three bedrooms and a pool downstairs. Isabel loves the pool because it is always warm.

Lila paid for Lucy when I had to go to court. Lucy worked very hard to get me out of the other place and to the Farm. She called the other place nearly every day. Allison told me that when I came here. 'Don't mess this up,' Allison said. 'You don't want all that work your lawyer did to go to waste. It's a privilege to be allowed to serve your last few months at the Farm—remember that.'

That's what we call it, the Farm, like that might make us forget what it really is. Still, it's better than real prison. And the best thing about it, the very best thing, is that once a month Isabel is allowed to come up and spend the weekend with me. I cross the days off on my calendar every night until the day she comes. The calendar is one I got free from the newspaper. It has pictures of baby animals on it. Isabel has named them all. Last month's baby animal was a tiger. She named it Billy.

In just one week I get to see Isabel for two whole nights and nearly two days. When she wraps her little arms around me we could be at the top of the Eiffel Tower or we could be on the beach. We could be anywhere. Lila has been to France and Mexico and Rio and England. She brings back lots of pictures for me and Isabel to look at, and one day she will take us both with her.

I hate being away from Isabel. She's in her kindergarten year at school and I know that every single day she is learning something new. Last month she wrote me a card that said *Miss you, Mum*, and she had covered the rest of the page with *x*'s. When I went into the other place she couldn't write her name. Kids change so quickly, you have to watch them all the time or you'll miss it. I'm missing so much. One day she will be smarter than me. Lila told me that she's already at the top of her class. Nothing makes my body feel peaceful and my heart feel warm like stories about Isabel. Before I was locked up I would count the hours until the end of my workday so that I could go home and be with her. I could watch her for hours, I didn't need to do anything else. I would watch her and I would feel filled with joy. That's how Isabel makes me feel—filled with joy.

Mum didn't want me to have her. 'Who do you think is going to land up taking care of the child?' she said to Lila on the phone. She thought I was asleep but I wasn't. 'Don't you think I've had a hard enough time? I know what it's like to have to raise children alone. Your father ran off and started a whole new life and we never heard from him again. This man doesn't want anything to do with the baby. I'm the one left to pick up the pieces, as usual.'

I didn't know what pieces Mum was talking about. There were no pieces, just me and a baby growing inside me.

'And what if the baby is like her? What if I have to take care of both of them? She hasn't thought this through, because she can't think it through, and you're not helping by telling her to do whatever she wants.'

I wanted to get out of bed and shout at Mum that my baby wouldn't be like me. My baby would be clever like her and Lila. I knew it would.

Lila shouted at Mum for me. Even though I was lying in bed and Lila was on the phone I could hear her because she was so loud. I didn't know what she was saying but she was very angry.

'Don't you dare call me selfish, Lila Grace,' said Mum. 'You want her to have this child, fine. I'll be here, but you need to help us with money. God knows you have enough of it.'

Lila has always helped me. When she knew about Isabel growing inside me she said, 'Tell me what you want to do.'

'I want to have a baby,' I said, and she said, 'Okay then.'

'Birdy, I feel like you're not with me today,' says Henrietta, and I remind myself to pay attention.

'Do you know that Rose Winslow came here yesterday?' I say to Henrietta, because I have nothing else I want to discuss with her. I have to be careful what I say to Henrietta. She doesn't have to know that Rose Winslow is just about the only thing I can think about right now. I ask her the question like I don't care about the answer, like it's something I just read in a magazine, but Henrietta is clever. She sits forward and puts her hands together, and I know that means she thinks she's onto something.

She did the same thing when I talked about how my father used to read to me every night at bedtime. I told her that he used to lie next to me on the bed, and she sat forward and said, 'And did he do anything else except read to you?' I laughed at her. I couldn't help it. 'No,' I said. 'He just read to me and then he kissed me goodnight and left.'

'She sees paedophiles under every rock,' said Jess about Henrietta. Then I had to ask Jess what that word meant. I didn't know there was a word for it.

When I laughed at Henrietta about my dad she was disappointed. She really thought she was onto something.

'I do know that she's been brought here—yes,' says Henrietta.

'Is she going to be seeing you?'

'You know I can't discuss that, Birdy. Even in prison, people are entitled to their privacy.'

'Do you think she meant to do it?'

'The jury in her trial seemed to think so. Why are you so concerned about Rose Winslow?'

'It's just interesting, that's all. You asked me how my week has been and that's how it's been. I looked after the birds and did my laundry and worried about Isabel and someone new arrived.'

'Someone new arrives here just about every week. Why are you so interested in Rose Winslow?'

I shrug. 'It's just interesting because she's, you know, famous.' I hope Henrietta can't hear the bubbling in my stomach. I can hear it.

'Are the others talking about her a lot?'

I shrug again and Henrietta sits back and sighs. I have irritated her.

'I spoke to your mother yesterday,' says Henrietta.

'I don't want to talk about that. I asked you not to contact her.' I asked her not to but I know that because I'm in prison she can do whatever she wants to do. Henrietta is allowed to speak to other people about me if she thinks it will help 'open up communication'.

'I know, but I feel that we would be able to move forward if you could just be open to a discussion with her or even to discussing with me what actually happened—and why it happened. I know you told your other therapist that you just got angry and that you were tired, but I think there's more to it than that.'

'There's no more,' I say. 'You can say it again and again but there is still no more to it.'

'And so I will continue to say, Birdy. People don't just hit for no reason. There was a reason, and if you can share it with me we can work through what happened and make sure that it never happens again. You don't have much time left here. Don't you want to go back out into the world healthy and healed?'

'Oh, fuck you, Henrietta,' I say, and then I stand up and open the door and walk out of my therapy session. I don't use that word often. I never used it before I got locked up. It is an electric word. It shocks people. It's the perfect word when you feel hate. I shouldn't have used it to Henrietta, but I could feel her trying to get me to tell her my secrets.

I've only said that word to Henrietta twice and I know that I can't get away with saying it too often, but Henrietta likes me to feel that I can decide when I want to talk to her. I didn't want to talk to her today. I can't stand her talking about me getting healthy. She is so pretty and so clever and she has a big diamond ring on her finger. It must be easy to be healthy if you have all that. She wants me to be healthy in my mind and healthy in my body, but I can't be healthy, not when I have to keep the secret of my bubbling anger and my agenda.

All I really want is to find out where Rose Winslow is going to spend her days. She's pretty smart so maybe she'll choose the library, but if she's still like I remember her she'll want to be in the garden. She was always in the garden—the front garden where all the beautiful flowers were.

One day I counted twenty-five different colours. I didn't count them alone—she helped me. I didn't count very well then. She used to wear a large straw hat with plastic flowers on it, and even though he used to laugh at her for it she kept on wearing it. 'I need to protect my skin,' she would tell him, and then she would smile. She never got angry with him no matter what he said or did. Never ever.

It's time to go back to my unit for breakfast but today I am not feeling hungry. I don't like seeing Henrietta so early in the morning. Talking to Henrietta makes me feel like I have something in my throat, and it makes me feel tired. I would like to go back to bed but it is time for breakfast and work. I don't go back to my unit. I go to the gardens instead in case Rose is already there. The gardens are empty.

'Fuck,' I say, because there's no one to hear me. Allison doesn't like us to swear. If Henrietta tells her what I said, Allison will give me a long lecture on behaving appropriately. Appropriately means correctly. I always behave appropriately. I don't do anything I shouldn't do but sometimes when the bubbling anger comes I worry that I will not behave appropriately. The bubbling anger makes me afraid of myself. I want it to stop.

Everyone is still having breakfast. I go back to my unit, where Jess has made toast and tea. We use white bread but it is cut so thin you feel like you are eating air. Jess and I sit on the veranda and I eat and eat while Jess gets through two cigarettes. When I swallow the toast it feels like it will get stuck but it goes down so I keep putting more into my mouth. I don't know why Jess doesn't get hungry. She only eats one piece of toast to my four.

'You're going to be sorry later,' I say to her when she has pulled off all her crusts.

'I'll just have another ciggie.'

'Have you got enough to get through until canteen?'

'Just. I'll have to slow down tomorrow.'

I don't smoke but almost everyone else does. Cigarettes are expensive but lots of the women here would rather go without food than without cigarettes. I understand that. Lighting up your own cigarette and taking your own sweet time to smoke it must feel like a little bit of freedom and space every time. I tried to smoke but it made me cough and then my eyes watered and Jess laughed at me.

After breakfast I go into my bedroom and have three small bites of my Mars bar. I hold them in my cheeks until they have just about disappeared. Isabel does that with her chocolate as well.

I go back out onto the veranda to wait for muster.

'That dickhead is on today,' says Jess. She's talking about Malcolm, who is only rostered on to work when one of the other guards is sick.

'Just ignore him,' I say, and then I move aside for Maya and Mina so that we can all be on the veranda. That's what Lila always told me to do when people at school said nasty things to me: 'Just ignore them.'

If Lila was there no one said anything. Lila would shout at them and say clever things and the boys wouldn't know what to say to her. 'Just ignore them,' Lila told me. You can ignore some things. You can't ignore everything.

We can see Malcolm walking slowly past the units, checking everyone off and talking all the time.

'Malcolm likes to think he's charming, but he's just an arsehole,' says Jess. 'He doesn't like it if whoever he talks to doesn't smile and giggle at the stupid things he says. He's such a dick.'

I've told Jess that I can make a complaint to Allison if she wants me to. We are allowed to make complaints if we think something is unfair. Malcolm being a dick is unfair, I think. I smile at him anyway. He has a nice smile. 'Don't rock the boat, Birdy,' Jess said when I told her I would complain. 'He's only here every now and again. Neither you nor I need to muck up now. One day I may see him out in the real world and then I'll let him know what we all thought of him.'

'Well, if it isn't the lovely ladies of unit seven,' says Malcolm, stopping to mark us off. 'Jess, you're looking stunning today. I can see you've really gone all out with that flannel shirt and those cute pants.'

Jess gives Malcolm a smile with thin lips. He knows we don't choose our clothes.

'Hey, Birdy, Birdy, tweet, tweet,' he says to me. I also smile.

He just nods at Mina and Maya and then he walks off. We know he will spend the most time at unit six where Paula is. 'He's screwing that girl and make no mistake,' says Jess as we watch Malcolm lean over the railings of the veranda at unit six.

'He'll get fired if they catch him,' I say. The guards aren't allowed to be friends with the prisoners. That's in the book of rules we all got. Allison helped me read through it.

'People like him don't get caught. Only people like us,' says Jess. 'Come on, off to work for us.'

I want to ask Jess if anyone new will be joining us in the gardens, but I can't think of a way to ask her so that she won't ask me why I want to know, so I chew my fingernail instead.

'Nothing left to chew, I would imagine,' says Jess quietly as we make our way towards the gardens.

'Sorry,' I say.

'Not my fingernails,' says Jess.

I walk over to the finch cages to get the water dishes. They need a good clean. Mould is beginning to build up on the edges. Mould is bad for finches.

I'm coming out of the cage holding the first one when I see her. Jess is explaining the gardens to her and she's nodding. She looks smaller than I remember her, but I suppose that's what happens when you grow up. When I was a child I thought she was perfect. I thought she could solve every problem I had, and that's probably why I'm angrier at her than at anyone else.

She could have helped me if she wanted to.

She could have saved me if she wanted to.

Chapter Six

The gardens here are obviously not really gardens. They are large, overgrown, scruffy vegetable patches. They grow everything from potatoes to corn, and I'm told it's all used by the cooking school or sold back to inmates through the canteen.

This morning I shared a nearly silent breakfast of tasteless cereal with Heather and Sal and Linda. Linda takes a long time to eat. She takes a long time to do anything. Halfway through her breakfast she spent a minute just staring into space.

'Linda, you'll be late,' said Sal.

Linda started and went back to eating.

'She's fried her brain,' said Sal when Linda left to go to the bathroom. 'This is the third time she's been in prison.

I think they're hoping that some time at the Farm will help her do better when she gets out. But nothing will help her. I think she'll just land up in prison again.'

'Poor thing,' I said, and Sal shrugged her shoulders.

'It's too late for her. It was probably too late after her first hit of ice.'

'How long has she been like this?'

'I don't know her from before, but she's only twenty-eight and she says she tried dope at ten, so she's been high for most of her life, I think.'

'At ten? How awful for her. What must her home life have been like?'

'Everyone's got their own sad childhood story,' said Sal and then she looked at me. 'Well, maybe not everyone.'

I'm acutely conscious of my difference to the women I am sharing a unit with. Regardless of what I've done or not done, most of my life has been lived worlds away from theirs.

This morning before she took me to the gardens, Allison gave me a password for the computer, which we're allowed to use once a day for twenty minutes. Simon never liked email, but I used to enjoy keeping in touch with old friends over the internet. I haven't emailed anyone for many months now. What on earth would I have said?

'Nothing compares to pen and paper, my dear. When you write you are connected with the words in a way that you never can be when you type,' Simon always said when I offered to teach him how to navigate his way around the computer. He had a computer himself but told me he merely kept it 'for the look of the thing'. 'I never go on it if I can help it. I'm not interested in what some child celebrity had for breakfast.' His computer is still in his study. I would like to check that it has no personal information on it and then throw it away, but I'm almost afraid of what it may contain. It's possible that he was an expert at using the computer but didn't want me to know, that he sat in his study all day long navigating his way through some sordid underworld. I now know that when it comes to Simon, absolutely anything is possible. Some days I shake my head at how many questions I have for him now, at how many truths I would demand were it not too late.

He used to write letters to the girls when we went away without them. Long, rambling missives about the colour of the ocean and the taste of the wine. I think it broke his heart a little when they did not reply in kind. I tried to get them to write to him, but Portia always scoffed at the idea—'As if I have the bloody time'—and Rosalind promised to do it but never got around to it. 'They are children of a modern age,' I consoled Simon.

People don't expect much from an email; they're happy with a few lines about your family and then they return a few lines about theirs. It helps you feel you are still in touch when in reality, I suppose, you're not in touch at all. I haven't heard from a lot of people this year—not even over email. Now it brings a smile to my face to think of typing *Hello from prison* to the ladies I used to lunch with.

The horrible wrong turn my life has taken must be the topic of every lunch date and dinner party in the country, especially those hosted by my 'friends'.

I find it remarkable that I'm still here, still living, that I have thus far survived all this. When the rumours about Simon first began I thought that I wouldn't be able to bear the awful humiliation of people speaking about me, discussing me and dissecting my life. I had little idea of what was to come. Now I know, sadly, that I can survive a great deal more than vicious gossip. Well, I have had to survive it. I have not consciously decided or made a choice about anything that has happened over the last eighteen months. I've simply held on as one would to a bolting horse.

Here at the Farm there is a central room with ten computers in it, and one of the guards walks around and around reading over everyone's shoulders. There are no secrets in prison. Depriving someone of their freedom is supposed to be the goal here, but I think the greater punishment is the lack of privacy.

'You can only access email,' said Allison. 'Everything else is locked, and it's only unlocked for those studying for things like their HSC.'

I hope that I will manage to get onto a computer tonight. I really want to let the girls know that I'm all right. I fret about them worrying about me. I would also like to know if Eric's had any luck with the appeal. It's inconceivable to me that I will have to stay here for three years. I am unable to conceive of it.

As Allison walked me to the gardens I noticed one or two heads turn, but I get the feeling that every new arrival is scrutinised the same way. I'm sure everyone eventually blends in together in their ugly shirts and baggy pants, and that is, obviously, the idea. I prefer it that way. I want to blend in and just be left alone. Since it happened I don't feel like I've been alone for a minute. In the weeks before I came here, either Portia or Rosalind was with me constantly, even at night. And the press were, of course, camped outside my house. No matter how many times they were told 'no comment' or simply ignored, they never gave up. They are tenacious individuals. I have to admire them for it.

'You mustn't even make eye contact with them,' Eric said when we discussed what to do about them. Every day when we left court, Eric would wrap his arms around me and guide me through the waiting throng. Robert would hold up his briefcase and almost use it as a battering ram to push his way through, and the girls would follow. We tried leaving by the back door, but journalists aren't stupid. They were there as well. I kept my head down and watched my feet. I understand their interest. If it had not been my face in the paper and on every television channel, I'm sure I would have been fascinated by the story as well.

'Just ignore them, Mother, and do what you want to do,' said Portia when we discussed the ones who had taken up residence outside my home. I suppose I should have just carried on as before, but it was daunting. The few times I did brave an outing I almost ran over one or two of them.

The women were the worst. They were so aggressive and seemed to have no concern for their own safety. They would leap behind the car when they saw the garage door opening and wait for me to practically nudge them before they got out of the way.

It is quite restful to be free of them. Now, of course, I am under an entirely different sort of scrutiny.

I was woken at some ungodly hour this morning to be counted again. Before I opened my eyes I had my regular few moments of peace before my life came crashing in. Those moments are the cruellest of all. For the last year I have woken and stretched and wondered why the aroma of percolating coffee was not drifting through the house. In all the years that Simon and I were married, he got up every morning to make me coffee. At first when we had little money it was just instant coffee, but our tastes changed with our income and status, and the machines we used to produce our morning beverage became more and more expensive. Despite the fact that everything was now automatic and only one button needed to be pushed, Simon would still get up early and make sure that my coffee was waiting for me.

'Good morning, my beautiful girl,' he would say, placing the cup next to the bed. When the girls were babies he would also bring me a wet and frantic bundle to feed and change, so I had to get up anyway. When Lottie and Sam were small, Rosalind used to yell at Jack for not understanding what it took to take care of a baby, but

I never expected anything from Simon. The babies were my job and I never questioned that.

'You don't have to do this anymore,' I told him a couple of years ago, because I wanted him to rest more.

'But darling girl, it is what I have always done,' he said.

Lately at home I had been drinking tea.

'Muster!' shouted Sal from the living room at six o'clock this morning, and I leapt out of bed with a dry mouth and shaking hands. There was no coffee smell and no Simon. I felt the familiar fist of grief and shook my head and lifted my chin. *Day one*, I thought.

'You got through your first night okay?' said Allison as we walked to the gardens.

'I did,' I said. 'Heather and Sal are—'

'Are not your friends. I don't want to sound harsh, but you should remember that. Getting close can lead to complications, and you all have to go your separate ways soon enough.'

'I understand,' I said.

There are quite a few women who tend the vegetables. Today I met Jess, who has close-cropped grey hair and the wrinkled face of a serious smoker. She also has that terrible smell about her that I've noticed on other smokers. She is friendly enough but very bossy. I think she's in charge, even though there are some other women who look a great deal more formidable than she does.

Still, I'm happy to get my hands back in the soil and I don't mind taking instructions from Jess, as she seems to really know what she's doing. She introduced me to Mina, who looks about sixteen but apparently is twenty-five, and Dana, who looks about Portia's age. I feel like I'm the oldest person in this place, and this feeling isn't helped by them all calling me Mrs Winslow.

'If Martha Stewart survived, you can too,' Portia said when we hugged goodbye before I was led away to prison. Rosalind didn't say anything. She didn't seem able to wrap her head around what had happened. She had assumed, we had all assumed, that my packed suitcase was a silly precaution at the sentencing.

'Probation,' said Eric when we discussed it.

'Or maybe home detention,' said Robert.

'You thought I wouldn't be found guilty,' I wanted to say but didn't.

'What on earth am I going to tell the children?' was the only thing Rosalind said.

'Oh good, Rosalind, give her something else to worry about,' said Portia.

'Now, girls,' said Eric. He has developed a habit lately of stepping in as Simon would have done. I don't think he knows he's doing it, but the girls responded as if their father had spoken.

I will miss my grandchildren most of all while I am here. Sam, at ten, seems to feel he is getting too big to spend time with his grandmother. Before all this happened he was already sighing and rolling his eyes whenever I said something he found ridiculous—like asking who 'Mario

Kart' was. He got on better with Simon, and I know he understands what I've done. I doubt he will ever forgive me. They used to play backgammon together. Simon was a patient teacher and he revelled in being beaten by Sam.

'Grandpa and I are going to turn the spare room into a model train room,' Sam told me on his last visit before Simon died.

'Really?' I said, feigning surprise. 'I didn't know that.'

'Well, it's not something girls are interested in. Lottie isn't allowed in unless I say so, and Grandpa says that I can choose the trains. They'll be replicas of real trains, not stuff for children. Grandpa has a book.'

I don't think Sam has directed more than two words to me in the last twelve months. I would like to have the chance to explain to him what happened, but I can't think how to do that without tarnishing his grandfather for him forever. I hope to have the time to win his love back. Simon does not have that luxury.

Lottie is only six and I don't think she really knows what's happened, or at least no more than Rosalind will allow her to know. I hope . . . I hope she does not know more than she should. Please God, let her not know more than she should.

'Has Lottie ever said anything about your father?' I asked Rosalind when we were in the middle of the trial.

'She misses him,' said Rosalind. 'I think she knows that he's dead but she still believes it's possible that he will be back from being dead.'

'Yes, but has she . . . did she . . .?'

'What, Mum?'

'Nothing. Never mind.'

Lottie plays on my mind all the time. She is so little, so innocent. I hope, I pray, that Simon was only ever a loving grandfather to her.

I believe Rosalind has decided to tell them both that I've gone away on a cruise. She'll get that past Lottie, but Sam spends all of his time on his computer. I have no doubt that he will find out the truth. I'm sure that children his age know more about the world than I ever did. Sam doesn't ask his parents questions anymore. He asks his computer. He did that when the allegations about Simon first appeared, and Rosalind and Jack had to try to explain what was being said. There will be snide remarks at school as well, I'm sure, as there have been for many months. I hope it dies down quickly. This generation is supposed to lose interest as soon as the story disappears from the headlines. I hope that Sam will soon be allowed to go back to being a ten-year-old boy and cease being the grandson of a criminal.

I wonder if it is easier to deal with your grandmother being accused and convicted of manslaughter or with your grandfather being accused of being a predator. If Simon was still alive and the investigation had begun, would Sam have turned against him? Would we all have turned against him? It's easy to flippantly remark that a person would rather lose their life than their reputation, but what if their reputation *was* their life? What would the answer be then? Would I have expressed indignation to police when they came to question him? Would I have held his hand to steady him as we walked into court, if things had gone that far? Would he even have survived being formally charged? His heart was strong, but his blood pressure gave him headaches in times of high stress. When it all began he would often retreat to the spare bedroom and lie in the dark waiting for his body to calm down.

'If you could just leave me be for a moment, my dear,' he would say.

'What can I bring you?' I asked. 'How can I help?'

'Oh, Rose dear, there's little you can do. Time will help. That's all.'

It was easy enough for all of us to discredit the first woman to come forward. Easy enough. She was an out-of-work actress desperate for a second chance at fame. The article appeared in a popular women's magazine and we only found out about it when Eric came over with the thing clutched in his hand.

'Have you seen this?' he said to me when I opened the door. He was dressed in his suit from the office with his tie straight and his shoes shined. He sounded agitated but appeared perfectly calm.

'What's that?' I said as he waved the magazine at me before even coming into the house.

'It's an article, it mentions Simon. Patricia read it at the hairdresser. Has anyone contacted you for comment? Has anyone contacted Simon?'

Simon came into the front hall holding the newspaper. His glasses had slipped down to the end of his nose and his slippers made a shuffling noise on the polished floors. He'd been doing the crossword. 'Rose, I have no idea what twenty-four down is. Do you know—Oh, hello, Eric. Have you come for an early drink? How nice.'

'No, Simon, I came to show you, to show both of you this.' Eric held up the magazine open to the page with the article.

'Who is that?' I asked Simon, feeling a slight twist in my stomach.

'I have absolutely no idea,' said Simon, glancing back at his crossword.

A woman was pictured curled up in an armchair with her hair falling over her shoulders in artificial waves. Her lips pouted and her eyes shone with unshed tears. In the article she talked about her financial troubles and how awful it was to find herself unemployed after all her years in the industry.

I had a wonderful career after being discovered on the talent show, but now it seems that the industry is only interested in young women with perfect bodies. Men never have that problem. Men are told they look distinguished. They can get work at any age.

'I have no idea what any of this has to do with me,' said Simon.

'Just read it to the end,' said Eric.

Simon held the magazine a little away from himself so that I could read at the same time. Her allegations about

Simon were almost a footnote. They seemed like something thrown in at the end.

'What a preposterous thing to say,' said Simon. 'I have
no idea who this is. I never met her. How can she say such
things about me?'

'She says she was on the show, Simon,' said Eric. 'I've put
in a call to the station so that they can check their records,
which I'm hoping they still have filed away somewhere.
Are you telling me that you had no idea this article was
coming out? Has no one called you to discuss it?'

*I have come across the worst type of men in this industry.
I met Simon Winslow when I was a child, and his behaviour
would now be called assault and he would be charged. Back
then he just got away with it. We all wanted to be famous.*

'Eric, we haven't heard anything about this,' I said.
'And she's not really saying anything, it's very vague. What
does she mean by assault?' I was irritated to have had my
afternoon interrupted with such silliness. I wanted to berate
Eric for bothering Simon when I liked him to remain calm.

'I know, but if they printed it she must have said a great
deal more to them.'

'We will sue,' said Simon looking at the article again.
His face was pale but I could see his ears turning red. 'Tell
me you will sue, Eric. People cannot be allowed to do this.
How can she make some vague accusation and expect to
get away with it?'

'I'll get hold of their legal department. I wanted to make
sure you hadn't heard from anyone before I did anything.

Don't worry, Simon, I'll sort it all out.' Eric grabbed the magazine and turned to go.

'What do we do?' I said. I still thought the whole thing ridiculous even as I asked the question.

'Do nothing. Do not talk to anyone who calls who may be in the media. If you find yourself involved in a conversation, just say "no comment". Try not to get into a discussion. Don't feel you have to defend yourself, just put down the phone. Leave this to me.'

'I think I need a stiff drink, my dear,' said Simon when Eric had gone. That was, perhaps, the first clue that the whole situation was not just something that would disappear with the next edition of the magazine. I should have tried to talk to him then but I left him to it.

'I'll call the girls. I think I need to warn them, don't you? Just in case someone says something?'

'Yes, perhaps that would be wise.'

And that was the end of the discussion between me and Simon. I understood immediately that it wasn't true. It was impossible for it to be true. Impossible.

'How could she not know?' they have asked about me in magazines and the newspaper. How could I not know? I want the answer to that as well but it was not something I thought to look for. How could it be?

'Would you want to know?' I would like to ask all these people with these firm opinions. 'Would you want to know that about someone you love?'

'Jealous bitch,' said Portia after she'd read the article.

'A complete lunatic,' agreed Rosalind.

'Why would anyone want to say such a thing about me?' said Simon.

We were, as a family, quite stunned, but determined. We were not going to let some awful woman tarnish his reputation with scandalous lies. Before now Simon had only ever been spoken of in glowing terms. In his entire career there had never been a bad article about him. Everyone who had worked with him described him as 'delightful' and 'charismatic'. Women described him as 'sexy'. He had been in the television industry for years and nothing negative had ever been said about him. Until now.

The magazine had only just come out that day. By the evening, Simon and I were both fielding calls on our mobile phones and the home phone.

Our friends were unanimous in their support.

'Shameful woman,' said Patricia when she called.

'Awful, jealous creature,' said Roxanne, who was part of my walking group.

'She should be ashamed of herself,' said Becca and Joan and Alice and all the others. Everyone we knew was absolutely certain that either the woman had made some ghastly mistake and assumed someone else was Simon, or that she was simply a vindictive liar.

The press did call and we followed Eric's instructions, eventually turning off our phones to get some peace. Eric released a statement to the press vehemently denying the woman's accusations and announcing our intention to sue her and the magazine for printing such lies. As a family we held up our heads and got on with our lives.

That was the first article, the first mention of any impropriety. The first article was easy to ignore and the furore died down quickly enough. What happened next was not so easily dismissed.

When I think about my concerns over the years they seem ludicrous to me now. I worried all the time about him having an affair. He was a devoted husband and never gave me a reason to doubt him, but he was a beautiful man in an industry filled with beautiful women. I had always feared that he would be drawn to another woman. It never even occurred to me to question his behaviour with children. Men who prey on children jump out of the bushes and steal them away to hurt them. Simon was not a predator. To accuse him of being such a man was, at the time, almost laughable.

'You shouldn't let it bother you,' I told him whenever he brought up the article over the next few weeks. I was always mindful of his health. He had already begun to stoop a little when he walked, and he was on medication for his blood pressure.

I had always been worried about him dying and leaving me alone to live out the rest of my life, but I understood that it was inevitable because of the difference in our ages. Sixteen years did not seem so much when I was fifteen and he was thirty-one, but once he turned seventy the age gap became more apparent to me. I still felt like I had so many things I wanted to do but Simon was ready to slow down.

'You want to make sure you get those seeds in quickly,' says Jess, pulling me back to what I'm supposed to be doing.

'Were you involved in this sort of thing before ... before . . . ?' I stutter as I try to find the words, struggling to bring myself back to the present with inane conversation.

'Before I came here? Yes, I was. I worked at a nursery. I've always preferred plants to people. People will give you crap, but plants just need a little love and attention and they'll grow for you.'

'You're right about that,' I say. 'I used to spend as much time in my garden as I could.'

'And you will again.'

'I don't know about that,' I say. 'I think when I do leave here I might want to sell the house, maybe live somewhere else.'

'Wish I had a house to sell.'

'Oh, I'm sorry, I'm just nattering on.'

'Don't worry about it,' says Jess. 'Why don't you come with me and I'll introduce you to Birdy.'

'Birdy?'

'Yeah, she's the last of the garden girls, although she doesn't spend much time here. She takes care of the finches in the aviary.'

'My husband used to have finches. We had a big aviary built at the bottom of the garden. I never liked them, but he seemed to find them calming. He could watch them for hours.' I bite down on my lip so I stop talking.

'I don't understand it myself. All they do is eat and fly around and shit everywhere, but Birdy likes them.'

'Is that her real name?'

'No, but don't call her anything but Birdy. She's pretty firm about that.'

I walk over with Jess to the large rectangular cages at the back near the shed. There are three of them butting up against one another to create one long cage. Jess and I walk in silence, listening to the gentle clink of the keys hooked onto her jeans. Everything here is locked up tight. I had to sign out a small hand spade. It feels like I'm back at school.

'Birdy, can you come and meet Mrs Winslow,' says Jess into the cage.

I can't see anyone at first, but then I tilt my hat forward and make out a large woman in the shadows. Her top is dotted with bird droppings but she doesn't seem to mind that. She angles herself out of the cage, still watching the little finches, who fly around hysterically as soon as she moves.

'Hello, Birdy,' I say, and the woman nods at me. Her thick black hair is tied up and is also dotted with the white leavings of the small birds. *She should be wearing a hat*, I think. The woman doesn't say anything once she is out of the cage. 'You have such lovely eyes,' I say, staring at the dark chocolate colour with flecks of green. I made a decision after breakfast that I would try to get on the good side of the women that I am to be spending I don't know how long with. I've been handing out compliments left and right.

'You have such beautiful nails,' to Jess.

'I like your hair colour,' to Sal.

'You're being so kind,' to Heather.

I didn't have to think when I looked at Birdy.

'So you take care of the finches,' I say when she doesn't reply. 'My husband had finches.'

'He did,' she says. 'I mean, did he?'

'Yes, he liked to watch them for hours. I didn't see much of them. They were in a large cage at the back of the garden, almost around a corner, behind the shed.' I stop talking. Birdy is watching me with her beautiful eyes. I shut my mouth firmly. I have a habit of speaking too much when I'm nervous. At every party Simon and I went to I would spend half the night in complete silence and the other half talking someone's ear off about my garden or my children. I always felt so unaccomplished when I was with other people in the entertainment industry. The women were so flawless that they looked plastic, and the men would quickly look me up and down, decide I wasn't worth talking to and simply ignore me.

'You mustn't let them upset you, darling girl,' Simon said whenever I told him what a horrible time I'd had. 'They don't know how wonderful you are, how special you are. You're my secret and I'm happy to keep it so. I wouldn't want you running off with someone from a rival network.'

'As if that could ever happen,' I said.

'What kind of finches do you have in here?' I ask Birdy. She's staring at me as though waiting for me to say something.

'Zebra and Gouldian,' she says.

I want to say something about the birds, but despite Simon going on and on about them I don't seem to have retained any information at all. He had shelves full of books on how to raise them and breed them. I couldn't fathom his interest in them.

'They are part of nature, my dear—they do not ruminate on their lives, they live them. All they care about is that they have enough food and clean water. It's peaceful to watch them moving happily from place to place, concerned only with a dip in the birdbath on a hot day.'

'I have lots of books on finches,' I say to Birdy.

'Enough chatting,' says Jess. 'Mrs Winslow, can you—'

'Call me Rose, please. Everyone should call me Rose.'

'Rose, can you help Mina with the weeding for a bit?'

'Of course.' I'm grateful to leave Birdy with her finches. Her silence is disconcerting.

Jess walks me over to Mina. 'Birdy's a bit special, Rose,' she says.

'Special?'

'She's not stupid,' Jess adds defensively. 'She's just not as quick as most people.'

'I'll remember that when I speak to her,' I say, and Jess nods and leaves me to get on with the weeding.

'You work over there,' says Mina, and I obligingly move a little further away from her. I can see that Mina isn't interested in having a conversation.

Jess uses the word 'special' to describe Birdy. Portia and Rosalind use the word as well when discussing some of the children Portia works with. Simon always said 'retarded', but people don't like that word anymore. I dig into the soil and try to remember if I've ever known anyone to whom the term 'special' applies. I think not.

Chapter Seven

She doesn't know me at all. That's okay. That suits me. I wouldn't want her to recognise me anyway. Not until it's time. Not until it's the end.

She looks the same even after all these years. Her hands are wrinkled but she is still the same. I'm the one who's different. He made me different and then I made me different. Sometimes I wonder who I would have been if I had never met him, but that's a funny thing to think. It's like thinking about who I would be if I didn't have Isabel or if I was clever like Lila. I can't think about that, because things are the way they are.

I watch her walk back to the vegetables with Jess and I put my hands in my pockets so that I won't do anything to let her know what my agenda is. She used to make toasted cheese sandwiches for lunch and put pickles and salty chips on the side. She would cut the sandwiches into perfect triangles. It was like being in a restaurant. Sometimes she would pour a glass of Coke and add a straw and an umbrella.

They moved in next door to us when I was four. Mum told me that. I was four and Rosalind was six and she liked to play with me because she thought I was cute. She didn't care if I was smart or not, because I was smart enough to do everything she wanted me to do. She was the mummy and I was the baby and I would listen to her when she read me a story. Sometimes she was the teacher and I had to write the letter A, but I wasn't very good at that. 'What's wrong with you?' Rosalind would ask.

'My mum says that,' I told her.

'Hello there,' he said the first time he saw me. Mum took me next door so we could introduce ourselves. Lila was asleep and Dad was in charge of taking care of her. Mum baked a chocolate cake and she put it on a pretty glass plate. I didn't want to go and say hello. I didn't like strangers, but I wanted a piece of the chocolate cake.

I was holding onto Mum's leg when he opened the door. He crouched down and looked at me. 'Hello there,' he said. I had never met a stranger who crouched down to talk to me. I didn't know what to say. I was shy. His eyes looked at me. They were dark, dark blue. I liked him right away.

'Your eyes look like my blue paint,' I said.

'Oh, Felicity, don't be silly,' said Mum.

'I don't think that's silly. Hello, Felicity, I'm Simon Winslow, nice to meet you.'

'Say hello to Mr Winslow, Fliss,' said Mum.

'Hello,' I said, because I knew how to be polite. Mum had told me over and over again how to be polite.

'Rose darling, the new neighbours have come to say hello,' he said, standing up.

'Oh, how lovely,' we heard someone say, and then she was there.

Mum and Rose had tea in the kitchen and Rosalind took me to show me her room. 'You're a baby,' she said to me. 'Don't touch anything.' I put my hands behind my back so I wouldn't touch. 'Sit down,' said Rosalind, pointing to a small pink chair. I sat down. 'Hold this,' she said, handing me a doll to hold. I held the doll. Rosalind smiled.

'Looks like you two will be great friends,' he said. I turned around. I didn't know he was standing at the door to her room. I didn't know he was watching us. I didn't know.

Mum liked me to go over there. If Lila had her nap and Mum wanted to nap too she would say, 'Go next door and see if Rosalind is home.' Or if she was cooking and I wanted to help and she wanted me to go out of the kitchen, she would say, 'Go and play with Rosalind.'

I liked playing with Rosalind but I didn't always like it. Rosalind was very bossy. Sometimes I said no and I didn't go. Sometimes I hid under the stairs and stroked Mum's lonely pet coat. But when I was five I always went when she told me to go.

Five was a bad year. When I was five I wanted to run away from everything, but I didn't know how. I wasn't allowed to cross the street. Five was a sad year. It was the year everything went wrong. Everything changed. Everyone changed.

It's funny the stuff that gets stuck in your brain even when you don't want it to. I remember the way my dad smelled. I remember the way he used to light a cigarette and breathe deep and then say, 'This will kill me one day,' and then cough. He made burnt scrambled eggs on cold toast on Sundays.

He didn't care about how smart I was. 'I will read to you for the rest of your life,' he told me. He used to lie on my bed at night and read me a story. Then he would say, 'Mum's turn,' and Mum would come in to say the poem. The poem was called 'Adventures of Isabel' by Ogden Nash. It's my favourite poem in the whole world. It's also Isabel's favourite poem. It's about Isabel, who is not afraid. She's not afraid of a bear, she's not afraid of a witch, she's not afraid of a giant, and she's not afraid of a doctor. Isabel is brave and she doesn't worry. I wanted to be Isabel. I wanted to be brave.

'What about something different?' Mum would say every night, but I needed to hear the poem over and over again. I needed to hear it so that it wouldn't escape out of the open door in my brain. I needed to remember it. I knew that if I could remember the poem then I could be brave like Isabel and then it wouldn't matter that

I couldn't tie my shoes or sing the alphabet song or make the scissors cut along the line, because I would be brave. Being brave was better than colouring inside the lines or drawing a circle.

'No, I want "Isabel",' I would say.

'All right then,' Mum would say, and her voice was tired but she always smiled.

Isabel met an enormous bear,
Isabel, Isabel, didn't care;
The bear was hungry, the bear was ravenous,
The bear's big mouth was cruel and cavernous.
The bear said, Isabel, glad to meet you,
How do, Isabel, now I'll eat you!
Isabel, Isabel, didn't worry.
Isabel didn't scream or scurry.
She washed her hands and she straightened her hair up,
Then Isabel quietly ate the bear up.

'More, more,' I would say, and Mum would go to the end of the poem. I was always afraid for Isabel. I knew she would be safe but each time she met a horrible thing I would feel my arms get bumps and I would feel cold. I was excited and scared for Isabel, but she always won in the end. I would go to sleep and dream about being brave and strong even though I didn't always know my colours. But then I turned five and Dad left and Mum wouldn't tuck me in or read to me or say 'Isabel'. That was when I needed 'Isabel' the most, and I would go over the words I could remember but I kept forgetting them and it wasn't the same.

'Please, Mum,' I said every night, 'please do "Isabel",' but she wouldn't.

'Leave me alone,' she would say, 'just leave me alone.' I didn't know why she wanted to be left alone. She wasn't busy. She just sat on the couch and stared at the television. Stared and stared. Sometimes she didn't even have the sound on.

'Your mother had a difficult time when your father left,' said Emily the therapist. 'You need to forgive her and move on with your life.'

'I had a bad time too,' I said, but then I said, 'I forgive her.' I wanted to come to the Farm. Forgive your mum, forgive your dad, forgive yourself and you can go to the Farm. But I'm done with forgiving now.

When I learned to read at my new school when I was eight I found 'Isabel' in the school library and I stole the book to keep behind my chest of drawers with my special things in case the bloody bank came again, even though we lived in the shitbox.

When we still lived in the big house and Dad went away, Mum wasn't Mum anymore. She was mean. 'Just get out of my hair!' she would shout, and I would run away next door where there were toasted cheese triangles and music played all day.

Rose always smelled sweet like a flower. She let me watch her cooking in the kitchen. I wanted to ask if I could help, but Mum didn't like me to help so I thought maybe Rose wouldn't like me to help either.

'I think I might need more salt,' she would say when she was tasting the soup and then she would look at me, but I didn't know if she needed more salt so I didn't say anything.

'Maybe it's time to go back to Mum,' she said when I didn't know if the soup needed more salt.

'Mum says that I must get out of her hair,' I said.

She shook her head. 'Oh, sweetheart, Mum is just having a bad day. You can come over here when your mum has a bad day. Even if Rosalind isn't here you can always come over here.' Sometimes Rosalind wasn't there. She went to visit a friend or to ballet or to piano lessons.

I remember how her hands moved in the kitchen, quick, quick. I remember her voice and her smell, but she doesn't remember me.

Maybe Rosalind will visit her here and she will recognise me. Rosalind looked like she did. They were both pretty with brown hair and brown eyes. I didn't play with Rosalind's older sister Portia. She was nearly eight when they moved in. 'Get out of my room, babies,' she would say to me and Rosalind, and then she would shout, 'Mum, they're in my room again!', and Rosalind and I would run and hide from mean Portia.

In the beginning Rosalind would also come to my house. The whole family came over for dinner and everyone listened when he talked because he was famous.

Rosalind told me that her dad was famous and then she told me that famous meant that everyone knew who he was, not just the people who lived next door but everyone in the whole country. It was because he was on the television. Mum liked to watch him on the television. 'She's a lucky woman, that Rose Winslow,' Mum said every time she saw him on the TV.

Mum smiled at him all the time when he came to dinner, but Dad didn't like him at all. 'Completely up himself with that fake English accent, like he wasn't born here,' he said to Mum after they were gone.

'How do you know where he was born?' Mum said.

'I just know. My bullshit detector was beeping all night.' Dad talked about his bullshit detector a lot. When I was little I thought it sat behind his ear, but I could never find it. Now I know it was just something he felt.

'You're just jealous,' Mum said, and then there was talking and shouting and Lila woke up from the noise.

Portia doesn't look like her sister. Portia was always tall and beautiful like a princess. She looked like nothing could touch her or hurt her. Sometimes I wished I was her. Portia had blonde hair and blue eyes—deep blue like her dad's eyes. She is the most beautiful of them all. Or she was. She might not be anymore. Maybe she is fat like I am now. Maybe she has changed the colour of her hair.

I wonder if he changed who they were as well. I haven't seen them for so long that they could both be different. But Mrs Winslow is still the same even though she's older now. 'Rose' is still the same, even if her face has wrinkles. She said that we must call her Rose, but when I was little I always called her Mrs Winslow. I called him Mr Winslow.

'Hello, Mr Winslow,' I said when I came to their house. 'Goodbye, Mr Winslow,' I said when I went home again. But I couldn't say, 'Don't do that, Mr Winslow.' I couldn't say that.

Now I watch her working in the garden. She wears gloves and an old hat without flowers and she laughs at jokes that Jess and Mina make and she talks about silly things like recipes for cakes and how to clean a rug.

'Oh, Ellie, you're a wonderful baker,' she said whenever she had some cake that my Mum had made. Mum didn't like to bake cakes after Dad left. She didn't like to do anything.

I think that she has not changed at all. I can see her pretending that she is anywhere but here. She is good at pretending, good at ignoring things that are right in front of her.

A few times in the day she looks up from her digging and weeding and catches me looking at her and she smiles and gives me a little wave. Stupid woman. Stupid, stupid woman. I have to swallow and swallow to keep the bubbling anger down. Mina is using a big spade to dig in the garden. I close my eyes and see my hands grab the spade and I hit and hit and hit.

I used to wish she was my mother.

One morning I woke up and Dad was gone and Mum said, 'Your father has decided to live somewhere else.' I was five and I didn't understand but I didn't know how to ask the right questions. 'Where is he living?' I should have asked, but I couldn't think of how to say the words.

'He has decided that taking care of two little girls is too much for him.'

'I'm getting big,' I said.

'Oh, please just go away and leave me alone,' she said, and she lay on her bed and only got up to make peanut butter sandwiches. 'I want toasted cheese,' I said.

'Then make it yourself,' said Mum, but I didn't know how to do that.

Mum was angry and crying about Dad and she was angry and crying about me and then she was angry and crying about selling our big house and I didn't feel like I had a mother anymore. Quick as a strike of lightning everything changed at my house.

I went next door. Rosalind was playing with her own friends and she didn't want to see me, and Mrs Winslow was in the front garden. 'You can help me dig if you like, or you can go and ask Mr Winslow for something to drink.'

He was the only one inside the house. He was often home when I went there. He went to the TV studio in the morning but he came home in the afternoon. Sometimes he was home for the whole day. He didn't go to work like my dad went to work. My dad used to leave early in the morning and come home late, late at night. Sometimes

I didn't see him for days and days, so he couldn't read me a story.

'You have a responsibility to these children,' Mum would shout at him, and then he would be home in time to read me a story for a lot of nights.

'My mum is angry and crying,' I told Mr Winslow.

'Why is she angry and crying?' he said. He wasn't like other grown-ups. He didn't pretend he hadn't heard me and he didn't say, 'Oh, I'm sure she's not.' He asked why and then he listened when I told him that my dad didn't want two little girls anymore.

'Don't worry, little one. You can stay here until your mum feels better,' he said, and then he poured me some Coke and put a straw in the glass. He took me to his study. He let me sit on his lap. He stroked my hair. His stroking made me feel sleepy and nice.

'My daddy has gone away,' I told him again.

'I know he has, angel. I know he has.'

'Are you going away?'

'No,' he said. 'I will always be here. Daddies shouldn't leave their little girls.'

I looked up into his eyes, his blue, blue eyes, and I smiled.

He put his hands on my legs and I was happy to stay on his lap forever. He read his letters and he wrote things down but he let me stay on his lap. Daddy had never let me stay on his lap when he was busy. But Mr Winslow's hand stayed warm on my leg. I didn't mind that my dad had gone away then. I thought maybe he could be my dad.

'Whatever is going on?' said Mrs Winslow. She was standing at the door to his study.

'Oh, my dear,' he said, and I remember he said that because he always said that. 'My dear, it seems Albert has left his family. Ellie is feeling unwell. Perhaps you could go over and see her?'

'Come with me,' she said to me, and she held out her hand and I had to go back to my house where Mum was angry and crying.

'Oh, Ellie, this is just dreadful,' she said to Mum. 'Is there anything I can do for you, anything at all?'

'Nothing,' said Mum. 'There's nothing anyone can do. The bastard has just ruined my life.'

'Shall I feed the children so you can have a rest?' Mrs Winslow said.

'Yes,' said Mum. 'Yes, please.'

I helped her find the plates. 'What a good little helper you are,' Mrs Winslow said, but I knew she was lying. If I was really a good helper then Mum wouldn't be angry and crying and Dad wouldn't have gone away because he didn't want two little girls.

'Birdy, it's lunch,' shouts Jess. I'm still standing in the cage. Sometimes I forget where I am and I have to remember.

I open the door of the cage slowly so the finches will stay calm and I walk out. I see Rose take off her hat and laugh at Jess. Sometimes Jess is funny, but I don't want Rose to laugh at her. I don't want Rose to laugh at anything.

Chapter Eight

Today we're digging up the potatoes. It's very satisfying. I wish now that I'd thought to have a vegetable garden at home. There was no reason why I couldn't have had one. Perhaps when I get back home I could plant one. The area where the aviary stood is probably a good spot. It gets enough sun but is also shaded by the large gum tree in the yard. Simon had a concrete slab poured to be the base of the cage, so I will have to get that pulled up.

'It's to stop the rats getting into the cage,' he told me. 'They come for the seeds but aren't above taking eggs and babies. Sometimes they bite the feet of birds that get too close.'

I sold all the finches back to the pet shop after Simon died. I couldn't bear to look at them.

'But Dad loved them,' said Rosalind. 'How could you have just got rid of them?'

'I didn't dispose of them, Rosalind. I sold them back to the pet shop. I'm sure they will go to good homes with people who know how to take care of them. They need a lot of care, and with everything going on at the moment I just don't have the time or the energy.'

'You could have asked me,' said Rosalind. 'I would have brought Sam over every day. He loved them as well. You can't just eradicate Dad from our lives, you know. Have you thrown all his clothes away yet? Have you?'

'Please, darling, I'm sorry I upset you. I can get the birds back. I haven't thrown anything away. I miss him too.'

'Do you?' she said. 'Do you really?' It was the first time she had seemed angry at me; well, the first time since it happened. Both she and Portia have been a great comfort. In the first few nightmarish days after it happened, Rosalind slept next to me in my bed, soothing me when I woke. 'It was an accident, Mum, you didn't mean it, you didn't mean it.'

It was inevitable, I suppose, that Rosalind would begin to question me. She has done her best not to, but I'm sure there are dark nights of the soul when she wonders about the truth. I could tell her. I could explain, but if I do she will have to know everything, and then it seems to me that I will be taking her father away from her again. To lose him to death was one thing, but to lose the memory she has of him would be worse, I think.

'Make sure you get all of them out,' says Jess to Mina and me.

I'm using a garden fork, pushing down hard with my foot and lifting the plant, and then Mina scrabbles around in the dirt finding the tubers. In the vegetable garden it's easy to pretend I'm somewhere else—somewhere far away from here.

I have to cook tonight. It will be pasta again because that's cheap and filling. I tried to think of a different sauce to use but so far I haven't managed to come up with anything. We don't have much to use for flavour beyond salt and pepper, and even though we have chilli I'm not sure I can use it. Everyone's tastes are different. I've been here for almost a week but I still haven't had a real conversation with any of the women in my unit. At first I thought it was because they were intimidated by my level of . . . of infamy, but now I think that they may just not be interested. Perhaps it is because women come and go so quickly here, or maybe they have their own concerns. I would like to have someone to talk to, but it seems it is not to be. I am so very different from these women. I'm pleased that I wear the same clothes as they do; at least until I open my mouth I am one of them.

Jess is happy to leave me to work on my own. She can see I know what I'm doing. I've always had an affinity for gardening. There's a certain peace that comes from touching the soft underside of a petal. Vegetables are more sturdy, more serious, but flourish the same way with the right amount of love.

Busy hands are good for contemplation.

Rob has lodged the appeal and he's certain we'll have you out soon, Portia wrote in last night's email.

Why are you calling him Rob? I wrote back.

Oh, Mother, she replied.

I know what that 'oh, Mother' means. Portia has fallen in love again. She has a habit of doing that, and of course she is so beautiful that men are happy to fall in love right back. There must be something illegal or immoral about falling in love with your mother's barrister, but I know there's no use in trying to persuade her to leave Robert alone. In truth, I'm a little jealous. I wouldn't have minded getting the chance to fall in love with Robert myself. I have to keep reminding myself that that part of my life is over. I'm still young enough to find someone else, I suppose, but I've never been with another man. Being touched by someone other than Simon is unthinkable. Rob and Portia will make a beautiful couple, and if they have babies . . . Silly of me to think like that. Every time Portia mentions a new man I imagine her having babies. I don't think she wants children. She is a dedicated social worker and sees 'exactly how fucked up families can get'.

Portia likes to swear. Most of her sentences are punctuated with the word 'fuck'. But she rarely swore in front of Simon. When she did so as a teenager, he would gasp and his face would flush a deep red. 'You were not raised in the gutter, Portia,' he said. He prided himself on never using an expletive, and I only remember it happening once, when he was very angry.

On that day the girls were both at school. I had left Simon inside the house talking to someone who, I had assumed, was from work, on the phone. I was on my knees pushing a new rose bush into place when I heard yelling from inside the house. I stopped, shocked. Simon never yelled. If he was angry he would lower his voice and speak slowly. There was a moment of silence and then the yelling started again. I got off my knees and threw my garden gloves onto the ground. Back in the house I hurried over to his study but when I got there I was confronted with a closed door. I hesitated for a moment, listening. His voice was loud and coarse. He didn't sound like himself at all.

'You tell that fucker to check his facts before he accuses me of anything. You tell him I'll fucking make sure that he never works in this town again. You fucking tell him that, you hear me?'

What alarmed me more than the swearing was his unfamiliar broad Australian accent. Even the pitch of his voice had dropped. He could have been an entirely different man. I touched the door and then turned away quickly and went back to the garden.

When I came in again an hour later he was seated in his favourite armchair in the living room with a whisky at his elbow and his collection of Shakespeare on his lap.

'A little early for a drink, isn't it?' I said.

'I suppose it is, my dear, but today has been a little trying.'

'What happened?'

'Nothing that you need to be concerned about—silly stuff from the studio, but it's all sorted out now. Shall we go out to dinner? Will it be possible to get a babysitter, do you think?'

I could have asked, could have told him I had heard his shouting and pushed for an explanation, but I didn't. I don't know why I didn't. It may have been fear of what his answer would be, or it may have been something else. Maybe I didn't want to know.

I liked to believe that everything at his work, after many years of struggling, was going well. I didn't want him to be like all the other men I knew, filled with some unexplainable rage from their forays into the world that had to be forever tempered by the women in their lives. I had watched my mother soothe and placate my father after an argument with his supervisor, and he was fairly mild compared to the fathers of friends. I watched my friend Joan pacify her husband through virtually every dinner we ever went to. I would see her catch a waiter's eye, pat Myron's hand and order him a drink whenever he began complaining about the food or the service. She never seemed to enjoy her own food and was visibly relieved when the dinner was over and Myron had not caused a fuss. Over lunch, we all agreed that the men we were married to were overworked. They came home tired and grouchy and needing to relax. They were, none of them, violent men. They just needed to be kept happy. They paid the bills. They went out to work while we

stayed home. I nodded along with everyone, sometimes . . .
how ridiculous I feel thinking about it now, but sometimes
feeling smug at Simon's equanimity.

It was a different generation, I suppose. But I didn't want
my husband to be like all the other Australian husbands.
I wanted him to be Simon. I enjoyed the picture he painted
of a fawning staff and high ratings. I struggled enough
with the balancing act between him and the children. It
felt exhausting to take on any problems he was having at
work. I remember thinking, *If he doesn't wish to discuss it
then it must not be a real problem.* Naive of me. Terribly,
terribly naive.

I let him be the man he wanted to be and did not think
to question who he really was, and on the rare occasion
when I did I quickly took my mind elsewhere. Maybe all of
this is my fault. My tacit acceptance of his well-constructed
facade may have allowed him to do the things he did, but
even now I'm not sure what good confronting him would
have done.

The truth is that my life was easier when Simon was
happy, so I cooked the food he liked, I dressed the way
he liked, I read the books he recommended and I guided
him gently through his relationship with the girls. Portia
and Simon didn't get along. Portia has been fighting the
world since the day she came into it. As soon as she was old
enough, she simply added her father to the list.

'Why must she fight me on everything?' Simon said
when she was a teenager. 'She's never quiet when she can

make a noise, never compliant when she can be argumentative. I simply have no idea what to say to her.'

'She's just being a teenager,' I said. 'All teenagers are obnoxious.'

'This is more than that, my dear. Every time she looks at me I can feel her judging me and finding me wanting. She is so different to Rosalind. Rosalind's eyes still light up when she sees me. She is so interested in what I have to say and she loves hearing about my day. Portia barely speaks to me except to fight with me.'

'Oh, Simon,' I said, and then I would go and find Portia and force her to apologise to her father for the argument they had just had. I didn't like to see him unhappy. Was that so very wrong? Does that make me an awful person? Not asking him about the incident in his study was just one more way of keeping him happy. He didn't want to discuss it so we didn't discuss it.

Portia is very perceptive, more so than either Rosalind or me. She reads people well, and now when I think back I wonder if she saw something we didn't. She was never able to articulate it—or at least she never did so to me—but perhaps Portia understood from a very young age that her father was not the man he presented to the world.

I think she misses him, I know she misses him but she doesn't want to talk about him at all. I know theirs was a fraught relationship, and I'm sure, I think I'm sure, that it was nothing more than a clash of personalities. Portia was as aghast as Rosalind and I were when the allegations about Simon first surfaced. If he had done anything to her, anything at all, I'm sure she would have yelled and screamed her distress at the time. It is perhaps a false level of comfort I allow myself, but I don't think Simon was anything other than a father to our daughters.

He was surrounded by children all day long, and I feel dreadful for thinking it but I do take a deep breath every now and again and say a little prayer of thanks that he chose to look outside our home. Self-preservation above all else, I suppose. Sacrifice is all well and good in theory, but in the end the pain of a stranger does not have the same impact that the pain of a loved one does. I know that for certain people—people like Portia—the pain of others motivates them to try to change the world. I am not that way inclined. I hope he never looked inside our home; I hope . . . I hope he left this world before that happened.

Portia cried almost nonstop for the first few months after she was born.

'Rose, is there nothing you can do about her?' Simon would say, and then I would cry too because I was so sleep-deprived and so out of my depth. I was only seventeen, after all. Far too young to be a wife and a mother. Especially a wife and a mother with no support. I had left my parents behind, thinking myself Juliet to Simon's Romeo. They were horrified at the age gap.

I met Simon when I was just fifteen. The first time I saw him I giggled, he was so unbelievably handsome. Not handsome like Robert, who has a strong jaw and permanent stubble, but softer, prettier, almost beautiful like a woman. He came to my school along with a whole group of actors to perform Shakespeare. He was Macbeth. I was standing at the back of the school hall because there were not enough seats, and he walked onto the stage and took my breath away. I remember running my finger over my lips, imagining how soft his mouth would be.

I was standing next to my friend Lulu, who at fifteen was almost a different species to me. Her breasts were large and her hips already looked as though they were preparing for babies. I was stick thin with two slight bumps on my chest. I hated everything about myself. My mother refused to let me cut my hair, so it hung straight down over my chest to my waist in a braid. I was an only child raised by overprotective parents who still carried thick Polish accents. They had never really adjusted to their new country. My mother found the heat too much and the Australian accent almost impossible to understand. They wanted to keep me safely wrapped up until they found a nice Polish boy for me to marry. I, of course, was desperate to escape.

'He's cute,' said Lulu as we watched Simon roar at the witches.

'Mmm,' I said, unable to trust myself to open my mouth.

The play finished in the blink of an eye, and when Simon took his solo bow I thought he looked straight at me and smiled. I felt a stone lodge itself in my throat at the thought of having to leave his presence.

'You can help serve tea to the actors,' said Mrs Bennet, the English teacher, to Lulu and me as we were herded out of the hall. I was often chosen to serve tea to school visitors, because I always managed to make myself unobtrusive. Lulu was only sent along because she was with me. She talked too much and laughed loudly. Perhaps Mrs Bennet thought I would keep her in line.

I was giddy with joy as Lulu and I ran to the staffroom. I almost clapped my hands at the thought that I would have more time to drink in the actor's beauty. I was going to say something to Lulu, but she spoke first.

'The guy who played Macbeth is all mine,' she whispered.

'He must be a lot older than we are,' I said evasively.

'Who cares? Not me,' said Lulu. I swallowed my disappointment. I knew I had no chance with him anyway.

I was put in charge of the rusty old urn, and Lulu went around the staffroom with the biscuits. 'His name's Simon Winslow and he's thirty-one,' she whispered to me after her first circuit of the room.

'He's an actor during the day but he works as a waiter at night,' she said as she passed me a second time. I had to bite down on my lip to keep from giggling. I knew that Lulu would keep going up to him until someone stopped her. He'd had five biscuits by the time the rest of the actors began to return their teacups and get ready to leave.

As he placed his teacup on the counter, I took one last

look at him, hoping to remember his features for future daydreams.

'Perhaps you could help us carry out some of our stuff,' he said to me. His normal voice was soft with a faint English accent. I actually looked around to see if he was talking to anyone else. 'I mean you, Rose,' he said.

My heart fluttered and I felt my hands get clammy. 'How do you . . .?'

'Know your name? Your friend Lulu told me. I think she wants me to talk to her, but I only have eyes for you.'

'For me?' I said, and my voice embarrassed me by coming out in a high-pitched squeak.

'Yes, for you,' he said in his velvet voice. I could have listened to him speak forever. His blond hair was long at the back, curling slightly at his collar, and he looked as though he was wearing makeup around his eyes, emphasising his long lashes and the bottomless blue of his irises. He could have taken home any woman in the room, including the teachers, who were much closer to his age. His beauty had transformed the staffroom. The teachers who had joined us for tea were all women and they stood straight-backed with their chests out, casting sideways glances at him. The air fizzed a little as Simon was admired.

I'm not sure how I managed to get any words out, but I asked Mrs Bennet if I could help and she said yes. I carried his sword and his crown. He hadn't really needed my help.

'Come and have a coffee with me,' he said.

'I'm not allowed to date.'

'It will be our secret, then.'

'My mother will be angry, and my father—'

'Don't worry about them. Tell me a place to meet you after school and I'll be there.'

When I'd turned fourteen I had begun a campaign to get my parents to allow me to walk home from school and stop at the shopping centre, which was only a block away from our house. 'No, absolutely not,' said my father. 'No,' said my mother, but they underestimated my determination. I raged and argued. In the end I used a very powerful weapon to obtain this small measure of freedom. I stopped eating.

They gave in after two days. My mother was almost beside herself, locked in the memory of her own mother trying to find food for the family during the war, but I had won. I was allowed to walk home from school as long as I was home by five. I was never even a minute late. I knew that the leniency I had been shown would be easily retracted if I made that mistake.

I gave Simon the name of the small cafe where Lulu and I sometimes shared a piece of cake and a milkshake. I felt daring and brave and petrified at the same time. I was never allowed to go out with a boy my parents had not met and approved of, and then I was only allowed out in a group. Simon was very definitely not a boy.

'I'll be there,' he said. 'I will wait for you forever.'

I barely remember the rest of the day. I know I was

chastised for not paying attention in every class until the final bell rang.

That afternoon he was already there waiting. I had dragged Lulu along with me without telling her about the planned meeting. *If he's not there I won't care, if he's not there I won't care*, I kept repeating to myself as we walked. When I saw him waiting for me, I wished I hadn't made her tag along.

She'd spotted him first. 'Oh my God, just look who it is,' she said, and she waltzed up to his table. She was always so bold, so sure of a favourable reaction from any boy she looked at. I hung back while they talked, certain that now he had taken another look at her he wouldn't want anything to do with me.

'Come and sit down, Rose,' he said to me, looking around Lulu, and I did so without thinking. 'I've asked Lulu if she could give us some time alone, and she has kindly agreed.'

I looked up at Lulu. Her cheeks were crimson and I knew from the way she looked at me that she was furious. 'Don't tell, okay?' I said. She could end things for me before they even began. Our mothers were coffee acquaintances. She nodded brusquely and left the cafe. I knew she wouldn't say anything. I had covered for her many times whenever she wanted some time alone with one of the boys at our school.

When she was gone I wished she had stayed. I couldn't think of a single intelligent thing to say.

'So, Rose, beautiful flower of a girl, tell me about yourself,' Simon said, and over chocolate milkshakes I did. He watched me as I talked, stumbling over words and giggling because his gaze was so intense.

'What did you see in me?' I asked him when we celebrated our fifth anniversary. I had held onto the question for years, never brave enough to ask it before then.

'Oh, Rose, you have no idea how beautiful you are. The moment I saw you I wanted to touch you. I liked the tilt of your head and the colour of your hair. You held yourself with so much grace and you were so serious. Even during the play I was looking at you. I wanted to unwind your braid and run my fingers through your hair. I wanted to be near you.'

I had kissed a boy before I met Simon, but only one. I was thirteen and at a party where we were playing spin the bottle. My parents would have forbidden me to go if they'd known what was to happen, but I knew to keep the true nature of parties to myself. I think the boy, Mark, was disappointed when the bottle stopped at me. He had probably been hoping for Lulu.

Simon had a car, a small Toyota that looked to be on its last legs. He drove me home and dropped me off a few houses away, and he kissed me. It was very different to be kissed by a man. It was different and wonderful and it made me think of things that had until then only been on the edge of my consciousness. I had thought of sex as something that would happen far into my future, but once Simon kissed me I knew it would happen soon. I knew it and I was also aware that Simon was now completely and utterly in charge of my life. It only took a couple of hours one afternoon, but then that's all it usually takes. He led the way, and he continued to do so all through our lives. I never felt bullied or pushed, but I usually acquiesced to his wishes. It is how we began, and it was only at the very end of our lives together that things changed.

It only takes a moment to fall in love. I'm sure Robert was in love with Portia two minutes after he met her. I had been making my way quietly through my life, reading books and doing as I was told to do. I stood no chance against the beauty and charisma of someone like Simon.

'You're just a child!' my mother shrieked when I announced one afternoon six months later that Simon had asked me to marry him.

We had continued to see each other in secret. I had not even thought of bringing him home. He was too old, he was not Polish, and my parents didn't know his parents. I couldn't even imagine a set of circumstances under which they would approve of him. I had grown adept at lying. Lying to my parents, and I'm sure lying to myself as well. Every time the question of what he was doing with me rose in my mind, I pushed it away. *I don't care*, I would say to myself.

Simon and I met every afternoon after school. Lulu kept our secret, thrilled—once she got over her pique—to be part of the drama, and Simon also kept her happy by sometimes bringing along another actor for her to meet. On weekends I slept over at Lulu's place; her parents were a little more lax than mine and were happy to leave the two of us alone on a Saturday night. Simon took me or both of us out to dinner—cheap places he could afford. Lulu made us up with lipstick and eye shadow, garish blues and pinks that made us look older.

'You don't need all that rubbish,' Simon said to me. 'I prefer you with no makeup on your beautiful skin.'

'I want to look older,' I replied. 'I don't want to look like a child.'

'You are far from a child, darling. You are a woman of exquisite beauty, and there is no need to hide yourself.'

We didn't do much beyond kiss and touch, but I yearned to go further.

'No, Rose,' he would say, 'not yet, not like this.'

My dreams were filled with sex. Sometimes I woke up in the middle of an orgasm and lay awake, shocked at what my body wanted. I whiled away hours in my bedroom thinking about what it would feel like to have his body on top of mine. My parents never noticed my abstraction. They worked long hours and if I brought home consistent grades—they thought everything was fine, just as it had always been. '*Moja piękna, mądra dziewczyna*,' my father would say whenever I presented him with an essay covered in compliments from my teacher. 'My beautiful, clever girl.'

I had moments of guilt and doubt at my betrayal of

them and of the values they had taught me, but I was happily drowning in Simon's eyes and his smell. I didn't take a breath without thinking of him.

Simon never pushed me, never asked me to do things I wasn't ready for, but one afternoon, sitting in his little car with the windows fogged from our breath, he said, 'I can't stand it, Rose. I need to be near you all the time. Our lives are meant to be entwined. You need to marry me.'

I giggled. 'Don't be silly.'

'Look at me,' he said, and he placed both hands on my shoulders. I looked into the depths of his eyes and knew that I would do whatever he wanted me to do. 'I love you and you love me and we should be married. Go home now and tell your parents about me, and we will be married soon.'

'What if they won't let me?' I said.

'Then we shall run away, far away, and be together.'

I was sixteen then. His words were honeyed, his hands made me feel things I had never felt before, and every night before I went to sleep I would run my fingers along my lips remembering the feel of his mouth. I was never going to tell him no.

I waited until my father was home to speak to them. I was so nervous I felt nauseous. All hell broke loose. I had known that it would. I didn't look at them as I spoke. We were sitting around the dining room table and my mother said, 'Rose, eat, eat, you need to eat.'

'I have something to tell you,' I said, pushing my fork through some cabbage, rearranging it into small piles on my plate. I spoke quickly, not letting my mother's gasp or the sound of my father pushing back his chair, stop me. When I was done I finally looked up. My mother had her hand over her mouth and my father's fists were clenched.

'You are making a joke, Rose,' said my mother. 'This is a joke?'

'No, Mama,' I said.

'I don't understand,' she said and she sounded genuinely bewildered, 'we have not met him and he is a man. How can you be with a man? You are a child.'

'I'm not a child. I'm grown up. I love him and I'm going to marry him.'

'It is illegal,' roared my father, 'It must be illegal. We will have him arrested.'

'I'll run away,' I said, pushing my hands under my legs so that they wouldn't see how hard they were shaking. 'You'll never see me again.'

'Don't you dare say such things,' said my mother. 'Do you know what we have given up for you? Do you know how hard we work?'

I knew they would drag out all their weaponry, and I was prepared. Growing up I had been told over and over again that they both came from large families where days without food were common. My father had arrived in Australia fresh from fighting in the resistance, which he had joined at the tender age of sixteen, and as an immigrant he had never progressed further in his job than the factory floor.

He and my mother had decided together to only have one child so that they would be able to feed that child, spoil that child, give it everything. But the truth was that it was too great a responsibility for me. Every time I walked into a test or sat down to write an essay I thought first of my parents and then what I had to do. Simon was going to rescue me from having to be the perfect daughter. It is no wonder that I grabbed at the chance of what I thought was freedom, and perhaps it is also no wonder that I was so suited to becoming the woman Simon needed in his life. I had already been trained well in the art of putting others before myself.

'If I'm married you won't have to work hard anymore. Simon will take care of me.'

'We know nothing about this man,' shouted my father. 'He's thirty-one. Do you know that he is nearly old enough to be your father? He is using you for your youth, for your body.' My father was forty, only nine years older than Simon.

'Oh my God, oh my God, please tell me you're not pregnant!' said my mother.

'No, I'm not pregnant. I'm in love. I don't care if he's older. I'm going to marry him and you can't stop me.'

'I will lock you in this house for the rest of your life!' spluttered my father.

'Peter, please,' said my mother. 'Calm down. We need to speak of this. Please stay calm. Rose, you cannot get married. You're too young. You need to finish school.

You wanted to be a teacher. You will regret this, my darling, you will regret it forever.'

'I want to marry him, Mama, I have to marry him. I love him and he loves me. I want you to meet him and like him, but if you don't then I will leave and you will never see me again.'

'How can you say such things to your mother? Go to your room. You're a brat, an ungrateful brat. Go, go now!'

I got up from the table, knocking over my chair, and ran to my room. I locked the door and threw everything I wanted to take into a bag. And then I waited.

All night long I heard my parents shouting at each other. I knew they had met when both were sixteen. I hoped my mother would persuade my father, but he would not relent. As dawn broke and my parents were finally silent, I unpacked my bag. I knew what they were going to do, but I had already formulated a plan. They would not keep me from Simon. That was the only thing I was absolutely sure of.

My mother came to my room an hour later and asked me to join them for breakfast. Her eyes were swollen, her shoulders rounded with the burden of my betrayal. I felt a pain above my ribs. I was hurting her and I didn't want to hurt her but then I thought of Simon and I didn't care anymore. They told me I was never allowed to see Simon again.

'You will not walk home from school anymore,' said my mother. 'I will drive you there and I will fetch you. You may not go out at all. If you leave the house to go to the shops or the dentist or anything like that, one of us needs to be with you. Understand that we do this for your own good, because we love you.'

I wanted to protest, to scream and cry, but I realised that there would be no point.

I packed as many of my things as I could fit in my school-bag and submitted to being driven to school. Once there I told the school secretary that I was feeling sick and asked to be allowed to call my mother. Instead, of course, I called Simon, and he came to fetch me.

You could get married at sixteen then. We applied for a licence and spent the weeks we had to wait moving from one friend's house to another. Simon lied to his friends about my age. It seemed the easiest thing to do.

My parents sent the police after me, but by the time they found us it was too late. I was Mrs Simon Winslow and I refused to leave him. Simon was thoroughly charming and explained it all so sensibly to the police that I'm sure my parents landed up looking slightly insane. My father had accused Simon of kidnapping me. 'You can see, sir,' said Simon, 'that I have done no such thing. Rose, you are free to go home. You can return to your parents and we can get divorced, even though we love each other and all we want is to be together.'

'I won't go,' I said.

'Sir, she is happy to be with me. Perhaps her parents do not like me because I'm not Polish, but this is Australia, isn't it? Here people are free to do as they please, and if you take her home I'm sure they will lock her up and never let her leave the house.'

'It's true,' I said. 'They will.'

'I'm sure you're both married,' said Simon. 'I'm sure you know what it's like to be in love with a beautiful girl.' And the police officers nodded their heads and laughed, murmuring something about young love.

My parents had underestimated Simon and the power he had over me. I loved them, but I was willing to give them up for him. I was willing to give up everything. I gave up school and my dreams of a future teaching children and I never even gave it much thought.

It's not as though I have just come to these realisations. I've always known that there was an imbalance of power in my marriage, always known and always accepted Simon as the master of my destiny. I'm sure that I would not be the first woman to be swept away so entirely by a man. My first year with Simon was a dream, and by the time I woke up and began to question what I'd done, I had a child and another on the way. And I still loved him, which is perhaps the most important thing. I still loved him—and despite it all, I still love him now. I don't think anything will ever change that, because even as I took his life in the knowledge of who he truly was, I could not let go of that love. I cannot out-think it. I cannot get it to dissipate. It is there, lodged firmly inside me, colouring everything.

He wanted me and he got me. I was young enough to be

groomed into being the perfect wife. I hadn't established an identity for myself and was happy for him to provide one for me. He gave me books to read and took me to movies and museums.

When he started making proper money, money that allowed us to buy what we wanted, he would come shopping with me. He liked to see every outfit I bought. He steered me away from anything that made me look older, always preferring me in clothes that emphasised my youth, my slight figure, the smallness of my waist. 'You are a delicate flower,' he would say to me. 'You should wear only the lightest, most beautiful fabrics.'

The week before I was convicted, I ventured out to a store to buy some new clothes to wear to court. I began my search for clothing among the lilacs and pinks that Simon always liked to see me in, but kept drifting back to black and grey. I realise that I prefer those colours, although I did not know that about myself until now, until the ripe old age of fifty-five.

He made me into what I am today. I'm sure he never expected me to turn on him. He never expected that.

He was very hard to disagree with. Sometimes I would be arguing with him about something and he would laugh and say, 'But my darling girl, why are you so angry? You are busy agreeing with me,' and I would realise that while I had started out on the opposing side, I had been manoeuvred out of my own thoughts and feelings.

When Portia was sixteen and still hating her teachers

and worrying about pimples, I found it hard to imagine her running away with anyone. She didn't even know how to use the washing machine. I was such a meek little creature. It is almost unfathomable to me that I sneaked around for months and then packed a bag and left my parents with broken hearts. People start wars over love, I suppose.

I made up with my parents before Rosalind was born. My mother had tried to contact me for a few months after I got married, but Simon convinced me to remain strong and stay away from her, and I did. 'Your parents need to understand that you are my wife now, Rose. Until they can respect me as the most important man in your life, the most important person, they cannot be allowed to see you.'

I understand the irony now. I had simply become someone else's child.

I struggled through my first year with Portia, and when I was pregnant with Rosalind I knew that I needed my mother. Besides, after having my own children I under-stood how devastating my betrayal of them must have been. Although I could not regret the presence of Simon in my life, I wanted them to have the joy of knowing their grandchildren.

'I'm going to see them,' I told Simon one Sunday. 'They've never met Portia and I want them to be part of her life. You can come with me or you can stay here, but I am going to see them.' I sounded resolute but inside I was trembling, and I knew that if he'd said, 'You may not leave,' I would not have gone. But I think he knew that they couldn't part us now. Once we had children there was no going back. A single mother was a shameful thing to be in those days. Now Portia knows quite a few women who have decided that a husband isn't necessary and have had children alone.

'I'll come with you,' said Simon, and he took Portia from my arms, an unusual gesture, and we set off as a family. He led the way into my parents' house, armed with his child, and I couldn't help but notice that his smile hovered somewhere between friendly and smug.

My mother was as charmed by Simon as I was, even though she would never have said that to my father, and then he became famous and she could openly adore him, and sing his praises to the whole neighbourhood. Fame meant that he was no longer the devious older man who had whisked away her precious daughter; instead he was the man everyone knew from the television. He was a catch. Now, despite my failing to fulfil any of the dreams she may have had for me, I had still made a wonderful choice. The whole street, the whole town, the whole country knew who her son-in-law was. What a prize for a struggling immigrant. What a prize.

My father, however, hated him until the day he died. He told my mother not to allow Simon to come to his funeral. (As it happened, Simon was away filming an advert anyway.) When he was alive, my father never came to our little flat or—later—our house, and when we visited my parents at home he would merely shake Simon's hand

and then disappear into the shed at the back of the house where a bottle of vodka kept him company.

'I don't understand, darling girl,' Simon said whenever we talked about my father. 'Can't he see how much I love you? Doesn't he know that I will give you everything?' Simon always found it difficult to comprehend when someone didn't love him immediately. The long journey he had to take to become successful disconcerted him. 'Can they not see my skills, my talent, Rose? Can they not see that?' he would ask me after every failed audition.

'They're jealous and ignorant,' I would reply, and then I would work extra hard in the kitchen or the bedroom to make him happy again.

I thought my father was just upset about losing me to a man so close to his own age, but with hindsight—oh, the delights of hindsight—I now wonder whether he saw something that my mother and I missed. We were both, as most women were, completely charmed by him. Simon would bring flowers to my mother, even when we couldn't really afford it. He would kiss her hand and he would look at her with those deep blue eyes as if there was no one else he would rather be speaking to. It was hard not to fall in love with Simon. Every woman he met fell under his spell, and I have no idea why that wasn't enough for him.

Simon's parents were never in the picture. He had left them behind long before he met me. 'My father had the temerity to suggest that I get a proper job,' he said. 'He's a boorish man who is vulgar and violent when drunk.'

'And your mother?' I asked.

'My mother,' Simon sighed. 'My mother is a transplanted English rose who has withered and nearly died living with him. I asked her to come with me when I left, but for some reason she loves him. She makes excuses for his behaviour, and I always felt that if forced she would choose him over me.' He was an only child, just as I was and after my reunion with my parents I felt deeply sad for Simon's mother to be without her son.

'Perhaps we should go and visit them. They would love to meet their grandchildren,' I said.

'I wouldn't want to subject you to my father, my dear. He has rages, you know. He gets drunk and lashes out. There were many times in my life when I went to school covered in bruises. Would you want to expose our children to such a monster?'

I had no desire to meet a man who could beat his child, or a woman who would let him, but now I wonder if his parents were the kind of people he painted them to be. He lied about other things—why not this? It is too late now to find the truth. Too late.

'Time for lunch,' says Jess.

'What?' I look up from where I'm crouching making sure that all the potatoes have been found.

'Thought you were a bit lost there,' says Jess.

'I was thinking about my husband,' I say, but Jess has already turned and walked away.

I try to stand up but one of my legs has gone to sleep.

'Oh,' I say, and look up again to see Birdy looking down at me. 'My leg seems to have gone to sleep.'

'Do you want me to help you?' she says. Her face is impassive and her tone flat. Although I am obviously struggling to get up she seems disinterested, as though she is merely asking the question to ask it. I find her strange, but then I remember what Jess said about her.

'That would be very kind.' I lift my arm so she can grab my hand.

'I can be kind,' she says

'Thank you—oh, that's fine, thanks. I'll be all right now. I'll just move it around a little.'

'You're old.'

'Older than I used to be.' I laugh.

'Yes,' she says. 'Older than you used to be.'

Chapter Nine

She came over to talk to me today. I think she gets tired because she has to work all day long. When she's working in the garden she keeps standing up and stretching. When she forgot to stretch last week, I had to help her stand up. She's light and small. I could have picked her up and thrown her over the fence.

No one knows I'm watching her. I know better than to discuss her, but the women in my unit talk about her a lot. Jess thinks she's nice, but Mina and Maya both think she's stuck up.

'She thinks she's better than anyone else because she has so much money,' says Mina.

'I bet she's not enjoying having to cook and clean,' says Maya. 'Sal says she's a good cook, but I don't believe that.'

'I think you should lay off Rose,' says Jess. 'She's doing her best.'

'Got a crush, have you?' says Maya.

'Fuck off,' says Jess.

'Her husband was really cute, when he was younger,' says Maya. 'I used to watch him on television. The girls in my year used to call him "sexy Simon".'

'Do you think he did what they said he did, I mean with that girl, with all those girls?' says Mina.

'Allison says we shouldn't gossip,' I say. I say it really loudly, but I don't mean to. I just want them to stop talking about him.

'Steady on, Birdy,' says Maya.

'Yeah, calm your farm,' says Mina, and then she and Maya start laughing, but I don't know what's funny.

We call Mina and Maya 'the twins' because they're both short and dark and their names both begin with M. And they both tried to kill their husbands. Mina didn't manage to kill hers, but Maya's is dead and under the ground. They're always together. They arrived on the same day, and even though Mina is Indian and twenty-five and Maya is Greek and forty they're best, best friends. I think they were friends at the other place as well. I don't know why they like each other, but maybe it's because they both don't like men anymore.

Mina hit her husband with a cricket bat and gave him brain damage so now he's stupid and slow, maybe even slower than me. She did it because he was hitting their little boy. He wouldn't stop hitting him even though Mina cried and cried.

'I knew he would kill him,' said Mina one night when she was telling us what had happened. 'My boy looked at me with his big, dark eyes and I could see that he thought there was no way I could help him. He'd peed his pants but it wasn't on purpose. He was scared of his dad. During the day he was as good as gold and he chatted to me and laughed and he never peed his pants, but when his dad came home he got all quiet, just waiting to get a smack.

'When Arjun came home that night I knew he was pissed off. He wanted to borrow money from my dad to open his own cafe, but my dad had told him no. I knew it was going to be a bad night because my mum had called me to warn me. Arjun just looked at the boy and he peed himself. "You do that just to spite me, don't you?" he said, and the poor boy just looked at him and shook, like a rabbit about to be eaten by a tiger.

'Arjun started hitting him and hitting him and it looked like he didn't want to stop. After a minute my baby wasn't even crying, just whimpering, and I thought that his dad wouldn't stop until he was dead. I couldn't let that happen. I knew that if he died I would have to die too, so I picked up the bat that we always kept by the front door for protection and I started swinging.'

When Mina told her story her eyes got all shiny and then she had to blow her nose. 'No one will ever hurt my boy again,' she said. Her boy's name is Suresh and he comes to visit her here. Sometimes he is here at the same time as Isabel, and they like to play together. Mina was only at the other place for a year before she came here, because she was protecting her little boy and the judge knew that. Her husband is in a special hospital and he will never be able to come home again. I'm glad that Mina's husband can't hurt Suresh anymore. He's a nice boy. He always shares his chocolate with anyone who asks.

Not everyone likes to tell their story. I have only told mine to Jess. But sometimes it will be nearly time for lights out and all the women will be talking and a story will slip out. That's what happened with Mina's story.

Maya drove into her husband with her car. She told us that on the first day she got here. She doesn't care who knows her story.

'Just so you know, I don't take any crap.' Maya was in the other place for years and years before she met Mina. 'I said to him, I said, "Christos, if I fucking catch you with that slut again, I will kill you." And he said, "Baby, you know it was just once. I love you and I don't want to hurt you. You know it's just you and me." But I followed him anyway. Gets himself all dressed up and then tells me he's going down to the pub to meet his mates. What did he think I was—stupid? I followed him and I saw them and that was it. I ran the bastard down.'

Her children are all grown up and they don't talk to her at all. That makes her sad sometimes. 'They don't under-stand,' she says. 'They don't know what it was like for me to always be worrying about whether he was lying, to always be wondering where he was and what he was doing.' Sometimes Maya cries, because she wants to talk to her daughter or her son but they don't want to talk to her.

'Don't worry about it,' Mina will say to her. 'You'll see them when you get out. You'll talk them round.'

'Damn funny friendship,' said Jess about them. 'Maybe they're lezzos.' Then she had to explain to me what that was.

'Killed the bastard, didn't I,' said Maya when she told us what she'd done. 'And I would have been free and clear if that bitch of a mother-in-law hadn't testified against me. I was watching him, but the old bag was watching me. When I get out of here I'll go over and visit and scare the shit out of her.'

'If you do anything stupid, you'll land up right back in here,' said Jess. 'In fact, it won't be here. It'll be the other place and they'll just throw away the key. The only way you'll know time has passed is if you mark it on a calendar.'

'Don't do anything stupid, Maya, please,' said Mina.

'Relax, I'm just talking. Talking is allowed, isn't it, Birdy?' she said, and I nodded and smiled because I thought she was making a joke. I don't always get the joke.

I think Mina is like a Gouldian finch and Maya is like a zebra finch and that's why they get along. I'm not friends with either Mina or Maya but we get along all right. They are both great cooks, and Jess and I are not very good, so I'm happy to share a unit with them. At the other place there were women who called me 'retarded' and 'brain-damaged', but here everyone is nice. I think Jess makes sure everyone in our unit behaves. She doesn't like us to fight. If Mina starts shouting at me because I don't understand, Jess says, 'Lay off, Mina,' and Mina stops shouting and goes to her room. Jess isn't much bigger than Rose Winslow but she seems to take up more space.

Both Maya and Mina think Mrs Winslow meant to do it and that she expected to get away with everything just because she has money.

'Who cares?' says Jess when Maya and Mina talk about Rose. 'I don't mind her. She knows her way around the garden and she does what I tell her to do—not like you, Mina, with all your suggestions.'

'Up yours, Jess, you're not the boss of the garden.'

'Know more about it than you do.'

'Oh, shut up, both of you,' says Maya.

I don't say anything, because I'm afraid that if I say even one single word then everyone will know the truth about me and Rose and then they will know my story, and not just the part that I've told Jess—the whole, whole story.

Jess doesn't like to talk too much about anyone or anything. 'If you keep your head down and your mouth shut, Birdy, there's a lot less chance of getting into trouble.' If Jess thinks I'm talking too much she looks at me and covers her mouth. Then I know she's telling me to remember the monkeys. On her desk she keeps a little stone sculpture of three monkeys. One is covering his eyes, one is covering his ears, and one is covering his mouth. 'See no evil, hear no evil, speak no evil,' said Jess when she showed it to me the first time. 'I made up my mind after the other place that the only way to get through this is to keep yourself to yourself.' Jess's daughter Chloe brought her the statue of the monkeys, and Allison said that Jess could keep it.

'Too bloody ugly to steal,' said Maya, but Jess didn't care.

'Keep yourself to yourself,' said Jess.

'Yeah,' I agreed.

Jess likes to tell me how to get through the day, and even though I know I don't have to listen to her—because I've only got to listen to Allison and all the guards—I still do. She needs to be listened to. It helps her figure it all out.

Jess's story is that she was sent to prison for theft and fraud. All she wanted was to keep her kids. Stolen credit cards seemed like the easiest way. 'People don't guard their stuff. It was so easy to walk past a shopping trolley and just grab the handbag sitting on it. Too easy, really. I would never leave my stuff unguarded like that.'

'I hold my bag close to me when I go shopping,' I said.

'It wasn't like it was my life plan, you know. I didn't wake up one day and think "I'll turn into a thief". I was just so scared of losing the girls. I was terrified that if all those nosy social workers knew they were going to school without food some days they would take them away from me. The last thing I wanted was to have them land up in the fucking system.'

Now her kids are in the system anyway. The foster system. I don't know if they're living with a bitch like Heather's kids are, but even if they're living with someone nice, no one likes to have their kids in the foster system. 'I could tell you some stories that would make your hair stand on end,' said Heather when she was talking to Jess about the foster system. Heather stays in the same unit Rose does, so maybe she is telling Rose her stories. Maybe Rose will listen to Heather.

When Jess's girls come and stay once a month I can see Jess trying to fit a whole month of being a mum into two days. She writes a list of things to tell her girls when they get here. I do the same thing, but I always forget my list and just play with Isabel.

'If that shit hadn't left me I would have been fine. If he'd paid me even the tiniest bit of child support I could have made it,' said Jess when we were looking at the monkey statue.

'Yeah,' I said.

Jess nodded and got a tissue out of her tissue box to clean all the little nooks and crannies on the sculpture. 'I keep it to remind me to just concentrate on my own stuff.'

Now she uses it to remind me to just concentrate on my own stuff as well.

I didn't say anything when Rose came over to the cage to talk to me today. I thought she was going to say, 'Thank you for helping me last week,' because that's polite, but she didn't say anything for a few minutes. I thought about the monkeys and I knew that even one word could get me into trouble.

I thought maybe she was just looking for a way to get out of the sun. The cage is the only part of the garden that has a little shade. It's important that the birds don't get too hot. If birds get too hot they open their wings to try and make themselves cool again. 'If you see a bird, any bird, with its wings open, angel child, then you know that that is an unhappy bird.' That's what he told me. On hot days I always make sure they have lots of basins filled with water. Every bird likes a bath on hot days. I like to watch them hop in and out of the water, shaking their tiny heads.

I thought she would just stand in the shade for a bit and then go away, but after watching me refill the seed tray, she said, 'How did you know how to take care of the finches?'

I shrugged my shoulders. I didn't want to speak to her at all. I wasn't ready. I need to think about what I'm going to say, but not what I'm going to do. I know what I'm going to do.

People's voices don't change. She looks different but she sounds the same, and when she talks her voice makes me feel hot all over.

'My husband used to have finches,' she said.

'I know, you said so before.'

'Did I? I must have forgotten. How many kinds have you got in here?'

'Just Gouldian and zebra finches,' I said. I really wanted her to go away.

'My husband used to have so many books on them. You wouldn't think such a small bird could have so much written about it. Have you read any books or anything? Or did someone teach you what to do?'

I emptied a basin of water that the birds had filled with poo and opened the cage to go and refill it. 'Someone taught me,' I said, and I looked straight at her.

'You remind me of someone,' she said, 'I don't know who,' and then she laughed a funny little laugh. 'I should get back to work.'

I was holding the water dish, so I couldn't use my hand to cover my mouth and I had to bite down hard on my lip instead. I nodded at her and kept my mouth closed. *Speak no evil*, I thought, but the words wanted to come out. Right there and then I knew that I could say something and she would realise who I was. *Speak no evil*, I repeated to myself, and she went back to her gardening.

When she'd gone, I was surprised to find my breath going in and out and in and out like I had been running, and my ears were ringing. It's not like I'm afraid of her. She's not the one to be afraid of in here. I'm the one she should be afraid of in here, so I don't know why I couldn't breathe.

'You're real quiet tonight,' says Jess before dinner. We're sitting out on the veranda waiting for muster.

I lift my shoulders up and down so she knows that I don't have anything to say.

'Always hard after the kids go home, isn't it?' Jess thinks I'm sad because I miss Isabel. I don't tell her what I'm really thinking about because it's my secret and my agenda. But I know she's waiting for me to say something, so I tell her I am sad about Isabel going home. It isn't a lie. I'm always sad about Isabel going home.

'Yeah,' I say. 'I miss her so much it's like my chest has something on top of it.'

'I know what you mean,' says Jess. 'But we had a good time, didn't we?'

'Yeah.' I did have a good time but it was too short. It's always too short. I watch the hands on the clock and I wish that I could hold them back and stop time going forward.

Lila brought Isabel up on Friday afternoon and came to fetch her on Sunday afternoon. At three o'clock on Friday afternoon I was allowed to stop work and go and pack my bag so I could stay in the mother and child unit. It's bigger than my unit. It has five big bedrooms and two bathrooms and each bedroom has three beds in it. Allison makes sure that there's always food in the unit so we don't have to buy any from the canteen—unless we want junk food, and we all want junk food. Jess and I put our money together and bought chocolate and sweets to give to our girls.

I only get to see Isabel once a month. 'Everyone needs a turn, Birdy,' said Allison when I asked her if I could see Isabel more.

'But Isabel is so little,' I said.

'And Jess's kids are big and Heather's kids are unhappy and so on and so on,' said Allison.

This weekend me and Jess were in the house together, and that made it fun. Suresh is coming next week. Also in the house were Anna and her baby boy, Liz and her daughters, and Esther and her son. I don't know the others very well. I hoped the baby would sleep through the night. Babies like to stay up at night. When Isabel was born she liked to wake up every two hours. Sometimes I would be so tired I wouldn't hear her, and then Mum would get up and bring her to me and she would be angry. 'I told your sister this would happen. I'm too old for this. I deserve to have some peace in my old age.'

'Sorry, Mum,' I would say. I didn't like waking up to feed Isabel, but when I was holding her and she was drinking from me I would feel my filled-with-joy feeling. Her little fingers liked to hold my hand. I wasn't very good at changing nappies at first, but Mum showed me and Lila showed me and the nurse who came to visit showed me and then I was good at it.

Jess and I waited and waited for our kids to arrive and finally they were there.

Lila isn't allowed to come into the Farm. She's only allowed to drop Isabel off and then leave. The first time she came Isabel cried and cried until she saw me. Now she knows about our weekend and she doesn't cry. She's really smart and she doesn't need to be shown things again and again.

'Mum, Mum, Mum,' said Isabel when she saw me. She jumped up and down because she was so excited, and I jumped up and down as well.

First we had to unpack her suitcase and make sure she had everything she needs, and then we sat on the veranda together watching the sun go down and Isabel told me all the things she was thinking about.

'I sit next to Bao in school. She's Chinese. Do you know how to spell Bao? It's B then A then O. She's my best friend and we play together at lunch. I can go across all the monkey bars and so can Bao. I can spell my name. I then S then A then B then E then L. My name is a long name. My teacher is Mrs Richards and she says I'm a good speller. I can spell Mum. M then U then M again.' Isabel talks and talks and never runs out of words. I listen to everything she says and I try to remember how she looks so that I can think about her when she isn't with me.

We had hamburgers for dinner. Jess's daughters are Chloe and Carla and they're eleven and thirteen so they helped with the cooking. Carla has pimples on her chin and she looks unhappy all the time. She didn't want to speak to Jess when she arrived, but after they made a cake together she was a bit happier and then she wanted to speak to Jess.

'It sucks being a teenager, love, I remember that,' I heard Jess say to her when they were sitting on the couch together.

I had the best sleep in the world because I was in the bed next to Isabel and I could hear her sleep noises all night long. Sometimes she sounds like a puppy. She sighs and squeaks all night. She still sleeps with her special blanket and her rabbit. I'm glad she does. She's still little and always happy to see me, and maybe when she's thirteen like

Carla she won't remember about seeing me at the Farm. Before she went to sleep she said, 'It's time for "Isabel", Mum,' and I said the Isabel poem for her. Lila says it for her every night and I say it to myself every night as well, even though she isn't with me. I don't want the words to go out of the door in my brain.

Allison came to get all the children on Sunday afternoon, and Isabel and I had to have five hugs because she's five. When she went with Allison to meet Lila, I had to clean up and go back to my unit. I was crying when I came back, and Jess was sad as well.

Maya and Mina are always kind to us after we've been at the mother and child unit. 'Why don't you girls watch some television and we'll get dinner ready soon,' said Maya.

Mina saw that I was trying to hold in my tears, and she said, 'Go on, Birdy, have a cry, get it all out, and then you can start to cross off the days until next time.'

I lay in bed before lights out and I counted how many days until I could see Isabel again, and then I counted how many days until I could go home.

Once a month we all have a meeting with Allison in the common room so we can talk about the Farm and all the things that are happening. When the meeting is over, we all stand up to pack away the chairs and Allison always says, 'Now, ladies, remember how close to the end you are. Remember that it's nearly over, and don't do anything stupid.' And then she leaves. She says the same thing every time to remind us to behave.

Lying in bed I counted the days till I could go home and I thought about what I wanted to do to Rose. Jess would say it was very stupid. She would be angry with me if I told her my agenda, but I can't change it. The feeling that she has to pay for what she did is stuck inside me. He can't pay because he's gone, but she's here, right here where I am.

Sometimes I wish that I didn't have my agenda, that it wasn't stuck inside me, but if I try to pretend that nothing happened to me I feel like the girl covered in flames. My skin burns and I can't breathe. I will never again be able to pretend that nothing happened. I was pretending for a very long time. I was happy to go on pretending forever. But on the day I hurt Mum I knew that I was done pretending.

The first night in the other place, I thought, *What if I've been pretending so long that I don't know the truth?* But the truth was there. It hadn't slipped away through the door in my mind. The truth was waiting inside, just like Rose and Mr Winslow were, just waiting somewhere in a corner, waiting for me to stop pretending.

When I was little I tried to tell the truth. I tried to say the words but they wouldn't come out right.

'Don't make me go there,' I said to Mum, but she didn't listen.

'Let me stay with you,' I said to Rose, but she wouldn't listen.

Maybe they would have helped me if I'd said the right words, but maybe not. Mum was angry about Dad, and Rose was busy.

When I was in the other place, Lila came to visit me and she told me about the stories in the newspaper. The stories were about Mr Winslow and all the things he had done. Lila didn't bring Isabel to visit me at the other place, because we agreed that it was a bad place for a little girl to be. Lila only came once a month. It was a long way to drive and she had to find a babysitter for Isabel because I didn't want Mum taking care of her. Lila would come and sit with me and tell me all about Isabel, and one day just before it was time for her to go and she had finished all her Isabel stories she said, 'Oh, and you won't believe what I read in the paper the other day.'

She was wrong about that; I did believe it.

I listened to Lila and watched as she smiled while she talked. 'Can you imagine that?' she said. 'To think that we actually lived next door to them for a few years. I thought they were nice, didn't you?'

'I don't remember,' I said. My skin was hot and I had to take deep breaths.

'But you used to play there all the time,' she said.

'I said I don't remember,' I said loudly.

'Are you all right?' said Lila. I didn't answer her and she was quiet for a long time and then she said, 'Fliss, is something wrong? Do you want to talk about something?'

'I'm fine,' I said.

'Look, don't worry about anything, okay? We're going to get you out of here as soon as we can. Lucy is calling all the time, trying to find a way to get you transferred to somewhere better.'

I started to cry then. Not because I wanted to be out of that awful place but because I wanted to tell Lila that I had stopped pretending about Mr Winslow and I knew the truth. But I couldn't make the words come out. I was glad that the women in the newspaper had found a way to tell the truth.

'Will he have to go to prison?' I asked Lila when she was standing up to leave.

'Who, Mr Winslow? I don't know. The police aren't involved yet. Some people are saying that it isn't true and some people are saying that it is.'

'It's true,' I said.

'How do you know?' said Lila, 'Did he . . . did he ever do anything to you?'

I shook my head. I couldn't tell her and then Lila had to leave, visiting hours were over. When she came to visit me the next time she had forgotten all about Mr Winslow because Isabel had been sick and she was telling me about taking her to the doctor and getting her medicine to make her better.

'Birdy, it's your turn to make dinner,' says Jess, and I stand up to go and do my job.

'I wish we could make hamburgers again,' I say.

'I know,' says Jess. 'They were good burgers.'

'When I go home I'm going to make burgers all the time,' I say.

'When I go home I'm going to sit in a restaurant and get someone else to serve me.'

'Will we see each other after we leave here?' I say.

'Of course we will,' she says.

I touch her on the shoulder because I want to give her a hug but Jess doesn't like hugs from anyone but her kids. I want to tell her about Rose and about my agenda but I cover my mouth with my hand.

'You right?' says Jess.

'Yep,' I say. 'I'm great.'

Chapter Ten

It's my turn to clean the bathroom in our unit today. I've been here for almost a month but have only just spotted my name assigned to this particular chore on the roster.

Time passes so slowly here that I feel as though I can see the minute movements of the clock hands, and yet the weeks seem to have gone by quickly. Perhaps that perception is more self-preservation than anything else. There are calendars everywhere you look, cheap ones with pictures of animals or landscapes. On every one the days are crossed off with strong black or red marks, tearing through the paper, almost eliminating the date. I understand the need to only look forward. 'How many months to go?' is a frequent question, because most of the women are at the tail end of their sentences. *How many months to go?* I think sometimes, and then I turn away from that thought. There is no point in that for me right now.

Very few of the women have been sent here straight from court. There is a woman named Julie who helped her husband die. He was suffering from cancer and in terrible pain and he begged her to end his suffering. 'If you had seen his eyes,' she says to everyone she meets. She doesn't introduce herself or explain anything, she just says, 'If you had seen his eyes,' and then she walks away. 'She's okay once she's told every new person that,' said Sal when I asked her about it. 'She just wants you to know.'

Her stepchildren did not see what she did as an act of mercy, and they forced an investigation into their father's death. Julie received a year's sentence and was sent straight here. She helps to run the cooking school. She is the only person here who is older than me, although there is a look of peace in her sixty-year-old face that sometimes makes her appear younger. Once she has said what she needs to say she smiles. I envy her that peace, that certainty that she did the right thing.

I'm aware that some of the women here view me as having been spared the time in a proper jail that I should have done. Each time I lose an hour here or there, involved in some task to the point where I forget where I am, I am grateful to Eric and his string-pulling. As the days go on I find it more rather than less bizarre that I'm still here, wearing my ill-fitting clothes, living with criminals. I feel as though in the latter half of my life I have become the actor in the family. I hope I'm putting in a good performance. I hope that I still know how to be Rose Winslow when I go home. I hope I still know how to be.

'We've been giving you a bit of a break, Mrs Winslow,' says Sal when she sees me looking at the roster of chores, and then she looks at Heather.

'Please, ladies, as I've said before, call me Rose. And there's no need to treat me any differently. I am here just like you and I will do what needs to be done.'

'It's just that you look a little tired, that's all,' says Heather.

I had no idea anyone was watching me so closely. My nights here have become difficult. I fall asleep easily enough but wake after a couple of hours to lie in the dark paralysed by fear over my future. I think about Lottie and Sam, who both have birthdays coming up that I will miss, and I think about my and Simon's anniversary next month. Families are tied together by celebrations, by the sharing of food and joy. I wonder what my daughters will think about on the day of my wedding anniversary. I worry that I may have broken my family, that I've taken away their innocence and that they will be pulled apart by grief and tragedy.

How will the grandchildren blow out their candles without Simon's baritone voice singing 'Happy Birthday'? One missing grandparent would have been terrible enough, but to be missing two seems a dreadful punishment. I have sent an email to Rosalind asking her to buy them gifts; she hasn't replied, although I'm sure she will get each of them something and tell them it is from me. I know that Lottie likes My Little Pony and Sam is interested in anything electronic. If I stay here for three years they will both be very different by the time I see them again.

I think about that as I lie in the dark. My heart rate speeds up and I cannot get back to sleep. If I eventually do, Simon is usually waiting for me. 'But darling girl,' he asks, 'how could you have done such a thing?' I find I miss him more as time goes on, not less. My loneliness makes his crimes recede and there is only my betrayal left.

At first I managed to convince myself that I was only here for a short time, but as the appeals process drags on and on and Portia's emails only say *No news* I've begun to feel quite marooned in this place. Yesterday we all had to line up in the hall while a dog sniffed us for drugs. It was beyond humiliating. I have no idea what the authorities think is being achieved by degrading human beings like this. The policeman handling the dog was very kind and professional, but it was hard not to imagine oneself guilty of something. We all stood straight-backed and silent, listening to the noises from the dog and I'm sure our own heartbeats. When it was over, there was some relieved laughter and then it was not discussed again.

'I am finding all the physical work a bit of a challenge,' I say to Heather. It seems to be the easiest explanation. 'But I cannot shirk my responsibilities. It's not as if I've never cleaned a bathroom before.'

'Didn't you have a maid?'

'Not at the very beginning. Not when we were first married. When I had my first child, I had virtually no money. Simon was working as a waiter.'

Heather nods. If not for Sal's presence, I suspect she would follow me to the bathroom to hear more about the life she imagines I have led. Heather spends all her spare change on women's magazines, and I can see that while her hands are busy working she lets her mind run riot imagining a different life. They cannot get at your dreams in prison—clichéd but true.

'I assume everything I'll need is kept under the sink?' I ask, and Heather points to the kitchen and nods again.

Heather used to drown out the more unsavoury parts of her life with alcohol. 'The usual bullshit,' she told me. 'Husband gone, no money, out-of-control kids, not the life I had imagined for myself.' Now that I know her better I can see that Heather wouldn't have been out of place living next door to me. In fact, at one stage there was someone much like her living next door to us. Someone whose life did not turn out the way she expected it to.

I think about her, Ellie, a lot these days, especially since Simon . . . After Ellie's husband left her and the kids I could have done more for her, helped her out more, instead of pretending to myself that she was coping I should have seen what was really going on instead of comforting myself that I was doing enough to help by babysitting when it suited me. I should have gone over to her house.

When Heather confessed her drinking problem I felt nothing but empathy. There was a time when I would have judged her, but that time is long gone. Profoundly shocking events in life can change a person. I understand that now. Before everything started with Simon I was content with one glass of wine every now and again, but as the months wore on and the press became more vicious I found myself turning to alcohol more and more. We both did. Two glasses of wine allow you to see a news article as a temporary thing. You explain it away and convince yourself that someone else will be the subject of the nation's opprobrium soon enough. Three glasses and four allow you to project yourself past what is happening in your life, and then you are tipped over the edge into sleep and nothing matters for a while.

He drank whisky alone in his study and I drank wine and watched bad television. The rosy glow that alcohol produces changed the direction of my thinking. I would go from believing that the police were about to arrive at our front door to drag Simon away to believing that the whole thing was a storm in a teacup, an overreaction by silly women who had misinterpreted Simon's friendliness. A few glasses on and I would grow bitter about being imprisoned in my house, and angry at the press who were attacking Simon and our family for no earthly reason. That would be followed by a thick, dreamless sleep that I woke from dry-mouthed and regretful. It didn't happen every night, but it happened enough for me to understand that I was only a step or two from the spiral downwards.

I'm sure there are people who can compartmentalise their problems and deal with them in a logical fashion, but during that time I found it difficult to think of anything but the accusations against Simon. Whatever I did and wherever I went I would be turning over the words of one woman or another. Five months after that first article in which his behaviour was just a footnote, I had a collection of phrases that I ran through over and over again. Phrases that brought to mind images that I didn't want to see.

He shoved his hand down my blouse.

He pushed against me and pinned me to a wall.

He whispered that I smelled like a summer peach and then he kissed me.

His fingers went inside me and it hurt so much.

I begged him to stop. Begged him.

'Preposterous,' said Simon every time. 'As if I would do something like that, as if I would say something like that.'

'No, of course not,' I would agree, and then I would bite down on the direct question: *But did you do this, Simon— maybe not in those words, not in that way, but did you do it?*

We had never spent as much time apart as we did in those last few months before he died. We were fond of the same television programs—or at least I was happy enough to watch what he wanted in order to enjoy his company. It had been our nightly ritual since the girls left home to take a small fruit plate and some good dark chocolate along with our cups of tea into the television room. There we would spend an hour or two chatting about what we were watching, about the girls, about our friends. We were such easy companions by then. We had so many years of memories to call upon. We never ran out of things to say. But when a new story began to appear every day about the things he was accused of, we became uneasy in each other's company. I think we were afraid to be in the same room for too long. He, because he was afraid I might ask him uncomfortable questions, and me, because I was afraid that if I asked those questions I would be given answers I didn't want to hear.

'How could she not know?' is a question asked of every woman betrayed by a man. 'How could she not know he was sleeping with other women, or gambling away all their money, or running a business that was going bankrupt, or cheating the tax office, or gay, or that he had a whole other family?' How could she not know, indeed?

The allegations didn't just mystify and disgust me, they were also a blow to my ego. Despite my curtailed education I had always considered myself to be relatively smart. I read voraciously. I kept up with the news and the world outside my home. I was capable enough, when I felt comfortable, of conversing on a wide range of topics. The idea that I had been so blind was difficult to accept. So I drank and ate away confronting thoughts about my lack of insight, and I waited for it all to blow over. It didn't, of course. My pants grew tight and my eyes acquired a red rim and the truth was eventually impossible to ignore, and so here I am.

I lost the weight soon enough with a court case hanging over my head, but I didn't really give up my three or four glasses of wine a night until I came here. I feel better for it, but certainly no happier. Wine-coloured glasses are much more pleasant than reality.

'The drink just makes life a bit better,' Heather told me when she explained why she was here. I didn't ask her for her story. I knew not to do that, but it came up over dinner. We were eating lasagne that I had made, and Sal said, 'I would kill for a glass of red.' I smiled at her, both of us sharing, I'm sure, the vision of an Italian restaurant, lit by candles throwing a warm glow on a rich, deep glass of red wine. Heather didn't respond; she was shovelling her food in quickly. Everyone eats quickly here. Our budgets are small and so food is not plentiful. Deprived of liberty and choice, people revert to a defensive, animal way of eating.

'I'll never drink again,' she said when she paused for breath.

'You only have a few months left,' I said. 'I'm sure you'll enjoy that first drink when you get home.'

Sal caught my eye and shook her head.

'No,' said Heather. 'Alcohol put me in here. I can't let that happen again.'

'Oh,' I said, and then because I know not to push I just went back to my meal.

'I had a car accident,' said Heather. 'I was drunk and I hit another car and there was a child in the back. I deserved to be punished. I did. I won't drink again.'

I had no idea what to say to that. I would have liked to ask if the child died and how old he or she was, but I could see the discussion was over.

Heather longs for the glossy life of a celebrity, but I'm sure she looks at me and wonders at the apparent perfection on the magazine pages. Celebrities and the wives of celebrities should certainly not end up cleaning toilets in prison. Strange how often they do.

I don't mind, really. I like to tire myself out. But when your hands are busy your mind is free, and there are days when that's not a good thing.

The last year and a half of my life has been the stuff of bad television.

It began, predictably enough, with wonderful news. Simon came back from lunch with his agent jubilant and triumphant. Lunch with his agent was a monthly occurrence, although they did little more than speak of Simon's glory days when he was the most famous man on television. Henry wasn't really working anymore but he enjoyed catching up with his only remaining client. They went to the same restaurant each time, and the maître d' had always reserved their favourite table and greeted them by name. They both ordered the steak with a side of potatoes au gratin; they split a salad and a bottle of red wine and whatever dessert was the special of the day. Simon would not sleep that night because his digestion was no longer what it used to be, but I didn't grumble at him about it. I knew that as he got older and the spotlight on him grew dimmer he clung to these lunches and discussions of the old days.

Usually he returned from the lunches a little drunk and with snippets of gossip about the industry he was no longer a part of, but his last lunch with Henry was different.

'My dear, I've had the most glorious news,' he said, and I obediently put down my book to focus on him entirely. 'I'm going to be inducted into the Hall of Fame. Apparently I was an integral part of Australian television history, and I'm to be acknowledged at the awards ceremony in September. They want me to make a speech.'

'Oh, Simon,' I said, 'that's delightful news! We must call the girls.'

'You'll need a new dress, and Henry said there may be interviews with magazines when the news gets out.'

He was the happiest he'd been for years. Simon was a performer. He revelled in being the centre of attention. Even when we were just out together he would behave as though a camera was focused on him. Once he had achieved a certain level of fame, I often had to chastise myself for thinking that his grand gestures of love were little more than performances for which he required my applause. He liked to hide gifts of jewellery in desserts and surprise me with tickets to Italy in the middle of dinner with friends. On my fortieth birthday, he bought forty roses and set them up in small vases leading all the way into our favourite restaurant, which he had hired out for the night. All our friends and family were waiting, and somehow the press had also managed to get wind of my surprise. In the pictures of our life that appear in magazines I am usually caught from the side or the back, always looking at or holding onto Simon. He doesn't look at me, he looks at the camera.

If I questioned his behaviour I always felt mean-spirited, and I was then especially effusive in my thanks.

'Did you have the most wonderful birthday, darling girl?' he asked me after the night in the restaurant. I had enjoyed the night, but secretly I would have preferred a small dinner with a few close friends and no flashing cameras.

'Oh, Simon, it was magnificent. You're so clever to have kept it so quiet.'

'You will be the envy of your friends, my dear. Look how much you are loved and adored.'

'I'm already the envy of my friends,' I said, knowing that it was what he wanted to hear.

The afternoon he learned that he was to be inducted into the Hall of Fame I watched him pace up and down the living room, talking and laughing about his lunch with Henry, and I saw glimpses of the young man he had once been.

It felt very glamorous to me at sixteen to find myself married to an actor; I had little idea of how scarce money would be. I was really still a child and had never had to think beyond making my pocket money stretch to cover a couple of shopping trips with Lulu. I'd never even had a real job. After we were married I left school, to the horror of my teachers and principal, who would gladly have allowed me to finish my studies if I agreed to keep my marital status a secret. Simon wouldn't hear of it. 'You're a married woman, Rose. You don't need to be at school pretending to be a child any longer.' I got a position at a supermarket, working at the checkout, and between the two of us we managed to pay the rent and keep ourselves fed, but then I discovered I was pregnant with Portia.

I was terrified. The first time we'd had sex had been shocking enough, but giving birth was almost beyond my comprehension. I was a child when I married him, and a child on our wedding night. I thought I was ready, but I can remember lying in bed after he had fallen asleep and thinking, *I'm never doing that again.* It was nothing like I had imagined, and there was no pleasure involved in the actual act. Lying there afterwards, I longed for my mother and my bed at home where my rag doll still lay on my pillow. I cried quietly, terrified that he would wake up and make me do it again.

Of course we did have sex again and of course it got better. Simon loved my body. He was always talking about how small and perfect I was. 'These breasts are just a cupful,' he said. 'The perfect cupful.'

What was he seeing when he looked at me? I think about that now. And if I was so perfect, why was I not enough for him? And would another woman have been better at being his wife, at keeping him from his transgressions?

He never wanted to discuss previous girlfriends. 'That is my past, darling girl, and you are my future and the rest of my life,' he said when I asked him. In all our years together I only met one of his ex-girlfriends, and she was much older than me—older than Simon, in fact.

'How is Lilly faring?' Simon asked the woman, Sarah I think her name was. It was at a Christmas party for the television studio. The woman was a makeup artist who had started out as an actor and changed direction.

'She's well, Simon, thank you. She has decided to stay in Europe. She loves it there, although I miss her. It was so generous of you to help her out with a ticket. Especially since you hadn't seen her for so long.' Sarah's tone was flat, distinctly ungrateful, I thought.

'It was nothing, Sarah, nothing at all.'

'Who's Lilly?' I asked as we made our way to the bar.

'She's Sarah's daughter. She was only about twelve when I met her, but she contacted me about a year ago. She needed money for a ticket to Europe. I gave her some, it wasn't much.'

'Why would she have contacted you?' I said. 'You have no relationship with her at all.'

'There will always be people from my past who want to get something from me. Last week someone I went to school with called me and asked me to invest in his

drycleaning business. Can you imagine? I haven't seen
the man for nearly thirty years but that didn't stop him.
I'm sure we didn't even get on when we attended school
together. When I knew Lilly I was a struggling actor, but
now I'm rich and famous. She and I were good friends.
It was a small gesture to an old friend, that's all.'

Red flags are not as easy to see as people might think.
Red flags can only be spotted when you are looking for
them. I thought it was terribly kind of Simon to give the
young woman money. I thought it was sad that people
thought they could use him for his money. I didn't think
anything else.

Simon was not pleased when he learned I was pregnant.
I had been hoping that he would find a way to make me feel
better, but he was horrified. I've often wondered whether
Portia felt his resentment for her in the womb and that's
why they've always been at loggerheads.

'It's not my fault,' I wailed when Simon yelled at me
for 'ruining his career'. 'Maybe that thing broke,' I said
referring to the condom, which was our only method of
contraception—and one that Simon didn't always use.
Simon smiled at me, 'Oh Rose, you're such a child,' which
made me even more upset. He seemed to be laughing at
me for being young, but it may be that he was pleased with
the obvious evidence of my naiveté.

'Now, Rose, darling girl, stop these tears,' he said. 'This is
a setback, but we will survive. I know there will be an extra
mouth to feed and it will be difficult, but we will manage.

I can get some extra shifts at the restaurant, and perhaps you can still work for a few more months.'

'Of course I will, Simon,' I said.

He kissed my forehead. 'There, see, it will be fine. All will be well. The only thing I ask is that you do not expect me to give up my dream. Please say you do not expect that. Especially now that I have Henry as an agent. He feels that at any moment now my big break will arrive.'

'I would never ask you to give up your dream,' I said. I had never really had dreams of my own. Being a teacher was an idea I absorbed from my parents. The only thing I had ever really wanted in my life was Simon.

'Of course you wouldn't, you're my darling girl and you know that when I'm famous we'll both be so happy. Now, you won't gain too much weight, will you? I can't abide women who let themselves go and turn into cows with bulbous breasts and fat stomachs.'

I worked right up until the week before Portia was born. By then I was exhausted. My stomach was a huge alien thing sticking out of the front of my body. Simon had stopped coming near me as soon as my stomach started to grow. 'I don't want to hurt the baby,' he said, and I had no one to ask about that. I wouldn't have dreamed of asking my doctor the question, and there were no women around I was close enough to to ask for advice. I wanted my mother every day but couldn't think of how to approach her. I also didn't want her to know how hard my life was. I was still young enough not to want to hear 'I told you so'. And Simon grew angry if I mentioned my parents, so I knew it was best to keep quiet. 'You have no idea how much it hurts me that they will not accept me, Rose,' he said if I brought them up. 'It pains me to think how much they hate me. How can you love people who hate me so much?'

After Portia was born, Simon worked every night at the restaurant and every day with one or another amateur theatre group. We were both so tired all the time that we only ever thought about sleep. Simon hated my engorged breasts and flabby stomach. He didn't say so, but every now and then I would catch him looking at me as I fed Portia and I would see the revulsion on his face. I tried to eat less so that I would lose weight quicker, but I was always so tired that I could not function without food. It broke my heart to see the way he looked at me, and even now when I remember it I am hurt anew, although there is some anger there as well. When Rosalind was pregnant with Sam I would watch Jack rub his hands over her belly, stroking and touching, trying to feel a foot or an elbow. His eyes followed her wherever she went, as though her mere existence as a pregnant woman was a miracle. It wasn't the same with Lottie, because he was so busy running after Sam, but he was never upset by her burgeoning body the way Simon was with mine. When I was pregnant with Portia I assumed all husbands behaved the way Simon did.

When the plays he was rehearsing for were performed he would stop working altogether and the money would disappear for a few nights or weeks. I never told him but I always held out hope of an early closing. He went to endless auditions. Henry always proclaimed that the next role he was auditioning for was 'just made for you, my boy. You almost don't even have to audition, just walk in and they'll give it to you.' Henry spoke like that to all his clients. Every one of them was, according to him, on the cusp of greatness. It was difficult for Simon to keep going back after each rejection, but he never lost faith. 'Henry will get me there, darling girl, I just know he will.'

By the time I was pregnant with Rosalind, however, he was beginning to play with the idea of giving up. I knew it was all talk, but I could see his despair at failing to become the star he thought he was destined to be. 'I'm a silly man with a silly dream,' he would say to me, and I, knowing that he had been made maudlin by cheap wine and a bad day, would reply, 'No, you're not, Simon. One day you're going to be a star.' But I privately longed for him to get a real job and become a proper husband.

And then one night everything changed.

One of our neighbours had offered to babysit Portia and Rosalind so that I could go and see Simon perform Hamlet. I was, by then, simply exhausted all the time. I had gone back to work at the supermarket the moment Rosalind started school. We were desperate for the money. Just keeping the rent paid felt like an enormous task. I didn't want to go out, but Simon was so excited for me to see him perform again and a night out did feel like a chance to remember that there was life outside of work and children.

When Simon was on stage I felt the same fizzing attraction to him that I had felt that first day watching him perform Macbeth. Despite my exhaustion and constant worry about money, I still ran my fingers over my lips, imagining the taste of his kisses that I knew so well.

Backstage afterwards I was over the top with my compliments, happy to see him enjoying the spotlight.

We were getting ready to leave when Henry came in with another man. Henry was practically frothing at the mouth, he was so excited.

'My name is William Hadley,' said the man and then he waited, presumably for us to recognise who he was. We had no idea. We couldn't afford a television because of the expense.

'Television, Simon,' said Henry. 'Television!'

William, as we would both later call him at dinner parties, stroked his neat grey beard, laughed and said, 'We have a talent show in the planning stage and we're looking for a host. We think you have exactly the right look for the project.'

I had no idea who 'we' were, because only William was present, but television people always see themselves as larger than life.

'I'm an actor,' said Simon. 'I don't want to host a show on television.'

'My dear boy,' said Henry, and I grabbed Simon's arm forcing him to look at me as I tried to silently communicate to him my fear about the overdue rent. I didn't know how much money such a thing paid but I was sure it must be more than being a waiter.

'Simon,' I said quietly.

'Of course there's no harm in talking,' said Simon, thankfully getting my message.

'No, no harm in that,' laughed William. He shook Simon's hand and nodded at me, and then he and Henry left. As they made their way out of the theatre, we could hear Henry listing the plays Simon had performed in.

The talent show was called *My Kid Can* . . . and each week it featured five children competing for a cash prize. They sang or danced or recited poems. Television had only just gone from black and white to colour. It was a medium that 'real' actors didn't take seriously. The stage was the place to be.

'Rose, I'm an actor. I've spent years honing my craft. I cannot give that up to be the host of some execrable talent show involving children.'

'I can't work any more hours than I am doing. I'm so tired. We can barely make ends meet. Please say that you will just go and talk to him—for me, for our children.' I whined the words at him, sounding more trucculent child than desperate wife, but it worked.

Simon gave a heavy theatrical sigh. 'For you, my darling,' he said, 'but only for you.'

Between them, William and Henry managed to persuade Simon to do just one show.

'Henry has asked me to do it as a favour to him,' he said when he returned from the meeting at the television station, 'and I have agreed.'

'Oh, Simon, that's fantastic,' I said, restraining myself from yelling at him about our lack of money.

The first night the show screened I invited some of the neighbours with whom I had formed tentative friendships to watch with us, but all I watched was Simon as he watched himself. Portia and Rosalind were beside themselves with excitement at seeing their father on television, but even his daughter's obvious delight had little effect on him. 'Make them be quiet or take them to bed,' he hissed at me when I went into the kitchen to refill a plate of biscuits. I had splurged on snacks and tidied the apartment, laying colourful cloths over our second-hand furniture so it wouldn't look so shabby. I had never invited the neighbours in before. Mr and Mrs Stein from next door who sometimes helped with the girls and the Leo family from downstairs joined us. Our landlord also came upstairs and presented me with a rose for the table. We were the only ones in the building with a television set at the time, because the television studio had kindly lent us one for the big night. 'They said if I continued on we could keep the set,' Simon told me when he brought it home. 'It might be worth it just for that,' I said.

Everyone who joined us loved the show. They laughed when I thought they should, they commented on each child and their various talents, and at the end they all applauded.

'You're a star,' said Mrs Stein, kissing Simon on both cheeks.

'Well done,' said her husband, shaking Simon's hand. Simon smiled and joked and performed for the little crowd.

When they had gone, I bundled my overexcited daughters into bed and then cleaned up. I knew that Simon was unhappy. Throughout the program I had watched the curl of his lip and seen him shake his head. I readied myself to talk him out of his mood. I wiped down the counter in the kitchen and practised the words I would use. When I was done tidying up, I found Simon in our bedroom, lying on the bed and staring up at the ceiling.

'I have humiliated myself, Rose,' he said.

Oh, I was so tired. Tired because I had spent the afternoon cleaning after being at work; tired because I knew that one or both of the girls would be up during the night with a nightmare or a stomach ache from all the biscuits I had allowed them to eat; tired because I knew that I would have to get up the next day and do it all over again. But mostly I was tired of my beautiful husband and his inability to see that I was drowning and needed his help. I knew that confronting him would achieve nothing. He was nearly forty-four and he was still prone to tantrums and shedding tears on his own behalf.

'No, you haven't. They loved it, Simon. They laughed in all the right places. They clapped when that little boy won.'

'Did you see how orange my skin looked? How ridiculous that suit was?'

'Maybe there's something wrong with the television the station gave us. We can get it fixed. It was a huge success, Simon, I promise you.'

'My career is over. One day you will look back at this and know that I sold out and ended my career.' It was clear to me from the way he spoke that the fault lay at my feet. I had forced him to take the chance by making him aware of our severe lack of money.

He didn't speak to me for the rest of the night. I was up and down dealing with Portia, who was prone to nightmares. In the morning he woke up determined to tell the station that he would never work for them again.

I was juggling both girls and trying to get ready for work. I didn't respond to his declaration that he was finished with television. 'Can you just get me some milk from the corner store before you go, please?' I said.

He walked out with his head bowed and his fists jammed into his pockets, but when he returned with the milk his whole demeanour had changed.

'She gave it to me for free,' he said, a light shining in his eyes.

'Why on earth would she do that?'

'She said she watched the show. She said her whole family watched the show and she thinks I'm a natural with the children and she can't wait for next week. She thinks it's the best thing on television. That's what she said—that it was the best thing on television.'

'Did you tell her there won't be a next week? Not with you, I mean?'

'Do you know, Rose, I think I could get used to this. I really think I could.'

I managed to hide my delighted smile until he left to inform Henry of the good news. 'Stupid man,' I said to the apartment after he'd left, and then giggled at my audacity.

'Who's stupid?' said Portia.

'No one, darling. Hurry up and brush your teeth or I'll be late.'

I went on with my day of work and laundry and cleaning while Simon had lunch with the producers of the show. He was kind enough to bring me back a dessert from the lunch. I believe it was a chocolate soufflé, collapsed by then but very tasty.

'Quit your job,' he said as he watched me eat the dessert.

And so it began. *My Kid Can . . .* was one of the most popular shows on Australian television. It ran for nearly ten years and set us up for life. The money got better and better, and I do remember at one point reading something about him being the highest-paid television host in history—only for Australia, of course, but it was more than enough. There were endorsements and public-speaking fees and it seemed that everywhere he turned people just wanted to hand him money.

He occasionally complained about having to work with children.

'The young girls can be very tiresome,' he always said, but otherwise he loved every minute.

That's what he called them—*tiresome.*

'You need to be patient,' I told him. 'Be kind to them, be friendly.'

A week after Simon had been told about being inducted into the Hall of Fame, a journalist from the local newspaper called about an interview.

'It has begun, my dear,' he said when he'd finished on the phone. 'I shall have one last hurrah before I shuffle off this mortal coil.'

'Please don't speak like that,' I said.

'Oh, Rose, darling girl. How I love you,' he said, stroking the back of my neck as he walked past me.

He was always affectionate. I thought that we shared a connection that I couldn't see in the other marriages around me. It's strange to find myself so wrong about something. He was not who I thought him to be, and because I was with him for so long, that makes me question who I am as well. Now that he's gone I cannot ask him, but I would love to have been able to say, 'If you're not the Simon I knew, then who am I? Who am I?'

I pour bleach into the shower recess. Bleach stings the eyes but it's important that everything smells thoroughly clean before inspection. If we can clean our units, presumably we can clean up our lives. Or something like that. Heather repeats Allison's words almost verbatim. She is holding tightly onto the rules and the lessons she has learned here. I hope she will still be able to hold on when she gets out.

The article in the magazine followed soon afterwards. We assumed that the woman had read about him and decided to grab at her own fifteen minutes. She was bitter and jealous, and Eric gave a statement telling the world we intended to sue. Privately he told us, 'It will cost hundreds of thousands of dollars. We will be up against the might of a media empire.'

'I don't care about the cost, Eric,' Simon said. 'I will have my day in court.'

Oh, he was so good, so convincing. Perhaps he really believed that he had done nothing wrong back then, or perhaps he didn't think anyone else would come forward. He huffed and puffed, and the girls and I tried to get him to see the logic of Eric's words.

'People always say negative things about celebrities, Dad,' said Rosalind. 'You need to just ignore it.'

'My reputation has been compromised, Rosalind dear. I cannot allow that to happen.'

Eric counselled and I argued and the girls persuaded and eventually he agreed to let it go.

There was a lull for a week or two and we imagined that we had put it behind us, but then overnight things changed. One woman after another began to come forward. The allegations mounted up and the accusations flew back and forth. 'Little whores,' shouted Simon about two women who came forward at once.

My hand flew to my mouth at his base expression, but I put it down to extreme stress.

Eric came over daily and went through newspaper and internet articles, television interviews and tweets that went around the world.

'Who is this woman?' Eric asked Simon each time one came forward. 'Do you remember this one? Do you know her? Do you know her, Simon?'

Simon was incredulous. He did not know any of the women. He couldn't recall their names or faces. He was stunned by the accusations, completely stunned.

He began to drink more. He debated going to the press with his own story, but Eric advised against it. 'Until they charge you with something, this is all just rumours, speculation and allegations. Stay quiet until it becomes absolutely necessary for you to speak.'

'Why are there so many of them, Dad?' asked Rosalind.

'Are you telling the truth about this?' asked Portia.

'Leave your father alone,' I told them. 'Can't you see he's suffering? Of course none of this is true. I have no idea why these women would want to hurt an old man like this. What kind of people are they?'

Yet all the time I wanted to ask him the question. It was on the tip of my tongue as I made him lunch and dinner. It hovered unspoken in the air between us. It followed us to bed and was there waiting for me in the morning. He would catch me staring at him, and instead of asking me what I was thinking, as he had always done throughout our marriage, he would lower his head and go back to his book or his crossword.

I wrote it down and tried to find different ways to ask it, but all I wanted to do was yell, 'Did you do this, Simon? Did you do these things to these children? Did you? Did you do this?'

In the bathroom I slump forward over my knees. It is too much to think about this. I can feel the tears on my face and I pull off the gloves to wipe my cheeks. The bleach smell stings my nose and it begins to run. I try to stand up but can't seem to move, 'Simon,' I call, 'Simon, I need your help,' and only when Heather comes into the bathroom do I remember where I am.

Chapter Eleven

Everyone has come to help me cover the back half of the aviary. It's getting cold at night now. I only have two months left here at the Farm. Two months is about sixty days. That's two more times that Isabel will come and stay with me and then we will live together all the time. Lila says that I can come and live with her. 'Isabel has already decorated her room,' she told me, 'but when you come we'll do yours together.'

What if you find a boyfriend and want to get married and have babies? I said in the email when we were talking about where I was going to live after the Farm.

I don't think that's going to happen, she said. *I have lots of friends. I don't want a husband.* Lila has always had lots of friends. When we were still at school together she would leave her friends and come and sit with me at lunch. Sometimes she would bring lots of girls with her and then I would feel like I was sitting with friends as well. School was hard for me, because kids are cruel. That's what Mum said if I told her that going to school made me feel sad. 'Yes, well, kids can be cruel, Felicity. You have to learn how to deal with it yourself. I can't save you from everything.' I didn't understand what Mum meant, because she hadn't saved me from anything.

I left school after year ten and finished up at a special college where I learned all the subjects but didn't write the exams. I also learned how to cook and go to the bank and take care of myself. I didn't mind the special college but I missed being able to sit with Lila at lunch.

Lila is a good little sister. I don't think I have been a very good big sister. I thought Lila would be mad at me because I hurt Mum. I had to stay in the jail cell while I waited for my trial, because Mum told Lila that I would hurt her again. I agreed that I would stay because I was also afraid of myself, of the bubbling anger inside me. I didn't know what I would do. In the jail I thought about all the things that I had been pretending didn't happen. I thought about Mr Winslow and about Mrs Winslow and about Mum not seeing me. I thought about Dad going away so I couldn't tell him about Mr Winslow, and then I thought about what Lester had done to Isabel and it was all too much. I cried and cried for all the things I'd been pretending about.

'What happened, Fliss?' said Lila when she came to visit me.

'I don't know,' I said. 'I just got so mad. My hand moved so quickly.'

'But why were you mad with Mum? I mean, I know she can be difficult but we don't hurt each other in this family. Mum never hit us, did she?'

'No,' I said. I chewed on the last nail I had left. I had chewed up all the others in the night. My teeth caught the end and pulled and I felt the sting and looked down to see the blood. Lila handed me a tissue. 'Hitting isn't the only way to hurt people,' I said. I didn't know how to explain things to Lila. I would have to use too many words.

'Did Mum say something to hurt you, Fliss? Did she say something about Isabel or Lester?'

I looked up. 'Did Mum tell you what Isabel said about Lester?'

Lila nodded. 'She did, and I know why you're angry at him, although I think maybe you should have spoken to him about it. Isabel is only four, Fliss, maybe she made a mistake and he was just, you know ... being nice and playing with her.'

I stood up and pushed my chair back. My hand was shaking.

'Everything okay?' said the guard standing by the door.

'It's fine,' said Lila. She held up her hand to show me that I had to stop. My fingers were pushing into my hand. My fist was getting ready to hit.

The guard started to walk towards me and I sat down again. 'He. Wasn't. Being. Nice,' I said.

'All right, Fliss,' said Lila in a low voice. 'It's all right. I believe you, I believe Isabel, okay? Did you hurt Mum because you wanted to hurt Lester?'

'I don't know.'

'I'm going to get you a lawyer, a good one, okay?'

'Okay, and you'll take care of Isabel and tell her that I miss her and I love her?'

'I'll tell her. She's living with me at the moment, don't worry about her. One of my friends is looking after her right now.'

'You mustn't let Lester near Isabel. You have to take Isabel away from Mum and take care of her and keep her away from Lester.'

'Maybe we should tell someone about Lester,' said Lila.

'Mum didn't believe Isabel. Maybe no one will believe Isabel about Lester.'

'Maybe,' said Lila, 'but if it's true then we have to tell someone. He's a teacher. He shouldn't be allowed around children.'

'I don't want Isabel to have to tell. I think it would be very scary for her and if people don't believe her then she will be sad. Don't make her tell, Lila. Please!'

'Okay, Fliss, don't worry about it, I'll think of something. I can look into it when Mum is taking care of Isabel again.'

'No, no, no. Mum can't take care of Isabel. She doesn't see her, she doesn't see anything.'

'Felicity, I have to work, I can't take care of Isabel. You know I love her, but I have to work. She's staying with me while Mum's in the hospital, but then she'll have to go back home.'

'Please, Lila, please, please, please don't let her go back to Mum,' I said. 'Mum won't listen to her. She won't listen to her and she won't see her.'

'Okay, okay . . . stop crying. I'll figure it out. I'll keep her with me, I will.'

I think Lila lets Mum visit Isabel now, but I don't want to go back and live with Mum. I don't want to hurt her again. I'm trying to keep all my bubbling anger for Rose only, but there's still some left over for Mum. I don't know if it will ever go away. I don't know why I'm so angry at Mum. I know what happened the day I hurt her, but I don't know why. The only thing I do know is that that was the day all the anger bubbled up inside me and I couldn't pretend things hadn't happened anymore.

That's what Henrietta wants me to talk about. Henrietta wants to know why. I'm afraid of why. Why is a secret that my mind won't let go of.

'I would like to try hypnosis,' said Henrietta the last time I saw her.

'What's that?'

'It means that I will help you relax, just with words, and you will feel sleepy and then maybe you can tell me what happened and you won't feel bad about telling me.'

'No,' I said. 'No, no, no.'

'Okay, Birdy, okay. We won't do it.'

In bed at night now I can hear the wind as it howls through the valley like a monster. It makes me worry for the finches. They don't like the cold. They're so small and vulnerable. I have to protect them. I wish I could bring the finches into my room where it's warm. I think they would like it. They could fly around and fill my room with colours.

'Quite a few of them died last winter,' Allison told me when I asked her to buy me some tarp for the cage.

'They don't like the wind. They're too small. We need to cover the back half of the cage so they're protected.'

'Okay, Birdy, I'll get you your tarp.' Allison listens when I tell her about the finches. Last month we sold some to a pet shop and made four hundred dollars. Allison let me keep fifty dollars because I'd done such a good job. Gouldian finches can sell for a lot of money. The ones with pretty colours sell for the most money. Allison was proud of me because I managed to make the finches breed and all the babies lived. The finches were safe and happy and they had clean water and food and that's why they wanted to have babies.

I also have some old blankets to put over the cage. They have holes in them but I think they will help keep the finches warm. And I had to take away the breeding boxes so they don't breed. I love finches but sometimes they're not very clever. They don't know to only go in the boxes to keep warm. You can't tell a finch something over and over again. Finches do what they always do. They survive by . . . by instinct. That means they are born knowing what to do and how to live. It's not the same for humans. We have to be taught, but you can't teach finches. If they try to breed in winter they can get something called egg bound. That means the eggs get stuck inside and then they die. They are only supposed to breed when it's warm.

Rose doesn't help much when we're putting up the tarp. Her job is to hand us the hooks to go through the metal eyes in the tarp and then into the cage, but she has to sit down after a few minutes. She looks thinner to me than she was when she came here a few weeks ago. She was never very big to begin with. Heather says she doesn't eat much at dinner, which suits her and Sal and Linda because it means more for them. I didn't ask Heather about Rose. She just told me. I would never ask about her. But Rose doesn't just look thinner. She looks like she's shrinking. I hope she doesn't get smaller and smaller until she disappears, not until I've done what I have to do. I will be the one to make her disappear. That is a bad thought, but it makes me feel strong to think it. I will be the one to make her disappear.

'My husband never did this with his birds,' she says while she watches the rest of us working our way around the cage.

'He had heat lamps,' I say, and then I have to bite my lip because I can't cover my mouth while my hands are busy with the tarp. Speak no evil.

'How do you know what he had?' says Rose. Her voice is high and squeaky.

I have to think fast and I'm not good at thinking fast but my brain does me a favour. 'Finches need to be kept warm. If he didn't do this, maybe he had heat lamps,' I say.

'I don't think so,' says Rose, and I can feel myself getting angry. I want to tell her, 'Yes he did, I saw them,' but I know that I have to keep quiet. She didn't come out to the finch cage. She stayed inside with Portia and Rosalind. Only I went out to the finch cage at the bottom of the back garden with him.

'What if you're doing the wrong thing?' says Rose. 'I'm sure my husband let them stay uncovered in winter. They need the sun. I know he told me that.'

'Yeah, well, he's not here now, is he?' says Jess. 'Birdy's in charge here and we do what she says.' Jess is using her bossy voice. I don't think Rose likes it when Jess uses her bossy voice.

'I think I may go and get some water,' says Rose, and as she walks away she rubs her eyes with her hands and I know she's crying.

'I'm such a bitch,' says Jess.

'You can go and say sorry,' I say. 'I'm just about done here.'

'Maybe?' she says, and we hang the last piece of tarp. Jess isn't big on apologies but she does the right thing when she has to.

Rose was right about her husband never doing this for his birds. Their cage had a wall built around half of it. The birds were always protected from the wind.

'Now, angel, you must remember that if a finch gets a chill in winter it can get sick and die.'

'They're so little,' I said.

'Yes, angel, little and perfect just like you, but even though you want to touch them you cannot. They're too fragile and their hearts would beat too fast if you tried to catch them, so we must always move slowly and speak softly when we're around them. No noise and no shouting.'

I was allowed to help fill the seed containers and to pick the grass that had been planted for them. I would press my face up against the cage and watch as they jumped from perch to stick to seed basin and back again. I would look hard at the colours and their quick little wings. Sometimes I would look so hard that my eyes would get blurry. The finches never stopped moving. They were light and free.

'Can you see them, beautiful girl? Can you see the wonderful colours?' he said, and I nodded and I looked and looked.

First his hand just rested on my back, then both hands would stroke my shoulders. It felt nice. Mum didn't like me to hug her too much. She had to save her hugs for Lila because Lila was little. 'Off you go now,' she would say when I tried to put my arms around her. 'You're too big for this nonsense.'

I didn't tell him that I was too big for this nonsense. I liked the stroking and the touching. It made me feel calm and sleepy. But after a bit he didn't just stroke and touch. Sometimes he did other things. One day his hand went under my skirt and tapped on my private place. Mum called it my private place and I knew it was the place that wee came from. Mum said, 'Have a bath and wash your private place.' Now I know it's also the place that babies come from. Grown-ups like to touch each other's private places. It can feel nice. It felt nice when I was Frank's best girl and it felt okay with Lester.

I didn't like it when I was little. It felt funny when his fingers went tap, tap. My tummy felt like there was something inside pulling it down. It wasn't a bad feeling but it wasn't a good feeling either. It was a confusing feeling. I didn't say anything. I looked at the finches.

'You're such a beautiful girl,' he said. 'You're going to be so lovely when you grow up.'

'I'm big already,' I said, but I was only six and seven and eight. After I turned eight we moved to the shitbox far away from him.

'Such a beautiful girl,' he said, and his fingers went inside my blue undies with pink flowers on them. His voice sounded strange because his breathing was all raggedy and he didn't seem like Mr Winslow who was nice. In my head I made him the raggedy man. The raggedy man with the raggedy breathing. He wasn't nice Mr Winslow. He was different.

I tried to say, 'I'm too old for this nonsense,' but the words wouldn't come out and his breathing was raggedy and raggedy and I felt pulled down and then it was sore and I wanted to say 'stop' but the raggedy man with his raggedy breathing was a stranger. The finches hopped from perch to perch and their wings were all the colours I loved. I watched the finches.

The fingers stopped their tapping and Mr Winslow was back and he said, 'Time for you to be off home, I think,' and his hands weren't touching me anymore. He smiled at me and patted my head. 'Come back tomorrow and you can help me feed them again. If you're very good I might even let you name one.'

He was nice Mr Winslow again, and I thought that maybe I had imagined his tapping fingers and his raggedy breathing, but then I didn't know why I felt so funny.

I went home but I walked slowly because I felt so heavy. I felt heavier than a stone. I didn't want to be heavy. I wanted to be light and free like the finches.

I lay on my bed until my mother came to find me. 'What's wrong with you?' she said.

'Nothing,' I said.

'Well, get up then and come and have dinner. I can't deal with one more thing from either of you today.

I had been next door the whole afternoon. I'd had lunch and then I went down to the finch cage. I hadn't been in the house. Mum couldn't see me. She couldn't see me when I was there and she couldn't see me when I wasn't there.

I couldn't eat dinner.

'Please don't tell me you're getting sick,' said Mum.

'I'm not getting sick,' I said, because that's what she said to tell her.

I didn't want to eat dinner. I didn't want to put food inside my tummy, because I knew it would make me feel even heavier. I wanted to be light and free like the finches. He couldn't touch the finches. He couldn't catch them, because they would fly away fast. I wanted to be like the finches.

In bed I thought, *What happened? What happened?* I thought about Isabel who was brave and didn't care. I thought about how she didn't scream or scurry. I tried to remember all the words, but lots of them had gone out of the door in my head. I wished for my dad. I wanted him to come and lie on my bed and read me a story and then say, 'Mum's turn,' so Mum would say 'Isabel'. I was heavy and sad and I felt the tears come out of my eyes.

'Isabel met an enormous bear,' I whispered into the dark. 'Isabel, Isabel didn't care.' I wished that Mr Winslow was a bear so that I could wash my hands and comb my hair and very quietly eat the bear.

After the first time his hands tap-tapped on my private place he did it every time I went next door. I would come home from school and me and Mum would do homework but I was bad at homework and Mum would say, 'Oh, for God's sake, I can't take this anymore, just go and play next door until I call you for dinner.' It took a long time for me to learn to read, and Mum didn't like to show me over and over again.

'C-A-T spells cat,' she would say, and she would point at the word with her finger. 'Now what does that say, Felicity?'

I would look at the letters and I knew they were letters but I didn't know what they said when they were all next to each other.

'It's C-A-T, Felicity. I've just told you what the word is— it's cat. Say it now, say cat.'

'Cat,' I said.

'How do you spell cat? Look at the letters here.'

'I,' I said, because I could remember I. I was for Isabel.

'No, Felicity, cat starts with C. It's C-A-T, see, look here, look at the letters.'

I looked and looked but the letters didn't look back. 'I remember I,' I said.

'Oh God, I can't take this anymore,' said Mum. 'I just can't take it.'

I only learned to read when we moved out of the big house to the shitbox and I went to a new school. Mr Watkins was my teacher in the new school and he helped me learn to read. I was in a class with Leonard and May. We all needed to be told things over and over again but Mr Watkins didn't mind. He laughed and smiled and said the letters so many times that Leonard and May and me all learned them and then we learned to read. Sometimes on a Friday afternoon Mr Watkins would say 'Isabel'. Not every Friday, because May liked the poem about the swing and Leonard liked one about trucks, but if it was my turn to choose I always chose 'Isabel'.

Sometimes after Mum told me to go away I would hide under the stairs and pat Mum's pet fur coat, but if she found me Mum would shout, 'What are you doing there? It's dirty and disgusting. Just go and play next door and give me some peace.' And then I would go because Mum couldn't take it anymore.

'Rosalind and Portia have homework,' Rose would say, 'but you can sit here with me.' I didn't call her Rose then. I only called her Mrs Winslow. She gave me hot chocolate with marshmallows on cold days and I watched her cook. She was happy when she made dinner. She would hum little songs. *Da dum da da dum.* She would talk to me and ask me questions, but she would talk very fast and sometimes I couldn't make the answers come out quickly enough. Then she would take a big breath in and let it out like she was sad.

And every time I went there he would come into the kitchen and say, 'Hello there, Felicity. I didn't know you were here. Why don't you come and help me feed the finches?'

I wouldn't answer him, because I didn't want to go. I was quiet and I hoped that maybe he wouldn't see me anymore.

'Felicity, Mr Winslow is talking to you,' Mrs Winslow said. 'Don't you want to go and feed the finches? You love the finches.'

'Not today, thank you,' I said. I knew how to say please and thank you because Mum had taught me over and over again.

'Come on, little angel, the finches miss you,' he said. 'I can hear them calling your name. They flap their wings and they say, "Fliss, Fliss, come and play with us."'

'Can't I stay with you, please?' I said to Mrs Winslow. 'Please let me stay with you.'

'Silly Fliss,' smiled Mrs Winslow. 'Pop off and help Mr Winslow and then I'm sure your mum will want you home for dinner.'

I had to go next door because Mum couldn't take it anymore, so I had to listen to Mrs Winslow because if she couldn't take it anymore then I didn't know where I would go.

I had to leave my hot chocolate even though I wasn't finished and I had to go and fill the seed trays and then I had to watch the finches while his fingers tap-tapped. I tried to hear their wings saying, 'Fliss, Fliss,' but I couldn't hear anything except my heart thumping and thumping and his raggedy, raggedy breathing. I tried to like what he was doing but I could feel my stomach pulling down so I was heavier and heavier. I tried to open my mouth to say, 'I'm too old for this nonsense,' but the words wouldn't come.

When I went back home, Mum would say, 'And what's the perfect family next door doing?' It was a question, but she didn't wait for the answer. 'I suppose you've had a lovely time pretending Rose is your mother and the famous Simon is your father while I've been dealing with your little sister all alone. I'm always alone. You're selfish like your father, Felicity—selfish, selfish, selfish.'

I would go and lie on my bed so Mum didn't have to tell me I was selfish. Selfish is a bad word. I knew when I was seven that it meant I was mean and greedy and that Mum couldn't take it anymore.

I would lie on my bed and stay quiet and then Mum would come and say, 'Oh, Felicity, I'm sorry, love. It's just been such a hard day. I don't mean to yell. Come and have some dinner and we can watch television together.' Then she would let me sit next to her on the couch after Lila was asleep and I would forget about the tapping fingers, but they always came back.

Always.

Sometimes I have a terrible dream about the tapping fingers. I dream that I am walking in the garden to the finch cage. I am small and the garden is big and I walk and walk and walk because the garden keeps getting bigger and bigger. When I finally get to the finch cage it is empty but Mr Winslow is there and then his hands go inside my undies and I want to shout but I can't shout because suddenly I am Isabel and Mr Winslow is Lester. I feel myself running and I am running and running to the cage to save

Isabel but the garden gets bigger and I run and I run but I know I will never get to her.

That's when I wake up, and I think about Mum and Mr Winslow and Rose and what I'm going to do.

Chapter Twelve

Eric has come to see me. 'Things are looking good,' he says. 'I have a feeling that we'll be granted a new trial.'

'On what grounds?'

'I've used the extensive media coverage as the main part of my brief. I've argued that the jury was prejudiced against you. There's no way they wouldn't have already formed an opinion about Simon, and about you for that matter. I think we'll get the chance to tell the story again. If it's only heard by a judge or judges we have a fair chance of getting a different outcome.'

'Thank God. I was beginning to think I would be here for years.'

'Is it very bad?'

'No, it wouldn't be fair to say that, but I miss my home and the girls, and of course I miss the grandchildren.'

I do not convey to Eric the true depth of my distress. I see no reason to burden him with it. He's doing everything he can and there would be no benefit in him worrying about me being here.

When I say that I miss my children and grandchildren, what I mean is that I ache with longing for them. I miss Rosalind's perfume and the way she runs her fingers through her hair, getting it out of her face. I miss Portia's rants about the state of the world and her ability to drink a glass of wine with me and laugh at nothing.

I think about my grandchildren all day long. It had been my responsibility, before Simon died, to fetch Lottie from school on a Wednesday and take her to her ballet class so Rosalind could get Sam to his swimming lessons. I would wait at the school gate for her and feel my heart lift each time I watched her catch sight of me and jump on the spot with joy because she realised it was Wednesday. We would stop off at the local bakery for a treat before class. Lottie talks to everyone, delighting them with her chatter and energy. Every Wednesday since Simon died I have missed that time with my granddaughter. Last week Rosalind sent me a letter from Lottie with a drawing of me on the cruise, lying on a deck chair. She wrote *Miss you, Nan,* and drew hearts all over the place. I sat and cried over it for ages.

There was nothing from Sam, and I can almost feel him pulling further and further away from me. He used to hold my hand as trustingly as Lottie did, but after Simon died his serious blue eyes held too many questions for me. I don't know if he will ever speak to me again. He has Simon's eyes—such beautiful blue eyes. I long to take both of my grandchildren in my arms and hold them until they squeal to be let go.

'Have you seen them?' I ask Eric, blowing my nose, swallowing my tears.

I hate the way I'm becoming prone to tears lately. I cried for Simon until I thought I would never be able to shed another tear. Getting convicted started me off again, and now I don't seem to be able to stop. All of us here, it seems, are walking an emotional tightrope. I'm not the only woman who aches. Perhaps it's the temporary loss of our children or perhaps it's because we're all locked up here together with no way out and no way to take the edge off, but most of the women are on the verge of bursting into tears at any given moment. Small memories of backyard barbecues, kindergarten concerts or spring days will render everyone in a room quiet, eyes glowing with unshed tears. It is, I think, punishment enough for most women to remove them from their children. More than enough, really.

Yesterday I studied Lottie's stick figure drawing and remembered her as a newborn, tightly wrapped with beautiful dark eyes. 'Oh, Rosalind,' was all I could say when I saw her. I had been waiting at home for Jack to call from the hospital, pacing up and down with the phone in my hand while Simon made me endless cups of tea and said, 'I'm sure all will be well.' Sam was asleep upstairs in the guest room with his hand curled tightly around his blanket. I had not been there for Sam's birth, because he arrived early and Simon and I were in Greece. I was so grateful to be there, to be able to help out, when Lottie was born.

The love I have for my grandchildren surprised me. I thought that I would feel a little removed from them, able to see things more clearly and to help Rosalind by dealing with things logically, but I was as overwhelmed by them as I had been by my own children. After Sam was born and we dashed home from our holiday, Jack had to kindly tell me to give Rosalind some space. 'If you're over here all day, every day, how will she learn to do it alone?' he said quietly.

'I did drop by Rosalind's house,' says Eric, drawing me back to our conversation. 'I had a drink with Jack. Sam knows what happened. Jack has tried to explain to him that it was an accident, but I gather that both he and Rosalind are having a hard time convincing him of that. Perhaps you should write yourself.'

'Perhaps I should, but I have no idea what I would say.'

'Well,' says Eric, 'it might be a good idea to write down what happened anyway.'

'What for? I've repeated the story hundreds of times. It's not going to change, is it?'

Eric doesn't reply. He shuffles through his briefcase looking for nothing in particular.

'Eric? Why do you want me to write it down?'

'Perhaps some things have come back to you, some things that you may have forgotten because it was such an awful time. You were grieving and stressed.'

Eric's impassive face doesn't fool me. I look at him for a moment and notice his eyes do a quick dart sideways. There's something else he wants to say. 'What do you think I may have forgotten, Eric?'

Eric sighs. 'Now, I know it's a dreadful thing to say, Rose, and please just hear me out, but if Simon was guilty of the things he was accused of it could sway things our way a little. You knew him better than anyone. You were closer to him than anyone. Perhaps there are things he said that you've forgotten, things that could tell us more about his state of mind. We've argued that it was his choice and that you were trying to stop him, but because the allegations will always remain just that, allegations, it's harder to prove. I think the jury probably wondered why, if Simon and everyone close to him so strenuously denied everything, he would then have been driven to do such a thing. So what I want to ask you is what happened on that night that you haven't told me yet?'

'I've told you everything, Eric, everything that happened.'

Eric smiles his slight smile at me and waits. I've noticed that he uses this tactic when he's dealing with someone he believes to be hiding something from him. He waits just long enough for the other person to begin to feel uncomfortable and to speak without meaning to.

I could tell him, I think. *I could tell him right now.* I try to imagine the look on his face if I revealed that everything that had been said about Simon was true, everything and more, in fact. Would he feel betrayed the way I felt betrayed? Would he question everything Simon had said and done over the years the way I now do? He and Simon were very close. They spoke on the phone every few days and often went out to lunch, just the boys. How would Eric feel if he found out that his friend was not the man he thought him to be? An important part of being a lawyer is, I'm sure, being a good judge of character. How would Eric feel if he knew how wrong he'd been about Simon? Would it lead him to question his whole life the way it has led me to question mine?

'There's nothing more to tell,' I say, and Eric drops his gaze.

'Visiting hours are over,' says Natalie from the corner of the room where she's sitting reading a magazine. Eric clears his throat and looks at me, and it suddenly occurs to me that he might know more than he has told me. It's possible that Simon confessed his crimes to his lawyer; Eric would have been legally compelled to protect him. I swallow, feeling a little sick. What if Eric knew all along and didn't say anything, and in keeping quiet allowed more and more little girls to be hurt?

'Do you know something you're not telling me, Eric?' I say. My voice is strained, strangled as it makes its way out.

Eric shakes his head. 'I only know what you've told me. I've gone over our conversations again and again, all those years of conversation, trying to figure out if he said anything to me that would lead me to believe he was capable of such behaviour.'

'And?'

'And I've come up with nothing,' he says. 'Perhaps he was a much better actor than anyone ever gave him credit for, or perhaps he was truly innocent.'

'I'm sorry, but it really is time,' says Natalie.

'Rose, please . . . just think about it, all right? If there's something that could help us, anything at all that will further prove his state of mind at the time, you need to tell me.'

'I'll think about it,' I say.

Eric nods and gets up to leave. 'There are several magazines who would like an interview with you. If you'd like to speak to them, I can arrange for a journalist or two to come here and see you.'

I laugh out loud. I can't help it.

'Yes,' says Eric, 'that's what I assumed your reaction would be. I told them so, but it's my duty as your lawyer to inform you of everything that's happening.'

'How are Patricia and your children?' I ask, holding onto Eric's presence for a moment longer, holding onto my life at home as long as I can.

'Doing well, doing well. Patricia's going in for some routine tests, but we're sure everything will be fine.'

'Oh, Eric,' I say, because at our age tests are never routine.

'Now, don't fret, Rose. She's fine. I've called both your girls this week. Portia seems very taken with Robert. I believe they're even speaking of moving in together— something I heard from Robert, because I'm sure Portia wouldn't want me to know. For such a robust-looking man I'm afraid he tends to wear his heart on his sleeve. I think he referred to her as "Poppy" in conversation.'

The news doesn't surprise me. Portia's emails are peppered with *Rob this* and *Rob that*. She tries to make the emails long and chatty, perhaps fearing that I'm losing my mind. I know that she and Robert went to the symphony but that Robert fell asleep, which made her laugh. They went to the mountains and they've been to parties together. She sounds blissfully happy but is toning things down so as not to upset me. It does upset me. I'm missing something special. I like to see Portia in love. Her face softens and her body relaxes. I would have enjoyed watching the two of them together. Beautiful people are always lovely to watch.

'Will there be a problem with them living together?' I say to Eric. 'I mean, is it a conflict of interest?'

'Oh, I don't think so. He's your defence barrister, not part of the prosecution. And even if things somehow go awry I know that Robert is the consummate professional. He would never do anything to jeopardise the case. Winning is everything with barristers.'

'I hope they're happy, I hope they stay happy,' I say.

'That's all we can hope,' says Eric, and then it's time for him to go.

At the door he stoops to give me a kiss on the cheek and then stops and straightens up, remembering the rule about not touching prisoners. 'We'll get through this,' he says.

'I know,' I say. 'And I will try to think if there's anything else that could help. But you know that he didn't discuss things that he didn't want to. I think you probably knew more than I did, especially after that phone call.'

'What phone call?'

'Eric,' I say, frowning, 'you called him that night to tell him there would be an investigation. You said that the police were involved. How can you not remember such a thing? It was the phone call that . . . It was the call.' An image from that night comes back to me, making me feel sick. Simon's face, drained of colour, and his hand on his chest, covering his heart.

Eric is shaking his head. 'I don't remember it, because I never called him. The police weren't yet involved. The allegations wouldn't have gone away so easily if they had been. Is that what he told you? That the police were coming for him? Is that why he . . .?'

I feel the full force of his words and sag into a chair by the door.

'Are you okay?' says Natalie, and I hold up my hand to let her know that I'm fine, although I'm so very far from it.

'You didn't call him?' I say.

'I didn't call him,' Eric confirms.

'Why would he have lied to me about that?'

'I have no idea,' says Eric, 'but it may be that he heard the information from someone else. Let me look into it.'

I walk slowly back to my unit. It's too much to think about. I don't know why he lied to me about there being an investigation. If he hadn't said anything, if he'd just shown me the pictures—those awful, sad pictures—then I might have been able to talk him round. He didn't want to be talked round. He wanted to make sure. He made sure.

It's nearly time for dinner, but I don't feel like eating. Allison is beginning to worry about my weight loss, but chewing and swallowing seems like it would take a great deal more energy than I have at the moment. 'You need to take care of yourself,' she said when she last saw me. 'If your appeal comes through you will need to be strong to go through the whole trial process again.'

Allison is very different from what I expected the governor of a prison to be. Her attitude to her prisoners is very maternal. She's surrounded by women who have failed to live up to the expectations of society, and yet she treats us all like we're capable of doing great things and living rewarding lives. She greets everyone by name, even new arrivals, and soon knows everything about them. She knows the names of all the children who visit once a month, and Jess told me that she sometimes stops by the mother and child unit for an afternoon of craft. 'There's not many in the system like her,' said Jess. 'She's one of the few who haven't given up on making a difference.'

Allison keeps encouraging me to take a class. 'It will make the time go faster,' she says. I've been thinking about doing something with computers, but I'm very tired. It feels as though the last eighteen months have suddenly taken their toll on my mind and body. I feel like I have lost the art of concentration.

Perhaps because I'm surrounded by women who have led such difficult lives, perhaps because I haven't seen my daughters for so long, or perhaps it's just age, but I find myself drifting back through the years, trying to solve the riddle of how a life that was so incredibly happy and joyous has landed me here. While we were dealing with the allegations, and then when Simon was gone and I had to deal with the police and the trial, I focused all my energy on just getting through the days. I fixated on what had happened and on what my future might be, but I didn't think much about the past.

At the Farm my hands are busy all the time but conversation is limited. I keep swallowing questions, mindful of touching on subjects that no one wants to discuss. I drift back into the past all the time, questioning my life, questioning everything.

I understand that I missed things, that I was blind to things, but I thought I knew Simon. I felt that I knew him. He was a wonderful man, a wonderful husband and father—and yet and yet and yet . . .

I could tell Eric what happened that night, I could tell him about the evidence that I've hidden, and I'm sure that a judge would be swayed. It's not concrete proof but it's close enough. I understood as soon as I saw it what I was looking at. But if I tell Eric and Eric tells the world, then the man that I was married to, the father of my children, will be gone forever. All those years he spent on television making people laugh, entertaining them, will be gone. All his charity work and the causes he donated his time to—just gone.

I have seen what happens when a celebrity falls from grace. Simon and I had once been friends with a couple in the industry. He was a newsreader and she reported the entertainment news. They had been happily married until he cheated with the woman who read the weather. It was a tawdry affair, exposed by the press and then chewed over by the magazines, and eventually it became too much for all concerned. He resigned from his role as news anchor, and his wife left her job as well. Only the woman who read the weather remained on television, and I watched her over the months become thinner and more brittle as accusations of being a 'home wrecker' were flung at her. Today I'm sure such a thing would pass almost unnoticed, but back then, in the early eighties, it was a huge scandal. When Simon and I woke to the news of the suicide of the young woman who had remained on television, we were not surprised. They wore her down, and then when she was gone everyone lamented her loss.

Fame is fickle. Simon loved the spotlight until it shone too brightly on him, potentially exposing his flaws for all to see. If I let Eric know what I know, Simon will be forever exposed and forever damned. And in exposing him I expose myself, the stupid woman who found herself married to a monster. I will be held up for ridicule and scorn, because who better to blame than his wife? He is gone and cannot give any answers, so why not look to me? I am damned either way so perhaps it is better to let the man rest in peace, better to leave his memory untarnished so that my children and I can also have peace.

I don't think the time at the Farm will be so arduous as to be unbearable. The years will pass quickly enough once I have adjusted to this way of living. I have already sacrificed a lot being married to Simon, a man who lived his life in front of the camera, a man a great deal older than me, a man who was so certain about the way we should live our lives. I turned myself into the kind of woman he was proud to be seen with and I never asked myself what I really wanted. I gave up any ambitions I might have had for myself so I could stand by his side and raise his children. Isn't protecting his reputation just one last sacrifice?

Last night I dreamed about the day I found out about our house. It was such a glorious day, and I remember that at the end of it I was acutely aware that my life had changed forever, that I would never again have to worry about money, or about explaining the choice I had made with Simon. I understood that I was living the dream. That's how it felt, that I was living the dream.

Once the show became a regular Wednesday-night fixture, the money came rolling in. Television stars were lauded and fawned over then, even more so than they are today. That was, I now see, part of the problem. Even then it occasionally made me uneasy. Simon was the star that drove the show's success; sometimes he would be relating an anecdote about the show and it struck me that his behaviour might be perceived as arrogant and even slightly abusive.

'I told them that if they thought I was going to continue to wear those dreadful cheap suits, they would have to take the time to find another host. They know they would be nothing without me. Wouldn't you know it, by the afternoon my office was filled with the most beautiful choices.' He thought he was untouchable. A dangerous presumption for anyone to make.

Wherever we went, Simon was asked for his autograph. I would stand next to him with a wide smile painted on my face as he made benign conversation with everyone who complimented the show and admired him for his work.

The regular pay cheque changed everything. I, who had stood in the supermarket selecting the cheapest cuts of meat, suddenly had enough for whatever I wanted. For the first few months I was constantly surprised to open my purse and find it filled with money. Now it wouldn't seem like much, but then it was a sum almost too magnificent to imagine. How proud Simon was. Our empty bank account filled up and overflowed. Simon and I would look through the bankbook and giggle like children.

One Sunday afternoon six months after the show started, Simon announced that he was taking me and the girls for a drive. It was a hideously hot day and I didn't want to go. Rosalind and Portia had been fighting all afternoon and the thought of being locked in a hot car with them while they traded sly slaps and kicks was very unappealing. 'Please, Simon, let's leave it for another day,' I said. 'I know you're enjoying the new car but I need to get the girls out into the fresh air for the afternoon. I want to take them to the park or something.'

'I'm sure we will find a park where we're going, Rose.'

'Where are we going?' I said. Simon winked at me, irritating me further.

'They both hate just driving around. I don't want them cooped up in a car, I really want a break.'

'Rose, I will brook no argument from you. Put the children in the car now. I promise you will enjoy yourself,' he said, his voice rising slightly with his impatience 'Portia, Rosalind,' he called and the girls came out of their bedroom. 'We are going for a drive and there will be no fighting. If you are well behaved young ladies there will be an ice cream treat at the end, but if you cannot behave there will be no dinner before bed and no treats for a week.'

I sighed, knowing that Simon would not be there to enforce any punishment he dreamed up but the girls nodded and both promised to behave.

'In the car now,' he said to the three of us.

I looked at my beautiful husband and saw a gleam in his eye and knew that arguing with him would serve no purpose. I imagined that he wanted to treat us all to an indulgent afternoon that would ultimately be a failure because we had small children. Since the money had begun coming in he was prone to extravagant gestures that often fell flat. The week before he had dragged home an enormous teddy bear nearly the same size as me and given it to the girls. They had both been unimpressed with the stuffed creature. Portia was nearly eight and too old for such things and Rosalind was terrified of it. The bear was now crammed into a cupboard, taking up space we could ill afford in the small apartment. Simon's devastation at his daughters' reaction to the gift had been almost too much for me. I hated to see him upset, especially when I knew he was trying to be kind.

He was not a natural father. When he came home at night he seemed dismayed to find me still tending to Portia and Rosalind, as though at some point during the day the children should have been dealt with and put away. He never seemed to want to spend too much time with the girls, and sometimes I can't help wondering whether he was protecting them somehow, protecting them from himself. When the allegations began I couldn't think how to ask my daughters the question that I wanted to ask. I took their incredulous reactions to the allegations, as proof that he had never . . . had never hurt them. Portia would never have remained silent anyway. It was not in her nature. If Simon had done anything to her that she didn't like she would have shouted and screamed. I hope. I hope she would have shouted and screamed.

'It will be a wonderful afternoon, darling girl,' he said, stroking my cheek, 'please put them in the car so that we can go for a drive.' He still made me liquid inside. Even after two children and operating on little sleep, his touch still affected me.

As it turned out, five minutes into the drive both girls had been lulled by the heat and the movement of the car into sleep. 'Peace at last,' I said.

'I told you this was a good idea.'

'Yes, you did. Do you mind if I nod off for a few minutes too? I'm just so tired.'

'Not at all. It's going to be a long drive but well worth the journey, I assure you.'

Thirty minutes later I stretched awake and turned my head one way and then the other to banish the stiffness in my neck. 'Where are we?' I said.

'On the north shore.'

I laughed. 'How very fancy!' The north shore was a semi-mythical place to me, though I did remember my father once taking my mother and me over the bridge on a Sunday afternoon to show us how the rich in Australia lived. It's all different now, of course, with millionaires everywhere in the city.

As Simon drove, I looked out of the car window, taking in the large houses and tree-lined driveways. We drove for a few more minutes until Simon turned into a street with several hidden mansions, then stopped in front of a house. It wasn't terribly big compared to what I could see of the others in the street, but I was captivated by its gabled roof and pretty front yard complete with fountain.

'Imagine living here,' I said.

'Yes,' said Simon, 'just imagine.' He looked like Portia did on Christmas morning when she saw all the gifts under the tree. He got out of the car and stretched, and then he opened the front gate and walked up the path to the heavy wooden front door.

'Simon,' I called, jumping out of the car and feeling my face colour with shame at his behaviour. 'I'm sure they don't want visitors. Have you any idea who lives here?'

'Yes.' Simon turned back to face me, and it was then that I saw he was clutching a key in his hand. 'We do.'

It never occurred to me to question why I had not been included in the decision. That was never how I had expected my marriage to work. I ran up the path and into his arms, kissing him all over his face and ignoring the girls who were climbing out of the car.

Inside the empty house, Portia and Rosalind ran up and down the stairs and in and out of rooms, shrieking with delight at the space. I ran my hand over the bright blue laminate kitchen counter tops and peered into cupboards, unable to take in all the splendour. Portia ran into the kitchen, chased by Rosalind, and pointed to the French doors, indicating the large garden complete with wooden climbing frame and swing set left by the previous owners. 'It's a park,' she said. 'Let's go to the park.'

Once I had let them out I stood in the middle of a living room, awed by its size. 'We don't have enough furniture to fill even one of these rooms,' I said to Simon.

'That's what a credit card is for, my dear. I'm not allowing you to bring a single dreadful piece from that terrible apartment. We shall start anew—whatever you desire will be yours.'

He chose most of the furniture for the house, of course. He laughed and joked with salesmen and women, charming them into discounts and signing his name as he went. I had no faith in my own taste. I would stand in the furniture store and feel myself close to tears at all the choices on offer and the terrifying expense. I had been brought up with furniture that was bought because it was cheap. Function was all that mattered. I had never learned to see the beauty in the wood grain of a table or the craftsmanship in the turn of a leg. But Simon had firm ideas of how he wanted the house to look. I've no idea where he learned it all from. I'm certain from the few things he said that his background was as humble as mine (albeit ruled by a violent not loving father), and yet wherever he went he never seemed out of place. I think now that he must have spent many years before I met him turning himself into the man he wanted to be. He shed his origins and dressed himself as an educated Englishman. Why then did he not let go of his most terrible flaw? Or had that only come later, with fame, success and power?

Simon loved the shopping, breezing in and out of stores, energised with every purchase. 'I should have grown up surrounded by beautiful things,' he said, 'and I would have if my mother had chosen the right man. She used to tell me about the great houses in London, filled with antique furniture that had been handed down for generations. One day your great-great-grandchildren may sit at the very table we just bought. Isn't it wonderful to know that?

'Your mother would love this house,' I said when we had been living there for a few months. I thought he would want to show it to his parents, to share his success. I thought it was a chance for him to finally reconnect with his mother, even if he did not want to speak to his father.

'My mother died,' he replied.

'What? When? Why didn't you tell me? Was she ill? How old was she?' I was deeply shocked. My mother was, by then, an integral part of our lives.

Simon delivered the news of his mother's death as though mentioning an incident he had seen on the news. He appeared to have no emotional connection to the words, no feelings for the woman who had raised him. It was disconcerting for me to see Simon so distant and cold.

'It's not something I wish to discuss, my dear. I'm sure you can understand that.'

I didn't understand, but when Simon did not wish to discuss something, it remained undiscussed.

In the months after his death I spent a lot of time wandering around the house looking for him, and I realised that there wasn't one piece of furniture in the house that I liked. Yet I had, when he bought them, thought that I loved them all. *I have no idea who I really am*, I thought. *What do I like? What do I feel?* If I had not been involved in the court case and then been sent here, it's possible that I would have sold everything off and started again, but probably not. I don't know what I will do when I get home, be it in a few months or a few years. Right now it's difficult to think past tomorrow.

'I will make all your dreams come true,' Simon had said to me on our wedding night, just before he pushed himself into me, hurting me one way but soothing me with his words. And he had. He had done exactly what he'd promised. He was such a showman, and I was happy to simply be part of his show. I was happy to bask in his reflected glory.

His last burst of fame had energised Simon. He stood straighter, he laughed more often, and his voice seemed to boom across a room again. I accepted congratulatory calls from friends and acquaintances across the world, because the news about his induction into the Hall of Fame was quickly all over the internet, and then in one day it shifted and everything I had known was thrown into question.

When Henry called to tell Simon about the article in which the second woman was accusing him of groping her when she was a contestant on *My Kid Can* ..., it took Simon three hours to tell me what had happened. It was two weeks after the first article had come out. I was standing in the kitchen with the fridge open, trying to decide between steak and chicken for dinner. Earlier I had heard the phone ring and known that Simon had picked up but I had not seen him all afternoon. I heard Simon come into the kitchen and turned, 'do you want steak or chicken?' I said. 'I can do a nice béarnaise sauce or I could just get some rosemary from the garden for the chicken.'

He didn't reply, instead turning around and heading for the living room and the bar where he poured himself a large whisky. I followed him, noting his pale face and the way his hands shook a little.

'You can't drink all that,' I said.

'Oh, Rose,' he said. 'My darling, darling girl ...'

'What is it? What's wrong?' By this stage the first article had been explained away and we had all moved on. Or so I thought.

'It's ... no, I cannot say.'

I was beginning to panic. 'Is it the girls? Is something wrong with Portia or Rosalind? You must tell me. Tell me now.'

'What?' he said. 'The girls? No, it's not the girls.'

'Then what, Simon, what?'

'You must give me time, my dear, I need time.'

I had no choice but to leave him alone. I called my daughters and both soon arrived at the house. We sat in the kitchen and waited for Simon to be ready to talk. Portia grumbled a little about how selfish he was being, but she understood that in our home his needs came first.

When she was a teenager and just beginning to push at boundaries she had once yelled at Simon for giving her what she thought was an unreasonable curfew. 'You're just a selfish old man!' she said. 'All you care about is what you want. You don't give a damn about me or Mum or Rosalind. You think because you're famous you can do whatever you want, but you can't, you can't!' Then she burst into tears and locked herself in her room. Initially I was shocked by the fury of her first teenage tantrum—something I would eventually be quite blasé about—but more than that I was struck by her words and the certainty with which they were delivered. She saw her father in a very different light to the one I did and was not afraid to point out his failures. I did not think of Simon as selfish and if I ever did I dismissed his behaviour as being caused by stress or fatigue. Pleasing him, feeding him, keeping the house the way he liked it, keeping myself in shape and always looking nicely put together when he came home was how I showed him how grateful I was for the life he had given me. It was a life I had never even conceived to imagine for myself. I'm sure I wasn't so very different to most of the wives of my generation.

My daughters and I waited for nearly an hour before Simon came to find us. 'Oh, my loves,' he said. 'You have no idea what I have had to face today.' He sat down at the kitchen table and grabbed my hand. His eyes filled with tears as he explained that another woman had come forward to accuse him of inappropriate behaviour. His hands trembled a little as he lamented the gross unfairness of it all, the vindictiveness of the woman who was obviously only using him for her own gain. We were distraught for him. We could not believe that someone would say such a thing. Simon sniffed and wiped his eyes and shook his head as though unable to comprehend such a thing.

Even then the show went on.

'Another one,' said Portia, and in her voice I heard a tinge of uncertainty and perhaps the beginning of accusation.

'She must have got the idea from the first woman,' said Rosalind. 'What's wrong with these people?'

'Why would anyone do this?' I asked. 'Do you know who she is?'

'Rose, do you know how many children were on the show over ten years?'

'It must be at least a couple of thousand,' said Rosalind.

'Exactly,' said Simon. 'And that doesn't include the thousands who auditioned and didn't get in. I cannot be expected to remember every young girl I came across. They have all blended into one unmemorable face for me. I do not know why this woman has come forward to tell these dreadful lies, and I certainly have no memory of her ever being on the show.'

'Maybe that's why they're doing it,' said Rosalind. 'Maybe both these women want to use this to extort money from you. They know you can't remember and they're hoping you'll just pay them off to make them go away.'

'Roz, you've been watching way too much shitty television,' said Portia. 'This is not some fucking detective show. Why would these women have come forward? What would their motivation be?'

Simon stood up from the kitchen table. He took a deep breath and I could almost see him grow taller with indignation. 'Portia, you are not suggesting with your foul words that I have done these things, are you? You simply cannot be implying that I have any interest in touching a child, in groping a child?'

Portia can be fierce when she wants to be, but even she was deflated by Simon's tone. 'No, Dad, I wasn't. I just—'

'You just wanted to trust a stranger over your own father,' said Simon, and he turned around and walked out of the kitchen with his head held high and his shoulders back.

'Why can't he have a discussion like an adult?' said Portia sullenly. 'I wasn't fucking accusing him, I just want to try and understand.'

'Maybe if you showed him a little support he would want to stay and discuss it.'

'Fabulous, you've managed to find a way to make this my fault.'

'You're such a bitch,' said Rosalind.

'Girls, please, this is hardly the time,' I said, as I had said over and over throughout their childhoods.

'It's never really the time,' said Portia.

'For God's sake,' said Rosalind, 'you don't actually believe what these women are saying about Dad, do you?'

Portia sighed. 'I don't want to believe it. None of us wants to believe it, but why are they saying it? The first woman, I agree, seemed to be using her accusations as a platform for her career, but two? What's that saying about once being a chance and twice being a coincidence?'

'Three times is a pattern,' I said, feeling myself grow cold in my sunny kitchen.

'Accusing someone of something like this is a big deal,' Portia went on. 'Why would anyone do that? I work with girls who have been sexually assaulted. It changes who they are. Most of them never report it. It's too hard to face and it's fucking hard to prosecute. Children aren't considered reliable and so they just keep quiet.'

'These aren't children,' I said.

'No, Mum, but they were when they're saying Dad ... did these things. I'm not saying I believe them over him, I'm just asking why they're saying it.'

'You *are* saying you don't believe him,' said Rosalind. 'That's exactly what you're saying. You've never got along with him.'

'Oh, for fuck's sake.'

'Girls, girls, please,' I said and I could hear that my voice was high pitched and strained. I was desperate for some silence so I could think through what Simon had said. 'I think maybe your father and I need a little time alone. If you could give us some space, I'm sure we can discuss this rationally.'

'No, Mum, I want to stay,' said Rosalind.

'Rosalind, you need to go now. The children will be finished with their activities soon. And Portia, I'm sure they're expecting you back at work.'

Reluctantly, they both left, exhorting me to call them at any time, and I sat on at the kitchen table, my beautiful kitchen table made of honey-coloured wood in my beautiful house, with my cup of tea growing cold, working through different ways to approach Simon.

There was no point in even trying to raise the subject with him, of course. If Simon didn't want to discuss something, it remained undiscussed.

Chapter Thirteen

Mina and I are in the mother and child unit this weekend.

Isabel and Suresh are building a house out of the pillows from the couch and some blankets. Mina and I have to wait until we are invited over to have some tea.

'You will wait, Mummy,' says Suresh.

'Yeah, wait there until we call you on the telephone and say, "Hello, would you like to come to tea?"' says Isabel.

Mina and I are waiting and watching our children. We don't talk much, but I can see in Mina's eyes that she has the same filled-with-joy feeling that I do.

There is a knock at the door and I look at Mina and we both look at the clock on the wall, even though we know it's still only Saturday and the children will not go home until tomorrow.

'It's not Allison,' I say.

'Who is it, who is it Mummy,' says Suresh and he looks a little scared. He knows that his father isn't coming home anymore but he is still worried. It makes Mina cry when she thinks about how afraid Suresh is.

I get up and open the door and Rose is standing there. My throat gets tight and I feel afraid like Suresh does, but I don't know why.

'I'm so sorry to bother you here, Birdy,' she says, 'but I think one of the finches is sick. It's sitting on the bottom of the cage and it seems to be sleeping. I know you're with your daughter, but I asked Allison if I could just come over and ask you about it. I can try to help if you tell me what to do.'

I hate it when the finches get sick. Allison won't call the vet for just one bird. 'Too expensive, Birdy, and they're not essential to us.' Calling the vet doesn't always help anyway. Sometimes when you finally notice that they're sick it's too late. He told me that.

'You have to pay very close attention to the birds, beautiful girl, you have to watch all the time, because they cannot tell you when they're sick. They get sick very quickly. If you see they're sick you must make sure they stay warm and try to make sure they keep eating.'

He told me things about the finches over and over again, and when his fingers went tap, tap, I would watch the finches and think about all the things he had said about them. 'Try to keep them warm and fed if they're sick,' I said to myself over and over again while his fingers went tap, tap and he turned into the raggedy man and I listened to his raggedy, raggedy breathing.

'Birdy?' says Rose and I realise that I am just standing and staring at her.

'I'll come and see,' I tell Rose, and then I close the door so I can tell Isabel where I am going. I ask Mina to watch Isabel so I can go and look at the bird.

'No, no,' says Isabel. 'I want to come with you.'

'Stay here, Isabel. Build your house and then when I come back we can have tea.'

'Take me to see the birdies, Mum, please, please,' she says. She knows that I'm in charge of the finches. She and Lila looked up finches on the computer and Isabel sent me a drawing of a Gouldian finch, only she didn't know it was that. She just liked the colours. She thinks it's funny when people call me Birdy. 'You're not a birdy,' she says, 'you're a mum.'

I can't say no to Isabel.

I think that Rose will have gone back to her work, but she is waiting for me outside the unit. I don't want her near Isabel. Isabel is little and she needs to be protected. Rose doesn't know how to protect her.

'Oh my, this must be your daughter,' says Rose when she sees us.

I try to push Isabel behind me but Isabel likes to say hello to everyone. She steps in front of my legs. 'I'm Isabel,' she says.

Rose smiles at her and then her smile disappears. She looks at Isabel for a long time and her skin turns white. I think she is going to throw up. She puts two fingers in front of her mouth. 'Oh,' she says. 'Oh ... you're so pretty ... so pretty,' and then she turns and walks away quickly. She looks back at us once and then she walks even quicker.

'What's wrong with her?' says Isabel. 'Is she sick?'

'I don't know,' I say. 'Maybe.'

Rose looked at Isabel like Isabel was someone who wanted to hurt her, but she's only five. A little girl of five or six or seven can't hurt a grown-up. A little girl of five or six or seven can't do anything to a grown-up.

I take Isabel with me to the finch cage. Rose is right, one of the birds is sick. It's sitting in the corner of the cage and I can see it breathing very fast. Its purple and yellow body is shivering.

'If you catch them early enough you can save them, Fliss,' he told me. Keep them warm. Feed them sugar water and take them to the vet. Don't leave it too late. Finches are delicate creatures and they will die if you leave it too late.'

It is too late for the bird in the cage. Its eyes are sad. It isn't looking at anything. I know it is too late.

'Can you help the birdy, Mum? Can you help him?' says Isabel. She stands beside the cage and puts her fingers in the little holes in the wire. 'Don't be sad, little birdy, my mum will save you.'

'Isabel, get away from there,' I say.

'Can you save him, Mum?'

'No,' I say. 'It's too late. He's very sick.'

'Take him to the doctor, to the vet, Mum, please. He's so pretty.'

'It's too late,' I say. 'There's nothing I can do.'

When I was nearly eight I stayed away from next door for two whole weeks. I had a cold that turned into the flu. I got sicker and sicker.

'I'm afraid this is now quite a serious case of the flu,' said the doctor who came to our house in the night when I was hot and cold and hot again.

'That's all I need,' said Mum.

I had to stay in bed and take lots of medicine, and Mum brought me soup and jelly because my throat was so sore. She sat on my bed and stroked my head and said 'Isabel' over and over again until her voice was tired. I felt bad all over my body, but I liked it when Mum sat on my bed and said 'Isabel'. I wanted to be sick forever.

I was in bed for five days. Mrs Winslow came over to see me. She brought me a colouring-in book and some pencils. The book was filled with pictures of animals. I found a picture of a bird and I coloured it purple and yellow like the finches in the cage next door.

'Get better soon,' Mrs Winslow said to me, and she smiled.

'This is such a bad virus,' she said to Mum. 'They sent Portia home from school yesterday. I think we should keep them apart until everyone is well again, don't you?'

'Oh, absolutely,' said Mum, and she nodded like she agreed with Mrs Winslow, but her voice sounded like she didn't agree with her at all.

'I'm sure I wouldn't want her precious children to get sick,' Mum said to me when she came back from closing the front door behind Mrs Winslow. 'Of course darling Portia and Rosalind are more important than anyone else.'

'Are you mad at Mrs Winslow, Mum?' I said.

'No, Fliss, I'm just tired,' said Mum. 'I'll get you some more juice.'

When I was better I still played at home after school. I tried to be a quiet little mouse. I didn't even squeak. I walked on tiptoes and I played with Lila when Mum had a headache and I went to bed without her telling me to. I thought that if I could be there but not be there Mum wouldn't send me next door again.

But then after two weeks I was tired of being quiet all the time, and Lila came into my room and bashed down my block castle and I hit her because I was mad at her. I didn't hit her very hard, but Lila screamed so loud she even made my head hurt.

'Oh, give me strength,' said Mum. 'Will you just go next door and play so I can have some peace, please!'

'I don't want to go next door. I want to stay here. Don't make me go, Mum, I'll be good.'

'Felicity, I'm sure Rosalind misses you. Go and play with her for a couple of hours and then we can get some ice cream.'

I loved ice cream, especially chocolate ice cream with sprinkles on top. 'I don't want ice cream,' I said.

'Just go now!' yelled Mum. 'Take Lila with you. I haven't had five minutes to myself for weeks.' Her voice was loud and sharp, and Lila and I were scared.

'Next door, Fliss,' Lila said. 'Next door, next door.'

I took her hand and we went next door. I thought I could stay with Lila and she would keep me safe from Mr Winslow even though she was my little sister. 'Well, we haven't seen you two for ages,' said Mrs Winslow when I rang the doorbell and she opened the door.

'Mum wants us to play here,' I said.

'Oh, I'm sure she could use a break. Your poor mum. Hello, Lila, it's not often we have you come over for a visit. You're such a pretty little thing. Just look at those curls. Rosalind!' she called. 'Felicity and Lila are here to play.' She turned to me. 'I think Rosalind is in her room, but as you can hear, Portia is practising the piano. Come with me, little Lila, and you can watch her play.'

'Lila needs to stay with me,' I said.

'Don't worry about that,' said Mrs Winslow. 'I'll take good care of her, I promise.'

I went up to Rosalind's room, but she didn't want to play. 'I'm reading,' she said.

'I'll be very, very quiet,' I said.

'No, I don't want you here. Go and play with Portia or sit with my mum.' Rosalind was nearly ten and she thought I was a baby and she didn't want to play the games we used to play. She didn't like to explain things over and over.

I left her room and went down to the kitchen. Mrs Winslow was giving Lila some juice. She was touching her hair and stroking her cheek and talking to her in a baby voice. Lila was pretty with golden curls so everyone loved her lots and lots. My hair was straight and brown. Mum wanted to cut it short so that she wouldn't have to worry about tangles. I always said 'Ow' when Mum brushed my hair, and then she said, 'One day I'm just going to cut it short so I never have to hear that again.'

'Mr Winslow is down by the finch cage, Felicity. Why don't you go and say hello?'

'Can't I stay here with you and Lila?'

'Now don't be silly. Off you go. Lila and I are having a lovely chat, aren't we?'

Lila didn't look like she was having a lovely chat. She looked bored.

'Off you go,' said Mrs Winslow. I had to do what she said. Mum wanted us to give her some peace, so I had to do what Mrs Winslow said.

I went down to the cage. He was sitting on a chair and watching the birds. 'Felicity, angel,' he said, 'are you feeling better?'

I nodded and I went to stand far away from him. I hooked my fingers through the cage and watched the finches hop from stick to perch to seed basin. Mr Winslow stood up and came to stand behind me. He put his hands on my shoulders. 'Do you know what happened when you were away?' he said.

'What?'

'One of the finches died. He got sick and I tried to keep him warm and I fed him sugar water but he died.'

'Oh,' I said. 'Poor finch. Poor, poor finch.' I started to cry because I loved all of the finches.

'Oh, now, don't be too sad,' he said.

I sniffed and wiped my nose on the back of my hand. Mr Winslow took a tissue out of his pocket and wiped my hand and then he wiped my nose.

'Do you know,' he said when he put his hands back on my shoulders, 'I think he would have lived if you had been able to visit him.'

'I was sick,' I said, and his hands went down over my chest and into my pants.

'I know you were, lovely girl, I know you were, but all the finches missed you very, very much, especially the one that died. Promise me you'll always come and visit them and keep them safe and happy.'

His fingers tap-tapped on my private place and his breath was raggedy. Mr Winslow was gone and the raggedy man was back.

'I promise,' I said.

'You love the finches, don't you?' he said. 'I know you love them and you want to keep them safe. Don't stay away again.' He spoke slowly because his breath was raggedy, raggedy.

'I won't stay away,' I said, and then I cried some more. I didn't cry about the dead finch. I cried because I knew that I would have to go to the finch cage every day. I would have to watch the finches and keep them safe and happy so they didn't die and I would have to let the raggedy man's fingers tap, tap on my private place.

'Good girl,' he said. 'You're such a good girl.'

He didn't care that I was sad and crying. He only cared about his fingers and his finches. I hated him. I hated him, hated him, hated him.

'Felicity!' Mrs Winslow called from the house. 'Lila wants to go home.'

'I have to go,' I said.

His fingers went away and he stood up straight and smiled at me. His teeth looked yellow. 'Don't stay away too long,' he said. 'Remember about the finches. You have to help me keep them happy.'

'Poor bird,' I say to the sick little finch sitting on the bottom of the cage. I pick up Isabel and we walk away from the cage. She starts to cry but then I tell her that we are going to bake a cake and she stops. Isabel loves baking. I had saved money so I could buy the ingredients to make a cake. Mina and Suresh were going to help as well.

I don't think about Rose or Mr Winslow anymore, even when I wonder why her face turned white and she ran away from me and Isabel. I just squish the thought down.

I am with Isabel She gives me a filled-with-joy feeling and thinking about Rose and Mr Winslow gives me a heavy feeling, like my legs can't move. I don't want to feel like that when I'm with Isabel.

Chapter Fourteen

When I was in the early stages of my pregnancy with Portia, I would get dizzy. I would be standing up at work and I would feel myself begin to sway back and forth; time would slow down as objects and people moved slowly past me when they should have been standing still. It was a combination of low blood sugar and nausea that did it. Margaret, who worked on the till next to mine, was always on the lookout for one of my episodes. She was sweetly overprotective, telling me what I should and shouldn't eat, despite never having been pregnant herself. Pregnant women are magnets for useful advice, and instead of finding it tiresome, I lapped up everything anyone said. I had little idea of what was happening to my body and was desperate for guidance.

Seeing me begin to sway, Margaret would say, 'Oh dear, Rose is about to go,' and then shout across the store, 'Bring us some juice for the young one, Kev!' The manager would come running with grapefruit juice and then watch me sip it slowly. The acid hitting my stomach brought everything back into focus and quelled the nausea. Any customers in the store at the time would wait patiently for me to be able to get back to work and would then dispense advice and old wives' tales. I never got dizzy with Rosalind, or perhaps I didn't have the luxury of giving into it because I had Portia. I haven't had that surreal, almost out-of-body experience since my first pregnancy.

But I remember that feeling when I see her child. I want to put out my hand and hold onto something to stop myself from spinning away. 'I'm Isabel,' she says, and as I look at her I know that I can remember the feel of her golden curls in my hands. Her hair smelled of baby shampoo and she let me brush it and tie it in ribbons so that she could admire herself in a mirror.

I feel the rise of bile in my throat and press my fingers against my lips, suddenly craving grapefruit juice. It isn't her, of course it isn't her, but there she stands right in front of me. 'I'm Isabel,' she says, and she smiles. There she stands, a reminder of Simon and his sins.

I walk away as quickly as I can and only turn around once, fearful that she will be following me. There is nowhere to hide. Even in here the ghost of my husband has found me. I am allowed no peace. I have not thought

about him for a few hours, just a few hours, but Simon
will not be forgotten. He does not care what I think about
him as long as it is only him I think about.

'Even bad press can be good,' he said to me once when
he had been photographed coming out of a party, me
holding him up as he smiled with inebriated joy. 'At least
I will be talked about, as speculation on my problem with
alcohol grows.'

'It's invasive,' I said. 'You were a little tipsy. I hate the idea
that you're always being watched.'

'Better to be looked at than ignored, darling girl, better
to be seen than not.'

'Don't worry,' I want to shout to the wind as I stumble
back to the vegetable garden, 'I will not forget you. No one
will forget you.'

In the garden I get down on my knees and go back
to inspecting the carrots, but I find myself unable to see
anything except her face. I don't know why it is so clear in
my mind since I have not seen her for more than twenty
years and by rights it is her sister that I should remember.
I saw a picture of her sister twelve months ago. Twelve
months ago on the night I killed my husband. There she
was, standing in front of Birdy and calling herself Isabel.
But her name isn't Isabel, her name is Lila. Lila Adams
from next door. Lila Adams, daughter of Ellie Adams, and
sister to Felicity.

Lila's smile and Lila's eyes and Lila's golden hair. Lila from
next door, whose sister was Felicity. Felicity, whose picture

lay on Simon's desk and whose solemn little face is now the stuff of my nightmares. The greatest question mark of all exists around Felicity. She and Simon spent so much time together, and he had, among all the other photographs, only two of children taken in the garden. All the other pictures he showed me on that awful night twelve months ago were taken in his office at the studio. He posed them in front of the painting of the sailboat riding the crests of rough white-capped waves, its sails filled with wind and movement. For twelve years it hung on the wall of his office at the studio. I remember going with him to choose that painting. We both loved how the blue of the water behind the boat was reflected in the blue of the sky above the boat.

Instant, now-fading snapshots of girls in their prettiest outfits, hoping to find themselves in front of a camera on the studio floor, but instead finding themselves alone with Simon in his office.

Every night until the day I came here I thought about destroying that painting. I would stand in front of it in his study at home, where it has hung since his retirement, scissors held tightly in my hand, and wait for the courage to slice through the canvas—but it never came.

The photograph of Felicity was taken in front of the aviary. She is dressed in a blue corduroy skirt and ruffled pink top. Her brown eyes squint at the camera and her head is cocked to one side. Half of her mouth seems to be attempting a smile as though someone has told her to 'smile for the camera'.

There is nothing sinister about the picture, nothing sinister about any of the pictures, unless you were there that night, as I was, unless you had heard the words he said. They are all just pictures of girls, ordinary everyday pictures. In most of the pictures the girls look quite happy.

Felicity doesn't look happy, but then I don't think she ever did. *Surely*, I have said to myself many times since that night, *surely he cannot have done anything to Felicity.* I believe she is seven or eight years old in the photograph. *He wouldn't have, he couldn't have,* I have said to myself whenever I am woken by a racing heart from stifling dreams that I cannot remember except for the appearance of Felicity and her hand reaching out for mine.

Lila only came with her sister to visit every now and again. Mostly Ellie kept her at home and sent Felicity over, but sometimes she would send them both. If both children appeared on the step I knew that Ellie was having a bad day. I should have gone next door to talk to her, to help her. I was not, in the end, a very good friend to her. Her desperation and despair cut a little close for me, I suppose. She had gone from being a woman who took great pride in her appearance and the immaculate condition of her house to someone whose sink was piled with dirty dishes, her grey roots showing.

'After everything I've done for him,' she said when she recounted the story of Albert's leaving. 'After everything, he just walks out to begin a new life. He has no interest in seeing the girls, you know. He wants me to sell the house so he won't have to pay the mortgage. I don't understand how it came to this. I don't understand at all.' Ellie persisted in her state of confusion and anguish for months, taking to her bed or yelling at her children. I shook my head along with Simon at her deterioration, but I could not look too closely at her failures. I was aware that should Simon decide to leave me, I would be in exactly the same situation as she was, scraping together money to get through the week, fighting with her ex-husband for support, and fending off the bank, who wanted the house.

Beautiful moths fluttered around my husband all the time, and in my most self-critical moments his endless reassurances meant nothing to me. I could not fathom his interest in me when I compared myself to the women he saw at the television studio. Sometimes I would go through weeks when every day was a question. *Is this it?* I would think. *Is this the day he's going to tell me that he's leaving me?* It wouldn't take much to set me off on one of those self-defeating spirals. I would see a woman look him over at a party or he would be declared the sexiest man in Australia by some women's magazine, and it would be enough for me to question everything about our marriage.

'But my darling, have I ever given you cause to worry?' he would say if I confessed the turmoil I found myself in.

'No,' I answered every time, because he never did. Clearly, obviously now I know I was looking in the wrong place.

As far as I had known growing up, once you were married you were married for life. Divorce was never discussed in our home, it wasn't even discussed when it happened to someone else; but watching Ellie I was all too aware that it could and did happen.

I had no qualifications and no way of supporting my children. They and I existed in our luxurious home thanks to Simon's largesse. The girls attended private school and took ballet and piano and even riding lessons because Simon wanted them to have everything, to be everything they could be. 'I want them to be at home in even the highest society,' he told me when we discussed what other activities the girls might be able to do.

'What societies are those?' I asked.

'Oh, my darling girl,' he said, 'sometimes you are so delightfully naive.'

Watching Ellie, I saw how quickly everything could disappear. Simon put money in my account and paid all the bills. He and Eric discussed investments and interest rates and I smiled and poured the drinks. With a snap of his fingers he could take everything away. He never said anything to indicate he thought like that, but I was always aware that he had given me everything I had. My life was entirely different to my mother's life, entirely different to my childhood. When she was alive, my mother would come to visit and sit, looking like an uncomfortable stranger, on the living room sofa. She was awed by the size of the house and the expensive furniture. She had no idea how to treat the cleaners and found it difficult to talk to her privileged grandchildren once they were old enough to be aware of her accent and cheap clothes (she adamantly refused anything I offered her until after my father died). The thought of trying to take my girls back to the place I had come from was at once laughable and terrifying. 'I will make your dreams come true,' he had said. 'I will give you everything. You will be the envy of everyone you know.' And he did, he did and I was. He had given it all to me, and by default he could also take it all away.

Ellie was my worst-case scenario, and so I looked after her child or children a few afternoons a week and convinced myself that I was doing my best as I maintained a polite distance from her tragedy. Lila only started appearing on my doorstep with her sister after she turned three and Albert left. She was a gorgeous child, with blonde hair and blue eyes and a delicate fairy grace that made her seem lighter than air.

Felicity wasn't so beautiful, more interesting looking, with her thick straight hair and brown eyes. But Simon adored her ... adored her. 'She's so sensitive to everything around her,' he told me. 'She wants to learn so much, and she listens so carefully to everything I say.'

It doesn't seem possible that he saw her as anything other than a little girl, younger even than his daughters. She was a child when they spent time together, just a little girl. All the women who came forward to accuse Simon of wrongdoing were older when he met them. They were thirteen and fourteen and fifteen, young women already.

Those who supported Simon when the allegations began—and there were many, many people who did— would often point to the age of the 'victims' as possible proof that either nothing had happened and it was more fantasy than fact or that if something had, it was most likely mutual. *He was a famous man who could get them onto the show—a show that could possibly change their lives,* one man wrote on a blog that had been set up to query every accusation. *Is it not possible that these young women used their sexuality to persuade Simon Winslow to give them what they wanted? Have we moved so far into the arena of political correctness that we cannot even entertain the possibility that a fifteen-year-old girl is aware of her own attractiveness? Teenagers are having sex earlier and earlier. We must allow for the fact that Simon Winslow may have been the victim of circumstance. It is very difficult for a man to resist the invitation of a beautiful girl. Certainly his behaviour may not have been morally correct, but it was not illegal in the truest sense. In 1942, the age of consent in Australia was fourteen for men and twelve for women. This has changed over the years, even though teenage girls reach puberty earlier and earlier and their exposure to various media from a very early age gives them a greater level of sophistication.*

'I don't understand this,' said Simon when Portia alerted us to the blog. 'I don't know who this man is. I don't know why this is happening.'

'I'll look into it,' said Eric. 'I think he's doing you more harm than good, despite his intentions.'

'I think he's just trying to justify his own perversions,' said Portia.

Simon cannot have had any interest in Felicity, I have said to myself over and over again. Because if he had an interest in Felicity, I'm aware that there is another young child he may have had an interest in. *It cannot be. I cannot think it. Too much, it is too much.*

I pray that he didn't touch her, that she was only his friend, that his paternal side came out and all he did was teach her about the finches. I pray but I do not know, and now I will never know. I should have protected her, kept her close to me, and then the question would never have to play on my mind. I shouldn't have let him spend so much time with her, but she wasn't an easy child to be with. Rosalind grew tired of the friendship because Felicity wasn't bright enough to keep up with her, especially with the age gap.

'She's stupid,' she pronounced one afternoon when I asked her to play with Felicity.

'That's a very unkind thing to say, Rosalind, and very unlike you.'

'But, Mum, she can't even read yet and she's seven. I could read at seven. If we play school and I draw an A she doesn't know what it is.'

I don't know if there was anything wrong with the child, but her speech was slower than I thought it ought to be at that age and she had a curious way of staring at me as if trying to absorb the movements of my mouth as I spoke.

She rarely spoke herself, just watched. I never asked Ellie about it and she never mentioned it. We weren't close enough for me to bring it up.

After Felicity's father left, she acquired a desperate look of her own. She would stand next to me, almost as if she was trying to feel the heat from my body, but if I touched her, her thin shoulders would stiffen and she would pull away. I let her spend time in the kitchen with me, but I was always aware of being studied. I felt claustrophobic, caught in her unwavering gaze. She didn't have that easy chatty spirit that most children have. She was older than her years but able to understand less. I never knew what to say to her. She grated on my nerves and so I was glad to be rid of her. I was always grateful when Simon came to find her to take her down to the aviary.

And she seemed to love the finches and spending time with Simon. She went with him willingly enough and always returned to me with some new fact about the silly little birds. 'Do you know they need shell grit to di . . . di . . . digest their food?'

'Don't you find her a little strange?' I asked Simon. 'I mean most of the time she doesn't say anything at all. I think there may be something wrong with her.'

'I suppose she is different,' he said. 'She's certainly slower than the girls were at her age, but I don't mind the fact that she doesn't talk much. I feel that she is listening to me with her whole being. She's very restful to be around. She doesn't interrupt me or argue with me, she's just quiet. I think if we were the same age we would be great friends.'

'God, can you imagine her at our age?' I said.

'Life is very difficult for her at the moment. Ellie is not coping very well.'

'I know,' I sighed. 'I feel like I should do more.'

'Rose darling, our door is always open to her children, and I'm helping out a little as well. There's no more to be done.'

How was I to know? How was I to know?

Unlike her sister, Lila was a delightful little girl, all smiles and energy, and when I was with her I was pulled back to the days when my girls were toddlers, but without the worry of sleepless nights. (After Rosalind turned two I had toyed with the idea of having another child, but Simon was against it. 'I could not bear to have you turn into one of those blousy women with great cow udders and stretched skin,' he said, 'and there is little enough money as it is.') I loved being with Lila. My girls were independent. They chose their own clothes and did their own hair. Portia would roll her eyes at most of my suggestions and Rosalind was fond of saying, 'you have no idea . . .' about everything. Sometimes I felt a little like my mother—uncomfortable and out of place when talking to my spoilt children. 'Make me pretty,' Lila would chirp, demanding my time without thinking about it, safe in her certainty of being adored.

When we heard Ellie yelling next door, her voice stretched to breaking point, it was mostly at Felicity. Lila was too little, but I'm sure Felicity understood that her father was gone forever and her mother was desperately unhappy.

Only Simon wanted to spend time with the child. Only Simon. I thought he liked her because she was interested in the birds, whereas Rosalind and Portia never even wandered down to look in the cage. I thought their friendship was good for both of them: he loved being able to tell someone about his passion, and her father was gone, seemingly never to return even for a visit. How was I to know?

Today, I was the one who noticed the sick bird. Mina and Birdy were spending the day in the mother and child unit, so I was in the garden with Maya and Jess and a woman named Paula. I walked over to the cage just to look at the birds and saw the little one sitting on the floor of the cage. Birds will not sit on the floor if they can help it. I know that much. They like to be up high on perches and they move continually.

'One of the birds is sick,' I said to Jess.

'Fuck,' she said. 'Birdy will be upset. What do we do?'

'Well, it's just . . . you have to get to them quickly or they'll die. It needs help.'

'I have no idea what to do,' said Jess. 'Don't you know? You said your husband used to keep them. Allison won't get the vet. He only comes for the cows.'

'I never really had much to do with them. Perhaps I should go and tell Birdy. Maybe she'll know what to do.'

'You can't leave your allocated spot unless you've been given permission. I'll ask Allison, but we have to wait until she comes around. It shouldn't be too long.'

'Yes, but . . .' I said, and then I saw Allison. She was on her way to a meeting but said that I could go over and speak to Birdy. It wasn't that I really cared about the bird, but I didn't want to leave it suffering if there was something I could do for it. Sometimes Simon used to have the vet out almost every week for months. He once spent a whole night sitting in the kitchen feeding a sick bird sugar water with a dropper to keep it hydrated. It didn't survive. They rarely did, but Simon was always devastated when he lost one.

I was glad that Birdy agreed to come, and I wanted to meet her little girl. Birdy shoved her behind her legs as if to keep her away from me, but the child wasn't having any of that. She reminded me a little of Portia, who was also unafraid of strangers.

I only gave her a cursory glance at first, but when she spoke to me I looked at her properly and I felt the world start to spin. It's not the same child, of course. It's not Lila, but oh, how much she looks like her.

Ellie and the girls moved away when Lila was four years old, and that would be around twenty-five years ago. Felicity was eight by then and she was a sad, grim little girl. Was it just the divorce and the change it wrought in her mother? Or was it something else?

'We're moving,' Ellie told me one night, standing on my doorstep with both her girls' hands clutched in hers.

'Oh, Ellie,' I said, 'I'm so sorry, so sorry that ... I couldn't...'

'Please don't worry about it, Rose. You've done enough, and Simon has been so kind, but it's time for me to make it on my own. I have no choice in the matter.'

I knew that Simon had given her money a couple of times. 'Just to tide her over and pay a few bills,' he told me. He was generous like that. 'My darling girl, we have so much,' he always said. 'I need to share it with those who have less.'

He wanted them to stay next door. He didn't want to lose the child—Felicity. I shouldn't call her 'the child'. That diminishes her and I shouldn't do that. He didn't want to lose Felicity. I can see that now.

But I can't think about that. If I begin to think of the things he might have done, I find myself hating him with such a passion that if he were here I would put my hands around his neck and squeeze. I want to kill him over and over, and then I want to kill myself.

That child is so familiar, so definitely her. So not her.

There have been times lately when I've been busy with my hands and just thinking about my grandchildren and I've managed to forget why I'm in here and what I've done. The face of that child brings it all back. I would have liked to ask Birdy about her, but I know better than that. I go over and over the child's features, trying to remember and compare it with the picture in my head, until eventually I don't know what I have and haven't seen. I want to have another look at Isabel, but Birdy is in and out of the birdcage quickly, and gone before I get the chance.

I've no idea where Ellie and the girls went after they sold the house. 'Some ghastly little hovel far away from here,' Ellie told me when I asked her where they were going. 'I'll call when we're settled.' But she never did. I think I heard that they later moved interstate, but I could be wrong about that. Now, of course, I would be able to look her up on Facebook and find out all about her life.

Simon was depressed for months after they left. I didn't connect the two things. Should I have connected them? There was talk about the show being cancelled. There was always talk about the show being cancelled, but this time it seemed quite certain, and it turned out to be Simon's last season. He spent hours in front of the finch cage, sipping a glass of whisky or a cup of tea.

'I'm feeling my age,' he told me. 'Who will want an old man like me?' He was only fifty-one at the time, but that was old for the television industry.

'Retire,' I said. 'Go out on a high. We can travel and you can write. There are so many things we can do. I can hire someone to look after the girls.'

'I'm not quite ready to be put out to pasture.'

He did work for a few more years after that. They tried him on one thing or another, but nothing lasted very long. He went on to become a spokesman for an insurance company and a health fund and some other things. It kept the money coming in, and despite the humiliation he felt in having come down so far in the world, he was always able to justify it to himself. 'At least my face is still on television. You never know when some executive will see an advert and think of me for something else.'

After an hour of distracted weeding around the carrots I decide that my mind is just playing tricks on me. Birdy's daughter probably doesn't look like Lila at all. The last time I saw the child I was in my thirties. I probably imagined the resemblance.

At dinner I am once again unable to eat. The child or what I saw in the child has forced me back into the circular thinking of the months before Simon's death. It never does me any good, but round and round my thoughts go. How could I have missed what he was doing? Who was he really? How could I have been so wrong? It is exhausting.

When the second woman came forward to accuse Simon of touching her when she auditioned for *My Kid Can . . .*, we waited for the interest to die down as quickly as it had after the first woman. But it didn't. This time the media grabbed hold of the story and it began to appear everywhere, and then more women came forward with the same allegations. Articles appeared in newspapers and on the internet. Websites were set up to condemn Simon, and an equal number of them were set up to support him. Journalists began to call the house, first during the day and then at odd hours, hoping we would pick up. We had to change our phone numbers. News vans took up residence outside the house. Letters and emails arrived, some wishing Simon dead and others wishing him luck.

'This is disgraceful,' Simon said to Eric. 'They cannot tell these lies about me. They must be stopped.'

'Why is this happening to me?' he said to me. 'What could I ever have done to deserve this?' It felt surreal, like some badly plotted movie where the protagonist is accused of something he didn't do and must fight to clear his name. I would wake up some mornings convinced that we would receive a call that very day from Eric telling us that it had all been a huge mistake.

I shook my head at what was being said. I shook it at the first article and the second. But by the time the whole country was interested, I found it harder and harder to shake off. *This is not my husband,* I thought when I read an article on the internet after he had gone to sleep.

In the article, the woman described him as a predator. *I was crying because I had failed at the audition and he pulled me aside into a corridor and gave me a hug. He said, 'You will make it next time, my dear,' and then before I knew it his hands were up the back of my shirt and then around the front, squeezing my breasts. I didn't know what to do. I was only thirteen and I was terrified.*

This is not my husband, I thought. *How can this be?* I read story after story, trying to find the one thing that I could use to tear each account apart, but the only thing I found was an eerie similarity. All the women were upset in some way. They were all nervous or sad about being passed over or unhappy that they had lost. All of them needed comforting and Simon was always right there. Right there where he needed to be.

Chapter Fifteen

I worry about the finch all night long. I know it's sitting on the floor quietly waiting to die. I want to run over to the cage and take it in my hands and keep it warm until its little heart stops beating, but I'm with Isabel and Isabel is more important than finches. Isabel is more important than anything.

In the morning I wake up and Isabel's nose is next to my nose. I laugh at her eyes going all crossed.

'I don't want cornflakes for breakfast,' she says.

'If there's bread for toast then you can have toast,' I say, 'but if there's only enough bread for sandwiches you have to have cornflakes.'

'I'll be mad,' she says.

I laugh again, and then she gets up to jump on the bed.

Isabel doesn't stay mad for very long. She's happy all the time. I look at her and I wonder what it would be like to feel like that. Isabel's life has changed because I'm here and she has to live with Lila, but she's still happy because she knows that we can see her. She doesn't try to be quiet and she doesn't try to be small and she never has to hide away. She can eat and eat and still feel light and free like the finches because there's nothing to pull her down.

'I saw Gran,' she says when we're eating breakfast.

'Did you?' I say, and I take a big sip of my too-hot tea so that it burns my tongue. I need to stay calm.

'Her face looks funny. It looks funny because you hit her.'

'Really?' I say.

'Yep. Aunty Lila says that it was a bad day and that's why you did it. Was it a bad day?'

'It was, Isabel. It was the very worst day ever.'

Isabel bites off a corner of her toast and chews and chews. 'Will there be more bad days?' she says.

'No,' I say. 'Not ever, I promise.'

'Is Lester gonna come and live with us and get married to you?'

'No. You never have to see Lester again.'

Isabel asks me about Mum and Lester every time she comes. I don't mind. I am patient with Isabel.

'Me and Suresh are gonna draw some pictures now,' she says, and she goes to the table where all the pencils and paper are kept.

I clean up the breakfast dishes and think about Lester. I got a letter from Lester last week. We don't get many letters, because we're allowed to use email, but sometimes Isabel sends me a drawing in the post.

When Jess came into the living room she saw me holding it and said, 'What's that?'

'It's from Lester,' I said.

'That bastard won't give up, I see.'

I shook my head. 'I didn't answer any of his emails so now he's written me a letter.'

'Yeah, well, if I were you I'd just chuck it in the garbage. He's lucky you haven't told the police about him.'

'Lila wants me to tell the police about him, but I'm scared.'

'What are you scared of?'

'I'm scared they won't believe me and they won't believe Isabel. I think they won't hear me and they won't hear Isabel.'

Jess sat down next to me on the couch and sighed a big sigh, 'I suppose you have to try, Birdy. Even if they don't listen you have to try. You said Lester is a teacher and if he does do these things then he shouldn't be a teacher. Kids should be safe at school.'

'I don't want to rock the boat,' I said. 'I just want to go home and be with Isabel and Lila.' When I said those words I knew that it wasn't the truth. I felt bad but I couldn't tell Jess about my agenda.

'Some boats need to be rocked,' said Jess and I wanted to tell her then but Mina came into the room and I couldn't talk in front of Mina.

If I told Jess about Mr Winslow and my secret agenda she would know that I'm very good at not rocking the boat. I know how to not rock the boat but sometimes I would like to jump up and down and maybe sink the bloody boat.

I took Lester's letter and threw it in the garbage. I didn't need to read any of his words. They would have said the same things that all his emails did. *I love you. I miss you. I don't know why you won't talk to me. What did I do wrong? Why won't you email me back? I want us to get married. I want you and Isabel to come and live with me.*

He tried to come and visit me at the other place but I wouldn't let him. The only thing we could decide on at the other place was whether we wanted to see people from the outside or not. They tell you when to get up and when to go to sleep and what to eat and what to do all day long, but you can say who you do or do not want to see. It's strange to think that when I was little I couldn't say who I did and did not want to see. I wasn't in prison, but if Mum said, 'Go and play next door,' then I had to go. If Mr Winslow said, 'Come down to the aviary and help me feed the finches,' then I had to go. I wasn't in prison but I couldn't decide about anything.

I met Lester when Isabel was three. I was still working at the fruit shop, but Frank had gone away. His wife was very angry about Isabel and she made him get another job.

'He needs to pay child support,' said Mum. Child support means money. Babies and children need lots of things and now Isabel likes My Little Pony toys and they cost money as well. Isabel is lucky that Lila likes to spoil her. Sometimes I wish that I was Isabel.

'This child is his mistake as much as it is yours,' said Mum, but I didn't think that Isabel was a mistake. I thought Isabel was my own special present. I didn't mind if I had to use all my money for nappies and toys for her. I didn't want Frank to get into more trouble with his wife, so I didn't ask him for any money for Isabel. I worked hard in the fruit shop and I made money for Isabel, and Lila gave me money as well.

One evening just before closing time a man ran into the shop. 'I'm looking for small red apples,' he said to me. 'Do you have any small red apples?'

I was standing at the till watching the clock. Closing time was at seven pm. The big hand was on the twelve and the small hand was on the seven already. 'It's closing time,' I said.

'Look, please, they're for my mother. She's in the hospital and she said that she wanted a small red apple. She's very sick, please help me.'

I felt sorry for the man with the sick mother, and so did Amina who was the supervisor. We told him about all the red apples we had and then I found him a bag of small red apples. They were very small because they were supposed to be for children to put into their lunchboxes when they went to school. 'They may not be very good,' I said. 'They're really small.'

'They'll be perfect, thank you,' he said, and I put the code into the till and took his money. He smiled at me and I smiled back. He had a nice smile and green eyes with lines at the side. He also had brown curly hair and he was a little bit fat.

'I'm Lester,' he said, and because I know how to be polite I said, 'I'm Felicity,' even though my name was on my badge. My badge said, *Hello, I'm Felicity. How may I help you?* I liked that the badge said things for me.

'You're very pretty, Felicity,' he said.

I was small then. I didn't eat much at all. 'You can't live on nothing,' said Mum all the time, but I hardly ever felt hungry. If I ate an orange for breakfast I could feel it trying to hold me down. I needed to be light so that I could fly away fast if I had to, but I couldn't tell Mum that. When we moved to the shitbox I made sure I didn't eat too much. I grew taller and taller but I stayed light. Mum took me to the doctor and he said, 'She's just a fussy eater, she'll grow out of it.'

When I was a teenager I still wouldn't eat and Mum took me to another doctor, who said, 'This is very common in teenage girls, watch her carefully.' But Mum had to work and I had to take care of Lila in the afternoons and cook dinner, and when Mum came home and asked if I had eaten I said yes and she didn't ask again. I ate, I just didn't eat a lot.

Some days I would get really, really hungry and then I would eat a lot. I would eat chocolate and cakes and biscuits, and then when I had finished the biscuits I would make myself pieces of toast with peanut butter. One day I had eleven slices of toast in a row. Then I felt sick and very, very heavy. I felt too heavy to walk even one step. I crawled on the floor to the bathroom and put my head over the toilet bowl but the toast wouldn't come out so I stuck my finger down my throat and it came and came and came. After that I knew that if I had a day when I needed to eat everything, I could make it all go away afterwards. I liked to vomit. I felt empty and light afterwards.

'You're very pretty,' he said again.

The big hand was on the five and the small hand was moving past the seven. 'It's after closing time,' I said.

'Sorry,' he said, and then he smiled at me again and left.

I was pretty. Everyone always said I was pretty. I dyed my hair black and my eyes were big and brown. Now my eyes look smaller but only because my face is so much bigger. I didn't like it when my hair was brown. 'Such beautiful hair,' Mr Winslow would say to me. 'Such a beautiful colour.' And he would run his fingers through my hair and then massage my shoulders and then . . .

Before I was sent to prison, Lila took me to the hairdresser once a month and she dyed it for me. Now I have to do it myself and Jess helps me. I make a really big mess otherwise.

The next day Lester came back into the fruit shop. He bought apples and grapes and bananas. The code for bananas is 3201. He came and stood in the line for my till even though that line was the longest because sometimes I am slow. I am slow but I don't make mistakes because I know all the codes.

'Come have coffee with me,' he said when he put all his fruit in front of my till.

'I have to go home when I'm finished working,' I said. 'I have Isabel at home.' I had to talk and do the codes, so I was slower than usual.

'Who's Isabel?'

'Isabel is my little girl.'

'Are you married?'

I shook my head to say no because I was taking his money and I needed to pay attention.

'Please have coffee with me, and I'll drive you home, unless you have a car.'

'I don't have a car,' I said. Mum didn't want me to have a car but I could have had a car. I could have learned to drive but Mum wouldn't teach me and Lila didn't have the time to teach me, and Mum said that lessons were really expensive.

I knew that I wasn't allowed to go in the car with strangers. 'Strangers may try to hurt you,' Mum had told me and told me and told me.

'How will they try to hurt me?'

'They will do things to you, touch you and things. Just don't get in the car with one, okay? Or go home with one. Stay away from strangers.'

'Will anyone else try to hurt me?' I asked.

'What? No, of course not. Now, just go and play next door or something, Felicity. I can't have any more questions today.'

I knew Lester was a stranger but I liked his green eyes. I let him take me for coffee, except I had a milkshake. I don't like how coffee tastes.

Lester talked about his mother who was going to die and he told me he was lonely. He asked all about Isabel and Mum and Lila, and then he drove me home and he came inside to meet Mum.

Mum wasn't happy about Lester at first but she said I could go to dinner with him the next night.

We went out to dinner lots of times. And we went to the movies and sometimes Isabel came with us and Lester would talk and talk to Isabel and she would talk back to him. I liked that Isabel had someone else to talk to.

One night Lester came to dinner and after we had eaten I went into the kitchen to get dessert plates and when I came back I opened the door slowly because I was carrying so much and I heard Mum say to Lester, 'I'm sure you've realised she's not exactly smart.' I stopped opening the door.

'I understand who she is, Mrs Adams,' said Lester. 'I know what to expect, but I really like her and I like Isabel. I think we could all be good for each other. I have experience with people like Felicity.'

Lester worked at a school. He was the special needs teacher. I didn't know why he wanted to be with me, because I was slow and I knew that he had to talk to children who were like me all day long. But then I thought that maybe he didn't care if someone was quick or slow. He liked me because I was pretty.

'I would be so happy to see her married and settled,' said Mum.

'Well then,' said Lester, 'we're on the same page.' I didn't know what that meant because they weren't reading a book.

After that, Mum and Lester were best friends. He came over all the time and he even helped to babysit Isabel. She liked him. He played all sorts of games with her. He knew lots of games because of being a teacher.

'It would be so wonderful to have a wedding,' said Mum. 'I don't know that Lila is ever going to take the plunge.'

'What does that mean?'

'It just means that I don't think she'll get married. But now with Lester around, you just might. Wouldn't that be wonderful? You could move out of here and have a home of your own, and Lester would take care of you and Isabel.'

'Lester didn't ask me to get married,' I said.

'Oh, I know, darling, but he will. He loves you and he adores Isabel. You're really lucky to have found such a man, and he seems willing to overlook your . . .'

'My what?'

'Just your ways—you know. You're very lucky to have him.'

'I don't know about him,' said Lila when she came to tea. 'He's just a bit funny.'

'Lila,' sighed Mum, 'you don't like anyone, and you're so protective of her. Let her have a life. You're not here with her all the time. I know this man, and he wants to provide for Felicity and Isabel. He should be admired for that.'

'Give it a rest, Mum. She's not a charity case. She doesn't need anybody to help her. She's got us. What do you like about him, Fliss?'

'I like his eyes,' I said.

'She doesn't know, Lila. She knows she enjoys spending time with him and he's kind.'

'Do you like being with him?' Lila asked.

'I do,' I said. 'He tells me jokes and he brings me nice chocolates.'

'What about sex?'

'Lila, really,' said Mum.

I shook my head and I felt my cheeks get hot. Sex with Lester wasn't like sex with Frank. He didn't say, 'Can I touch there?' or 'Do you like that?' It was quick and sometimes not nice, but afterwards he would ask me about the fruit shop and about what Isabel was doing at day care and he would hold my hand. I liked that bit.

'If you're happy, then I'm happy,' said Lila.

'Oh, thank you, Princess Lila,' said Mum, and I laughed because Lila wasn't really a princess.

That feels like it happened a very long time ago.

'Look at the picture me and Suresh drew, Mum,' says Isabel, and I have to stop thinking about Lester. It's hard to think about bad things with Isabel around. 'This is me and

Suresh and you and Mina and Aunty Lila and Gran and we all live together on a farm with chickens and ducks but not cows because cows stink.'

'That's a lovely picture,' I say.

Together we tidy up all her things and pack her bag. I'm sad and I want to make the hands of the clock go backwards but I know I can't do that.

'Bye, Suresh,' says Isabel when he leaves to go home with his aunty.

'I can't believe all this is nearly over,' says Mina. Mina's going home in three weeks and she will be able to see Suresh every day. I'm happy for her but a little bit sad for me even though I'm going home soon as well.

'One more visit and then I'll come home,' I tell Isabel when we hug goodbye.

'One more, one more, one more,' sings Isabel.

I hope that I'm telling her the truth. I hope my agenda won't get in the way. I need to make sure I don't get caught. That's why I have to plan it. I want to go home to Isabel but I have to make sure Rose understands what she did. People shouldn't be allowed to get away with doing the wrong thing.

I go to the finch cage before I go back to my unit. The little bird is lying on the floor, all stiff and dead. I pick it up gently. 'I'm sorry, little one,' I say. 'I'm sorry I couldn't protect you.'

I find a spot at the back of the cage and dig a hole with my hands. The soil is cold and dry so it isn't easy, but

I don't want to find Jess and sign out a spade. I dig and dig until there's a hole big enough for the little bird and I put him inside and cover him up.

'Fly away now,' I say to him, but I know his body isn't going anywhere. I don't know where finches go when they die. Humans go to heaven. I learned that at school from Miss Bradley, who was the religion teacher. Good humans go to heaven and bad humans go to hell. Heaven is up in the sky and hell is down under the ground, deep under the ground. When I walk back to my unit I stamp on the ground really hard, hitting Mr Winslow on the head.

'Isabel met an enormous bear,' I say as I stamp and stamp. 'Isabel, Isabel didn't care.'

Chapter Sixteen

'Rob and I are moving in together,' says Portia. She's sitting opposite me in the visitors' room. The visitors' room looks as though someone was given the brief to 'make it cheery'. In contrast to the rest of the prison which is painted in the utilitarian colours of grey and green it has sunny yellow walls and a deep blue carpet. There are red and blue and yellow bean bags dotted around the room and a large, worn leather sofa. Wooden tables and chairs complete the look. It is quite jarring on the senses but was obviously styled this way in an attempt to make visiting children feel comfortable. Two of the walls are completely obscured by children's drawings depicting 'mummy' in various poses and locations. Parks and beaches feature more than anything else.

When Portia arrived, I had to hold my hands together tightly to prevent myself from touching her. Prisoners have to remain a certain distance apart from visitors at all times. I have not been touched by another human being for eight weeks now. Everyday contact with my daughters went unnoticed before I was sent here, but now I find myself rubbing my arms a lot, warming myself, soothing myself.

'I'm pleased, Portia, really pleased. He's a nice man. I hope you'll be happy.'

'I am happy,' she says, and she pushes up the sleeve of her leather jacket to show me a small tattoo of a snake on her wrist. 'It's identical to his, but his goes all the way up to his shoulder.'

'What a giddy schoolgirl thing to do,' I want to say, but I can only bask in the reflected joy radiating off her beautiful face. 'Do you think he's the one, then?' I ask instead.

'I do, Mum, I really do. We're . . . we're trying for a baby.'

'Oh, Portia,' I say, and then I have to stand up and get myself a tissue from the box on the coffee table.

'Don't cry, Mum. It's a good thing.'

'Of course it's a good thing, my darling. It's a wonderful thing. I thought it wasn't something you wanted, that's all.'

'I didn't before Rob,' says Portia, and then she shrugs her shoulders as if that explains it.

'I hope that it happens for you, and I hope to be there when your child is born. I really, really hope to be there.'

'Eric says any day now.'

'I know, but he's said that a few times. I just wish they would tell us yes or no. I'm so tired of waiting for an answer.'

'We'll be granted an appeal, and if we aren't we'll keep fighting until we get one.'

'I know, I know. How's Rosalind?'

'She's good. She's fine. Jack's been offered a partnership in his firm, they're both excited about that. Jack's working really hard to make sure he keeps on top of the extra work and they've been having dinners with all the partners to celebrate so I've been helping her a little bit with the kids. I'm taking Lottie to ballet every week, just . . . just until you get back.'

Portia's tone is indulgent and patient. Something has shifted in her, in the way she sees her sister, in the way she deals with her. I can see it. Jack making partner in his accounting firm has long been a goal but Portia always used to roll her eyes when Rosalind talked about it. 'How much more money can you possibly need?' she asked Rosalind. Now she sounds almost proud of Jack and very happy for Rosalind. The change in perspective is welcome but also a little disconcerting. I have always wanted them to get on better, but I can't help feeling that Portia is stepping in for her younger sister where I have failed.

'It's lovely that you're helping her,' I say, not quite managing to conceal a tinge of bitterness in my voice.

'Oh, Mum,' says Portia, and she shakes her head.

'I miss . . . I'm missing everything,' I say. 'I feel like I haven't spoken to her properly for weeks.'

'I know that you two aren't emailing much, but it'll be better once you're out.'

'I am emailing her, every chance I get, but she rarely replies, and if she does she just talks about what the children are doing. I felt like she was on my side all through the trial, but now I'm not so sure. I think she believes that I meant for it to happen, that I deliberately . . . that I did it deliberately.'

'She misses him. You know how close they were. She doesn't think your actions were deliberate. It's just that the verdict hit her very hard.'

'Harder than it did me? She has no right, Portia. She told me she believed me about what happened. She cannot now be questioning what I told her just because the jury didn't believe me. It's wrong.' Even as I speak it occurs to me that what I want from both my children is unfailing loyalty. I need them to accept my version of the truth without question. Their certainty is a stepping stone towards my own. Rosalind's unspoken blame makes me question myself even more than I already have done. In this I realise I am not so very different from Simon, who also wanted to be believed by those closest to him despite what everyone else was saying.

'I don't think she's doing that. I think it's all just sunk in now. The months after his death were absolute chaos. Things have quietened down now and that's given us both the time to think about what happened. She misses Dad so much, and I know that Sam is giving them a bit of trouble.

He wants to go over and over what happened. I think he's just trying to put it all into perspective, but Roz is finding it a bit much. You know her—she looks like she's keeping it all together, but underneath she's a bit of a mess.'

'Oh God,' I say. 'Everything is such a mess. I can't believe our lives have come to this. I miss him too. I miss him every minute of every day.'

'I know you do, and I know it was an accident.' Portia leans forward and puts her hand over mine. The guard in the corner of the room coughs discreetly, and Portia sits back. My hand is warm where she touched me. 'I just want you out of here so that you can get on with your life. You deserve to be able to travel and make new friends, maybe even male friends.'

'Oh, Portia, you're in love and the world seems filled with endless possibilities. I'm not sure what kind of a life I'll have when I get out of here.'

'You never know, you just never know, and there's no reason to think that it won't be a good life,' she says, and then we both study the drawings on the wall for a minute, staring at all the mummies and children playing in the sunshine.

Portia laughs. 'You won't believe it but a publishing house contacted me. They want me to write a book.'

'You said no, I hope?'

'Of course I said no. I wouldn't know what to write about anyway. The more I think about him, the less I think I knew him. He wasn't like anyone else's father, and I've never known another person like him. All my friends at school used to envy me. They thought that our lives were perfect because he was famous and there were always pictures of you two in magazines, but I remember feeling like none of it was really real, like *he* wasn't quite real—do you know what I mean?'

I nod my head slightly as I try to process what she's saying. 'You've never told me this before,' I say.

'I know. I'm sorry, I shouldn't have said anything.'

'Don't be sorry. It's how you felt. You can't help that. I hear what you're saying. He was an actor, a very good actor. I suppose it was hard for him to turn it off, but I do wonder now if I missed something about him.' I speak slowly, feeling as though I'm stepping onto a tightrope. I don't want to say anything that will give away what I know about Simon. I don't want to find myself in freefall, unable to take back the things I have said, but I desperately want to talk to someone.

'Rosalind doesn't feel that way. She really believes he was the perfect father. She still thinks that everything that was said about him was bullshit, even after so many women came forward. She doesn't think it's possible that he did any of the things he was accused of.'

'And you, Portia? What do you think?'

Portia looks down at her wrist and rubs her finger gently over the small tattoo. 'I don't know, not really. Before the television interview with that woman I was looking for a reason to dismiss the women's stories. Even when all that stuff started going around on the internet I still thought it was possible that a lot of it was made up. It was all rumours and speculations. I would read one article that said he was definitely guilty, and then I would read another that questioned if the women could remember exactly what had happened. At work I encourage all the girls I meet to stand up for themselves, to say something and not to let anyone tell them that they've remembered it wrong, but with Dad, I don't know . . . Maybe I just didn't want to believe it. One of the girls I work with asked me about him the other day.'

'She did?'

'She said, "Isn't your dad the one that felt up all those girls on his show?"'

'That's pretty direct.'

'They don't mince words. They've been through too much.'

'So what did you say?' I shift forward in my chair and I realise that I'm holding my breath. I want the answer, not because I care what she told the girl but because I have a feeling that Portia has the answer I'm looking for, the answer to the question I have been too afraid to ask my own daughters, in case I had missed not only what Simon was doing to other children but what he was doing to my own children as well.

'I told her that yes he was, and I explained that he was dead now, and then she asked me if he'd ever touched me.'

I just nod at her. I don't trust myself to speak.

'You never really asked us that, did you? I thought you would. When the stories seemed to appear overnight on the internet I thought you would want to make sure. I was upset about that at first.'

I sit back in my chair and am forced into a memory of a terrible night during the trial. It had been an awful day. I think it was my third day of testimony or maybe my fourth, I can't really remember. The prosecutor, a sharp-eyed woman named Mary Kirk, had begun the day gently enough—seemingly concerned for how I was doing. 'I understand this is difficult Mrs Winslow,' she said. 'We're nearly done now.' But as the day wore on she grew claws. She asked about Simon's life insurance again and again. The same question kept coming back with different phrasing. She would not give up.

'You knew about the insurance, didn't you, Mrs Winslow?'

'When you found out about the insurance you realised he was worth more dead than alive?'

'You knew the insurance would make you comfortable for the rest of your life didn't you?'

On and on it went until I shouted across the courtroom, 'No, no, no. I didn't know, I didn't know.'

Robert leapt to his feet and the day was declared over. I was completely exhausted.

'I think I'll stay with you tonight,' said Portia on the way home.

'No, I'll be fine, really,' I said.

'Don't be ridiculous,' said Portia. 'You look as if you can barely stand.' She was right.

Portia made dinner and she opened a bottle of wine, and then because it was a Friday night she opened a second bottle as well. The day drifted away.

In bed I found I could not sleep and so, despite knowing it was a bad idea, I took one of the sleeping pills I had been prescribed.

I dreamed of Simon, an appalling dream. I saw myself in the house, holding a laundry basket, making my way downstairs and I stopped to see if Portia had left anything on the floor of her bedroom. I watched my hand push open the door just a little and then stop. My eye went to the bed where Portia and Simon lay together and I watched him push his hand down her pants. I was there, standing right in front of them but they could not see me. Simon smiled and Portia laughed and I opened my mouth to scream but it was one of those silent dream screams.

I woke as if surfacing from underneath water and struggled out of bed. I stumbled over to Portia's room and shook her awake.

'Portia,' I said, 'Your father . . . did he . . . your father . . . was he?' Even in my half-awake state I knew my words were coming out garbled with sleep and wine. I kept shaking her.

'Mum, stop, please stop,' she shouted. She pushed me away and stood up and then she wrapped her arms around me. 'Shhhh,' she said. 'I know, he's gone, I know.'

She led me back to my room and tucked me into bed, making me her child. 'Your father,' I tried again.

'Go back to sleep, Mum,' she said—she rarely called me mum, only mother. 'Go back to sleep.'

'Mother,' says Portia. 'Did you hear what I said?'

'I did,' I say, 'and you have every right to be upset about that but I ...'

'I know, you couldn't. I talked to Rob about it. He has a way of seeing the other side of everything. He said that if Dad had ... done anything to either of us it would have been more than you could bear, especially since there was nothing you could do about it now.'

'He's right about that, but I should have asked. I was so afraid of the answer. I question everything in my life now, and I know that you and Rosalind are doing the same, but at least I've been able to hold onto the fact that I was a good mother. I think I was a good mother. If he did something to you girls and you tried to tell me and I didn't listen or if I missed it, then ...'

'Then what?'

'Then I wasn't really fit to be your mother, was I? And then what have I done with my life, Portia, what have I done with it?'

'Oh, Mum, please don't cry.'

I grab another tissue for myself and blow my nose, taking deep breaths. I bite down on my lip, pulling myself together. Portia does not need to hear all this. She may be an adult, but she is still my child. 'I'm just being silly,' I say, 'don't worry about me. What did you tell the girl?'

'I told her the truth.'

'The truth . . .?'

'That he never did anything to me or Rosalind.'

'Never?'

'Never. In fact, when Roz and I talk about it she remembers him as being physically kind of distant with us. He never brushed our hair or lay on the bed next to us to read stories, and he didn't tickle us or even hug us much. I suppose that's why it was so hard for me to believe it at first. He was always so reserved, so English. It didn't fit with who he was.'

'None of us wanted to believe it.'

'Before the interview I would go back and forth about it, but afterwards . . .'

'Afterwards you stopped coming over. He noticed that, you know. It broke his heart.'

Portia sighs. 'I can't keep apologising for that. I couldn't look at him. I'm surprised you could. I'm surprised Roz is still defending him.'

'He was my husband, and he was your father. There has to be some loyalty to the people you love. All those girls that you support through their court cases would be nowhere without some loyalty from you. You cannot simply abandon someone because of their failures.'

'It's not the same thing. The girls I help are all victims. Whatever crimes they've committed were done out of fear or desperation.'

'What would you have had me do? He was an old man, and as the months went by he got quickly older. If I had left he would have had no one at all. I'd been with him for most of my life, and until you find yourself in the same situation you have no right to judge.' I'm surprised to find myself so angry at her. I spend so much time missing her now that I forget how stringent she can be. The world has always been fairly black and white to Portia.

She stands up. 'I didn't come here to fight with you. I'm going to go now, because I love you and I miss you and I don't want you to get upset.'

I stand up too and we walk to the door together, watched by the guard, close but not touching.

'I'm sorry,' I say.

'I'll email you tonight,' she says, and then she's gone. It takes two hours to drive back to the city from the Farm.

I don't know why I defended him, once again, since there's nothing to be gained from going down that particular path. The television interview was revolting. Afterwards I came close to telling him to leave; close, but not close enough. Perhaps if I had told him to go he would still be alive today.

We only knew the interview was coming a few hours before it aired. 'They wanted to prevent me from having time to get an injunction,' said Eric when he came over to warn us about it.

'But they must be stopped,' said Simon.

'It's too late,' said Eric. 'There's nothing I can do, and

they're obviously sure they have legal right on their side. Watch it carefully, Simon, make notes. Write down anything you can think of that will refute what the woman is saying.'

'Who is she?' I asked.

'They wouldn't tell me. They're going to protect her identity.'

'Monstrous,' said Simon. 'This is monstrous.'

I called the girls, feeling the need of their presence.

'But how does Eric know it's about Dad, and who is it?' said Rosalind when she came over. She had arrived in a flustered state with her hair in a mess, after calling her mother-in-law to look after the children for the rest of the day. Our lives had always been so ordered, so predictable, but that afternoon it felt like we were descending into chaos.

'I don't know, darling. Eric just said that it would be airing tonight and that he cannot stop it. It must surely be connected with what is being said about your father. Please stay. I'll make dinner. We need to stick together now. Your father is so distressed. He's been locked in his study for the last hour and he won't open the door to me.'

'When is this ever going to end?' said Rosalind. 'Don't worry, Mum. I'm not going anywhere.'

'This is getting ridiculous,' said Portia when she arrived from work.

'We have to find a way to stop all this rubbish, all these lies,' said Rosalind.

'Oh, Roz, how can it all just be lies?'

'Let's not discuss it,' I said.

Jack was working late, so we were once again a family of four for the night. I cooked, taking some solace in the domestic act of seasoning the chicken and chopping vegetables for the salad.

What are people going to think? What are they going to say? I thought as I laid the table for dinner. The girls had opened a bottle of wine and were sitting in the kitchen, supposedly helping me but mostly trying to distract me with talk of the grandchildren and Portia's latest boyfriend. 'He's always on call at the hospital, so we've never even had a full dinner together,' she said. 'I think I like him, but I haven't been with him long enough to know.'

Simon was still in his study and I was pleased to just have to deal with the girls. I thought about calling a few people to warn them about the program, but I didn't want to draw anyone's attention to it. When the first article appeared, our friends were supportive of Simon and indignant on his behalf. They were still upset for us when the second woman came forward, but everyone had gone strangely quiet since the true media storm began. What could they say, after all? 'So sorry your husband is being accused of being a paedophile, shall we make plans for dinner?'

I laughed out loud in my quiet dining room. 'Are you okay?' called Portia from the kitchen.

'No,' I said, going in to sit at the small round table we had eaten breakfast at for years and years. 'No, I don't think I am at all.' I opened another bottle of wine and poured myself a large glass. It wasn't even five o'clock yet but I had taken to having my wine earlier and earlier in the day.

'It's a party,' said Portia, and she clinked her glass against mine.

'Jesus, Portia,' said Rosalind.

Of all our friends, only Eric and Patricia had really stayed true. And Eric had no choice but to support his old friend. He was, after all, being paid.

Simon had barely left the house for weeks. Our lives felt as though they were getting smaller and smaller. I had stopped going to bridge and my water aerobics, and Portia had shown me how to order groceries online. She had even organised for a hairdresser to come to the house. If I did have to go out, I had to run the gauntlet of the journalists outside the house and they terrified me. Portia and Rosalind don their sunglasses and charge through the waiting pack with their heads down, almost daring them to try to stop them.

When will it end? I thought, echoing Rosalind.

'Both my daughters for dinner, how pleasing,' said Simon softly when I had coaxed him to the table.

'I would appreciate it, my dears, if you left your mother and me to watch this vile trash alone. I'm sure you understand,' he said over a dessert of fruit and ice cream, as the time for the program grew ever closer.

'Of course, if that's what you want,' said Rosalind, but Portia would not be swayed.

'I'm staying, Dad. If you want to go to a different room, that's fine. But I'm watching it with Mum.'

For the first time I saw a small chink in the armour of disbelief and indignation that Simon had wrapped himself in. He met Portia's gaze and then quite suddenly he dropped his head and mumbled, 'Very well, Portia, my dear.'

After dinner we settled in front of the television in a state of nervous expectation. The music for the current affairs program began and the male reporter explained with barely disguised glee that yet another woman had come forward to accuse Simon Winslow of inappropriate touching.

'When Monica Rundle was sixteen years old, she auditioned for and won the chance to appear on *My Kid Can* . . ., then the most popular show on television. Monica didn't win, but her enthusiasm and love of the industry led producer Matthew Evans to offer her a part-time after-school job as one of his assistants. It was while working for the show that Monica became yet another victim of Simon Winslow. Monica does not wish her face to be shown on television and so we have agreed to disguise her appearance and voice and use low lighting. Rundle is not her real surname.'

The woman in question appeared on the screen. I couldn't make out much more than long dark hair. 'I thought I had found my dream job,' she said in a low, evidently altered voice. 'All I did was make coffee and tidy up the food table and things like that, but I loved being around television people. It was all I wanted to do with my life, and I was so grateful for the opportunity.'

'What was your first experience of Simon Winslow's behaviour?' asked the reporter.

'I hadn't seen him much when I was on the show except when we were on stage together. All the kids on the show had to call him Mr Simon and he was really nice to all of us. I liked him a lot. I even had a bit of a crush on him. When I'd been working there a few weeks I overheard two of the makeup women talking in the bathroom. I don't think they knew I was there. They were laughing about Mr Simon, calling him "Mr Handsy", but I didn't really think anything of it.

'Then about a week later, Mr Evans asked me to take a cup of coffee into Mr Winslow's office. I was quite excited because I really wanted to see him again and thank him for giving me a chance to be on the show.' The woman sniffed and reached to pull a tissue out of the shadowy tissue box in front of her.

'Take your time,' said the reporter, oozing sympathy and patience.

'I knocked on his office door and he told me to come in, so I opened the door and went inside and put the coffee on the coffee table. He was sitting there, on the couch. He had his feet up on the table next to this big jar of lollipops. "Thank you," he said, and I said, "I just wanted to tell you how much I love the show and how happy I am to be working here."

'"Oh yes," he said. "You're the lovely Monica. I'm pleased that you accepted the job. I see a very bright future for you in this industry. Come and sit down and tell me all the things Matthew is making you do." So I sat down next to him, because, I mean I wanted to, I really did, but I thought we would just talk. I sat down a little bit away from him but then he shifted right next to me. "Have you seen any stars wandering the corridors?" he asked me, and I said, "No, only you," and then he smiled and put his hand on my leg. I thought he was just being friendly so I didn't say anything, but then his hand moved up higher and higher and I got scared. I remembered the women in the toilet calling him Mr Handsy and I wanted to stand up and get out, but his hand was kind of pushing me down and the next thing I knew he was touching me all over and I couldn't move, I just couldn't move.'

I don't remember what else the woman said; by then the only thing I was listening to was the ringing in my ears. When it was over we all sat in silence. I stared straight ahead, not trusting myself to look at Simon.

'What the fuck?' Portia said, breaking us all out of our stunned spell.

'Must you sound like a peasant, Portia?' Simon said.

'*That's* what concerns you about this? You're worried that I swear too much? What's going on here? You have to tell us what happened, Dad. If she's making this up we need to sue her, we need to make her pay. She can't say these things about you. This is fucking unbelievable.'

'It's not true, is it, Daddy?' asked Rosalind. 'None of it is true, I'm sure. Do you even remember a girl named Monica who was an assistant? Did he ever mention her, Mum?'

'No,' I said. 'He never mentioned her.'

I looked over at Simon and he caught my gaze. The blue of his eyes had faded a little over the years, but I could see the anger flaring in his body. He held my gaze until I felt compelled to lower my eyes. He knew I was questioning him in my heart and he was furious.

He stood up. 'You will forgive me, ladies,' he said as though he were addressing strangers. 'I'm very tired and my back is aching. I'll go to bed now.'

'Wait, we need to discuss this,' said Portia.

'Let him go, Portia,' said Rosalind.

'Simon . . .' I began.

'You will forgive me,' he said again, and the coldness of his tone silenced us all. 'I'll sleep in the guest bedroom, my dear. That way I won't wake you if I need to move about to get comfortable.' And he left the room, touching each of his daughters briefly on the head.

I felt my mouth working as my brain tried to form a coherent thought, but nothing would come.

'It's rubbish, all of it,' said Rosalind. 'It's disgusting to think she would do this to an old man. What on earth can she be thinking?'

'Why would she make it up?' said Portia quietly. 'Why would all these women be making this up?'

'I'm not getting into this again with you,' said Rosalind.

'Bury your head as always, Roz. This is too much, there are too many. We can't ignore this anymore. It's not going to go away.'

'Portia, just because you are surrounded by girls who have experienced this doesn't mean that every man is a paedophile. He's our father, our *father*. How on earth can you believe this of him?'

'Girls,' I said, interrupting them. 'You need to go now. Thank you for being here, for always being here, but I think I need to speak to your father.'

'If it's all the same to you, Mum, I think I'll spend the night,' said Portia.

'If you need me to stay I can call Jack,' said Rosalind. 'I'm sure he can manage.'

I shook my head. 'Please don't make me ask you again. I think it would be best if we were alone. That way I might be able to get him to talk to me.'

They left reluctantly and I went to the guest bedroom to speak to Simon, but he had locked the door and would not respond when I knocked.

I was worried about him, worried for him, worried for all of us, but he wouldn't speak to me; and until his very last day on earth, that was how he handled what was happening to us.

'Please let me in, Simon,' I called, only to be answered with silence. 'Please let me in.'

Chapter Seventeen

A funny thing happened today. Not funny so that it makes you laugh but funny so that you feel strange.

'Only two weeks before you're off,' said Jess to me last night. Jess has to stay here for one month without me. I think she's worried that she'll be lonely. Even though I will be with Isabel and Lila when I go home, I think I'll be lonely for Jess as well. I have given her Lila's phone number and my mobile number and I hope she will call me when she gets out.

I nodded my head but I didn't say anything. I want to be happy about going home, but when I think about what I'm going to do I know I need more time. Even after what happened today I still have my agenda. In fact, my agenda is more important than ever, because now I know that

Rose is small but strong and she could have helped me if she wanted to. Now I know that the only reason she did nothing was because she didn't care and didn't like me. She liked Lila because Lila was pretty and cute and talked and smiled, but I was quiet and she didn't like that. She protected Lila but she didn't protect me. That's not fair. People like that shouldn't be allowed to live.

Malcolm was here today. He was here because Natalie is sick. I like Natalie. On her birthday she brought in cakes. There were enough cakes so that everyone could have a slice, and we all sang 'Happy Birthday', and Natalie laughed and it was a good afternoon.

We saw Malcolm at first muster. We were all standing out on the verandas, jumping up and down because it was so cold.

'Oh shit,' said Jess, 'it's him again.' Last week Jess told us that when Malcolm is here he likes to come up to her and say rude things to her.

'Like what?' I'd asked.

'You know, stupid stuff about how he could rock my world if I would just let him. I don't know why he's after me. I'm old enough to be his mother.'

'What do you do when he says things like that?'

'I tell him no, and I say it loud and clear so anyone who's nearby can hear me.'

'He'll move on,' said Maya. 'He's just looking for another friend because Paula's going home.'

Paula's gone now. I saw her leaving. She was all dressed up with nice clothes and makeup. I don't know if the clothes I wore to get here will still fit me when I go home. I think I'm getting bigger every week. When I email Lila tonight I'll have to tell her to bring me some more clothes. In her last email she said that Isabel is really excited and that she has made a sign that says *Welcome home, Mum.* Isabel is really clever. Sometimes I worry about what she will think of me when she gets big like Lila, but Lila loves me so maybe Isabel will too.

Yesterday I watched Rose in the garden and she looked so sad that I felt bad for having my agenda. I got bigger and bigger when I came here, but Rose is getting smaller and smaller. I've seen Allison looking at her with worried eyes. Rose looks like maybe she is sorry for everything in her life. Maybe she is sorry for not helping me, but I think she is just sorry that he is gone and she killed him.

She was digging with a garden fork and she had to push hard because the soil isn't soft anymore and I thought about going over to help her because I'm strong now. But then I remembered that she could have helped me, that she could have saved me, and just like that the bubbling anger came back. Sometimes it comes back so fast I feel like I can't breathe. I would like to tell Henrietta about the bubbling anger but I'm afraid that then she will say, 'You can't go home and be with Isabel, Birdy.' I don't want that. I want to go home and be with Isabel, but maybe the bubbling anger will make me a bad mother. I don't want to be angry and crying like my mum was when I was little. I want to be a happy, kind mum to Isabel.

I have to get rid of the anger before I go home. I don't want to go back to the other place, but she has to be punished. People can't do the wrong thing and be allowed to get away with it. I'm going to be smart about it and I'm going to be quiet. No one is going to catch me. Mum was punished and he is gone. There's only one person left. Lester is . . . Lester is something I have to think about. Lila is right. He shouldn't be allowed to teach kids. Maybe he's already feeling punished because I won't read his letters or talk to him. When I think about Lester I can't remember his face very well. When I count on my fingers all the people I'm angry at there is only one finger left now. He is gone, and Lester is not in my life anymore and I know that if he tries to come near me or Isabel he will be very sorry. I can make him sorry. I am big and I can protect Isabel. I can protect her from anything. The finger for Mum has also been pushed down, so now there is only Rose. She's the last one left.

'Well, well, if it isn't the lovely ladies of unit seven,' said Malcolm.

'Hello,' I said, and I smiled at him because Mum taught me over and over again to be polite, especially to police-men. Malcolm isn't really a policeman, or maybe he is. I don't know. Jess looked at me and I could see her lips go thin. She doesn't like it when I say hello to Malcolm, but he has a nice smile.

'Birdy, Birdy, tweet, tweet,' he said, and then I stopped smiling. Malcolm checked us off and walked away. We went back inside to have breakfast. I like to have toast and hot chocolate, but I'm only allowed cornflakes now because canteen isn't for another two days and we need the bread for sandwiches.

'He's going to be pissed because his fuck buddy has gone home,' said Jess. 'He'll be a real prick today.'

'What's a fuck buddy?' I asked.

'It's like a friend that you have sex with,' said Mina.

Mina is going home tomorrow and Maya is sad about that. Someone new will come and live in the unit soon and none of us feel happy about that. We all just got used to each other and now everything is going to change. 'She's going to turn into a real bitch,' said Jess about Maya when we talked about Mina going home.

'When I get out of here,' said Mina, 'that's all I'm going to have—fuck buddies. I'm never getting married again. It'll just be me and Suresh, and the only time I'll go near a man is when I feel like a bit of a ride.'

I didn't know what Mina was talking about but I didn't ask her to explain. Jess is patient and she explains every-thing, just like Lila. Mina is sometimes patient, but some-times she says, 'Fuck, Birdy, get a clue,' and then I know she's finished being patient.

'Your parents won't be happy about that,' said Maya.

'I don't care,' said Mina. 'I married Arjun because my parents said it was the right thing to do. They hated the idea of having an unmarried daughter of eighteen. I was too young to know what to look for in a man but I knew there was something about him I didn't like. I never would have gone ahead if they hadn't forced me. When he started giving me a smack every now and again my mother told me to just put up with it because "you cannot bring the shame of divorce on your 'family'." When he started hitting Suresh, my dad sat him down and had a talk to him, because no one in my family believes in hitting your kid, and he cried and promised to be a better husband and father. He was so full of shit and he just went back to hurting the poor kid and then blaming me, like I made him hit him. I tried to tell my parents how bad it was but they didn't listen, and eventually every time I complained my mother just offered me some food or tried to discuss the weather. I'm not doing anything they say ever again. I don't care if I have to be on welfare for the rest of my life, I'm not getting married again.'

'Aren't you talkative today,' laughed Jess.

'I guess so,' said Mina. 'I'm getting kind of nervous about going home. I hope Suresh is okay being with me all the time. My parents aren't going to want to give him back to me, I just know it.'

'They'll give him back,' said Maya. 'It's the law.'

'Hopefully,' said Mina, and then she got up to make herself a cup of tea. 'I don't know if I should take him to visit his dad or just leave it.' She was standing at the kettle with her back to us, so I couldn't see her face, but her voice was nervous. I think she has been thinking about Suresh's father for a long time.

'You should take him,' said Jess. 'He can't hurt him anymore, so you should take him until he's old enough to decide. If my arsehole ex wanted to see my girls I would let him. I hate him but he's still their dad.'

'It's stupid because I know he's harmless but I'm still scared of him,' said Mina.

'You won't be when you see him again. You'll know that you're stronger than he is,' said Jess.

'You'll be fine,' said Maya. 'I'll be out in two months and then we'll get a place together and live with Suresh and there'll be no shit from any men.'

'And lots of nice food,' I said, because Maya and Mina are the best cooks.

Maya laughed. 'Maybe we can invite you and Isabel over, and Jess too.'

We all thought that was a good idea but I don't know if I will see any of the women I have met here ever again. 'Don't get too close to anyone,' Allison told me when I got here. 'For some women a condition of parole is that they don't associate with anyone else who has been in prison. Be careful.' I had to ask Allison to explain what she meant. Allison is also patient.

I was careful, but Jess and I became friends and I'm not sorry about that.

After breakfast this morning we all went to do our jobs. I took all the seed trays out of the aviary to refill them.

Sometimes I just blow the seed husks off the top. They're so small and light that they fly away in the wind and then the good seed is left underneath. But every two weeks I throw out all the seed and wash out the trays and then give the birds new seed. They like that. They hop onto their perches and bob up and down like they're happy. I'm always careful to move slowly when I go into the aviary. Sometimes if I stand very, very still one of the finches lands on my shoulder for a bit and then flies away again.

I was in the shed washing the seed trays when Malcolm came in. 'Hey, Birdy, Birdy, tweet, tweet,' he said softly.

'Jess isn't here,' I said, because I thought he wanted to count the spades and garden forks. Jess is in charge of that. 'She's gone to get some manure for the garden.'

'I don't want to see Jess,' he said. 'I want to see you. I hear you're going home soon.'

'Yes,' I said.

'I was thinking, Birdy, that maybe we could be friends— until you go home, I mean. You'd like that, wouldn't you? I'm going to be here for a few days and we could make the time go faster for each other.'

I turned around to look at him, because I didn't understand what he was saying. He was smiling at me with yellow wolf teeth. He doesn't have a nice smile at all. 'Allison says we mustn't make friends,' I said.

'Oh, Birdy, don't listen to her. You're really pretty, you know, or you would be if you weren't so fat. I mean not fat, you're not fat. You're just pretty, really pretty.'

I filled up one of the clean seed trays. 'I have to go,' I said.

'No, wait,' he said, and he grabbed my arm, making me tip the tray, spilling the seed.

'Look what you made me do,' I said.

'Sorry. I'll help you pick it up,' he said.

We crouched down together and started to pick up the seed. 'I won't be able to use it. It's got dirt in it.'

'Don't worry about that,' he said. I looked up at him. 'I could make you really happy if you just give me a chance. You must be lonely in here with all these women. Come on, what do you say? Just a little kiss?'

'No,' I said in a big voice, because that's what Jess did. But there was no one nearby so no one heard me.

'Ah, come on, don't be like that. I'll get you something extra from the canteen.'

'No,' I said again, but Malcolm didn't want to listen. He leaned forward and kissed me. I pulled back as hard as I could and I fell over and spilled all the seed I had just picked up.

'What are you doing?' I heard someone say and I looked up and saw it was Rose. She had used a big strong voice, just like I had, but Malcolm hadn't listened to me.

Malcolm jumped up and away from me. 'Nothing, Rose. Don't worry yourself. Me and Birdy were just having a chat, weren't we, Birdy?'

I didn't say anything. I just started picking up the dirty seed again.

'You were . . .?' said Rose.

'Muster soon,' said Malcolm. 'You ladies don't want to be missed in the count, do you?' He walked out of the shed.

'Are you all right? Did he hurt you?' said Rose.

'I'm fine,' I said. 'He just wanted a kiss but I said no.' I put all the dirty seed in the bin and filled up the tray again.

'You should report him,' said Rose.

'No, I don't want to rock the boat. I'm going home soon.'

'Why does everyone here keep saying that?' said Rose. 'You *should* rock the boat. You should tell Allison. He can't treat you like that, it's wrong. Guards aren't allowed to fraternise with prisoners. It's in the rule book.'

'Allison won't believe me,' I said. 'He'll say we were just having a chat.'

'Yes, she will, she has to,' said Rose. 'I'll tell her what I saw. I'll support you.'

'That's not how it works. I'll tell, and then Malcolm will say we were just having a chat.' My face was hot even though the air was cold. I was angry because Malcolm made me spill all the seed and I was starting to get angry at Rose as well.

'Has he done that sort of thing before? Tried to . . . to have a chat?'

I shook my head and went back to filling the seed trays. Rose waited and I knew she wouldn't go away until I looked at her and answered her. 'He hasn't done it before,' I said, 'but maybe he's lonely because Paula went home. Jess said that Paula was his fuck buddy.'

Rose's face went red. 'You shouldn't, um . . .'

The siren sounded. It was time for muster.

'We have to go,' I said.

'Okay.' Rose turned around to walk out of the shed and then she stopped at the door. 'Birdy,' she said, 'if you want to go and have a chat to Allison I could come with you. I saw that he was in the shed and I can tell Allison what I saw.'

'I don't want to talk to Allison,' I said.

'Okay . . . I mean it's up to you, but if you did want to talk to Allison or to someone, I mean if you wanted to talk, I'm here to listen, if you want.'

I nodded my head so that Rose knew I had heard her, and she went out of the shed.

My heart was beating very fast. I was glad that Rose came in and saved me from Malcolm. I didn't want him to try and kiss me again and I didn't want to be his fuck buddy. Up close Malcolm smelled like cigarettes and eggs. Isabel would have said, 'He smells yuck.'

I put all the seed trays back in the aviary and then I went back for muster. I was almost late but I couldn't leave the birds without food. They eat all the time.

'Rose said that the dickhead started with you,' said Jess.

'No, he didn't. We were just having a chat,' I said.

'But Rose said that—'

'Rose talks too much!' I shouted, and Jess was quiet. I don't like to shout at Jess. It makes her sad.

I was angry with Rose but I was also happy with Rose. That was a funny feeling. Not funny so that I wanted to laugh. Funny strange. She shouldn't have told Jess, but I'm glad she came in and saw what Malcolm was doing. She saved me from Malcolm and his yellow teeth, but I got angry at her. While we were waiting for Malcolm to come past and check us off his list I thought about why I got angry with Rose in the shed.

'It's good that she was there anyway,' said Jess softly.

I nodded, to let Jess know that I'd heard her, but I didn't say anything. And then I knew why I got angry with Rose. It's because now I know that she could have helped me; that she could have made him stop what he was doing. Now I know she really could have saved me.

Malcolm was scared of her because he was doing the wrong thing. Rose is right about it being in the rule book that he's not allowed to be friends with me. Maybe Paula didn't read the book, but I did, even though it took me a long time and Allison had to help me.

Mr Winslow would have been scared of her as well. All she had to do was walk down to the bottom of the garden and she would have seen and then she could have used her big, strong voice and told him to stop. Sometimes his hands would be in my pants and I would be staring at the finches and listening to his raggedy, raggedy breathing and I would wish for Rose to come down to the bottom of the garden. I would stare hard at the colours until I couldn't even see the birds anymore and I would call to her in my mind. 'Mrs Winslow, please come,' I called. 'Please come.' I thought that if she came she would say to him,

'What's going on here?' and then she would take my hand and take me back to the kitchen and I would be saved. But even though I called her and called her with my mind, she never came. I knew Mum wouldn't come, because she was always angry and crying, but Mrs Winslow was so nice and she made toasted cheese triangles. I thought she would come.

She could have come. She could have told him to stop. Even if she didn't say the words, she still could have made him stop the way she made Malcolm stop and go away.

'Too little, too late.' That's what my mum would say.

Too little, too late.

Chapter Eighteen

'Are you absolutely sure about this?' says Allison.

I found Allison in her office just after lunch. I'd fretted all the way through my dull cheese sandwich about what to do. Birdy had asked me not to say anything, but I found that I couldn't keep silent.

Over lunch, Heather and Sal were talking about Linda, who was in the hospital in town. She'd cut her hand making dinner; we had assumed it wasn't a big deal, but the wound had become infected.

'She did it to herself,' Heather said. 'I'm telling you she did.'

'How do you do something like that?' said Sal.

'I don't know. Maybe she put some dirt in the wound or something. She just wanted out. She wants to be near all the drugs in the hospital.'

'But there'll be a guard there, surely?' I said.

Sal shrugged. 'Druggies can always get what they need.'

'Poor girl,' I said, and then I threw away half my sandwich.

'You're getting too thin,' said Sal.

'Oh, I'm fine, just not really hungry right now.'

Once we'd been checked off after lunch I went to find Allison.

Allison is finishing off her lunch of what looks like leftover Chinese takeaway. My mouth waters at the smell. I'm finding the endless repetition of the same dishes hard to stomach. I tried to interest Heather and Sal in some different foods, but they don't want to try anything new or different, and anything other than basic ingredients costs too much anyway. I have never eaten so much pasta in my life, not even when Simon and I spent five weeks travelling through Italy.

Heather and Sal will both be leaving in a few weeks. I find it galling to look around the prison grounds and know that of everyone here I'm the only one not in the last few months of her sentence. I understand that the Farm is an easier place to be than some others, but it's no less a prison.

'I saw it with my own eyes,' I tell Allison.

'Listen, Rose, you have to understand that this is a very serious allegation. If it's true, he'll lose his job with us. I won't have my women treated like that. But if Birdy denies it there's really no point in pushing it.'

'Birdy's scared. She's going home soon and she said she doesn't want to rock the boat.'

'Yeah, everyone here is big on not rocking the boat. What exactly did she say happened?'

'She said it was only a kiss, but maybe it was more. I think it would have been more if I hadn't come in when I did.'

'But you did come in, and he left?'

'Yes, but what if I hadn't?'

'Did she look scared?'

'Not scared, more, I don't know … more irritated, I guess.'

'Well there may have been no real harm done, but I'll call her in and have a talk with her,' says Allison.

'No,' I say. 'She asked me not to say anything. She just wants to leave it.'

'I'll have to think about this,' she says.

'You have to do more than think about it,' I say, only realising after the words are out of my mouth that I have sounded a little imperious, forgetting where I am and who I am talking to.

Allison picks up the uneaten parts of her lunch and throws them roughly into the bin.

'Shit,' she says when a few bits miss and land on the floor.

'Look, Rose,' she says while she cleans up, 'you're putting me in a difficult position here. If she just wants to leave it and I bring her in, she'll deny it happened and he will too and then both of them will be angry with you.'

'I know, and I don't want . . .' I hesitate.

'You don't want what? This is a serious accusation. You cannot make it and simply go back to the way things were.'

'I just didn't want to keep quiet about it. It's wrong. Birdy is . . . well, she's like a child, isn't she?'

'Birdy is capable of defending herself. I know that.'

'That's not really the issue.'

'I know it's not the issue, Rose. I'm not going to ignore the problem but I need to be able to handle it the right way. If Birdy came to me and told me about the incident herself, it would be a different story. But as of now she hasn't accused Malcolm of anything so I'm going to ask you again to leave it with me. I've said I'll look into it, and I will.'

I nod my head, feeling suitably chastened.

'Anyway,' says Allison, changing her tone, 'I'm glad you're here. I wanted to see how you're going.'

'Oh, I'm . . . I'm fine,' I say, and I'm surprised by a lump in my throat. Her concern takes me by surprise.

'You've lost a lot of weight. Are you feeling all right?'

'It's just hard to eat, I suppose. I'm adjusting.'

'Hang in there.'

I nod my head and leave Allison's office. I've still no idea why I chose to tell her, especially when Birdy asked me not to, but it seemed like the right thing to do.

Alison said that there might have been no real harm done, but what does that mean? How do you measure how much harm was done? It was such a small thing, a tiny incident that my arrival prevented from going further. I may have even interrupted something that Birdy wanted, although she didn't seem happy about Malcolm touching her. There was seed all over the floor and I know she's careful with her seed. But even if Malcolm did come on a little strong, by tomorrow Birdy will probably have forgotten all about it. He didn't grab her or hurt her. He kissed her, and she—or my arrival—stopped him from going any further. There really wasn't any harm done.

Women's lives are filled with little incidents of that nature that mean nothing. Situations that could have turned ugly but didn't and leave one with only the fading memory of having been slightly uncomfortable. Portia has spent most of her life ignoring men who call out to her in the street. 'Hello, beautiful! Hey, baby! What about a smile? Jesus, look at that!'

'Dickhead,' I've heard her mutter when I'm out with her. Although Portia can be fierce, even she doesn't have the energy to address every remark thrown her way. She usually just lowers her head and keeps walking. While she was at university, a professor invited her out for a drink; when she declined, he failed her in an exam. Portia was incensed. She reported him to the chancellor. I admired her for it, but Simon seemed to think she'd overreacted.

'It's one exam, Portia. You've hurt his feelings. Move on with your life. He's been humiliated enough already, and I'm sure he won't let you fail the course.'

'There are so many things wrong with what you just

said, Dad, that I can't even be fucking bothered to explain it to you.'

'Must you use an expletive, Portia? Is it really necessary?'

I said nothing when Simon and Portia were speaking, but that night I went to find her in her bedroom. 'I think you were very brave,' I said. 'I'm glad you didn't let him get away with it.'

'Then why didn't you say that when Dad was giving me shit about it?'

'Oh, Portia,' I said.

'Yes, yes, I know, "oh, Portia",' she said. I wanted to chastise her then, to tell her that she had no right to tell me what to do, but I knew that Portia saw something when she watched Simon and me. I had raised her and her sister, just as my mother had tried to raise me, to expect more for themselves from their lives. I preached education and success and rarely mentioned that they should think of getting married and having children. I congratulated them for standing up to teachers and bullies at school and encouraged them to one day travel the world with friends. And yet when Simon was home everything revolved around him. I never contradicted him on anything, even when he was clearly wrong as he had been about Portia's reaction to her professor. Portia saw this and it frustrated her but there was nothing she could do about it. I wasn't ready to stand up to him. I was never ready to stand up to him. Not until the very end.

It has, perhaps, taken me far too long to learn to stand

up for myself. At fourteen, I had travelled into the city by bus one day with my mother. It was an exciting day for both of us because we were having lunch and then going shopping for a dress for me to wear to a cousin's wedding. I can still remember that dress. It was green taffeta with ruffles on the bottom. My mother and I even found a pair of matching green shoes to accompany it. Hideous by today's standards, but the height of sophistication in my fourteen-year-old mind.

It was the middle of the school holidays, so the bus to the city was crowded and there were people standing in the aisle. When it came to our stop, my mother and I had to squeeze past some men standing by the door, and as we got out, one of them pushed his fingers against my breast. It happened very quickly. The doors closed and the bus pulled away and I said nothing to my mother. I wasn't even sure if it had actually happened—and if it had, whether or not it was an accident. I soon forgot about the incident, but for some reason it comes back to me every now and again and I try to picture the man who may or may not have assaulted me.

There was no harm done to me. I went on to have lunch and a beautiful afternoon tea complete with petits fours and cake, and I enjoyed shopping with my mother, laughing with her over some of the clothes we saw. I wasn't upset then, even though I found myself throughout the day absentmindedly touching the breast that had been touched. But what is 'harm'? What does it mean? How do you measure how much harm has been done? Some of the women who came forward spoke of lifelong depression after their encounters with Simon. One of them told the newspaper that she was addicted to prescription medication, but in the next breath mentioned a bad car accident. Would all of those girls have led happy lives if not for Simon? How much harm did he do, and how will anyone ever know the answer to that?

Matthew Evans had used the words 'no harm done' when he talked about Simon. Matthew was the producer of *My Kid Can . . .* He was older than Simon by about five years and had been in the television industry virtually since it began in Australia. He became a close friend to Simon. A close friend and, I'm sure, a protector. For nearly all of its ten years on television, *My Kid Can . . .* always rated in the top five shows. High ratings meant advertising dollars. Advertising dollars meant survival. Simon's appeal was a big part of those ratings. Who knows what Matthew was willing to overlook to keep things ticking over?

When more and more women began to appear with their stories Matthew gave an interview to one of the major newspapers. In it he vigorously denied that Simon was ever anything but a model human being. His memory wasn't what it used to be, he said, but he did remember one of the girls who had since come forward to say that Simon had exposed himself to her in his office. (*He took out his penis and asked me if I wanted to touch it. I wanted to be sick.*) She had been thirteen at the time. She had tripped over during her dance routine for the audition and never made it onto the show. Her name was Alexandra—I'd always liked that name, but Simon was adamant about naming the girls. 'Ever since I first began performing Shakespeare I have dreamed of naming my children after some of his greatest characters.'

'I remember that child,' Matthew was quoted as saying. 'She was very pretty, with long red hair, and she was very upset when she failed. She wanted the chance to perform her dance again, but we wouldn't allow it. It wouldn't have been fair to all the other children. She got quite hysterical and we had to work hard to get her to just sit down and let us continue with the rest of the auditions. The rules were the rules. Her mother had left her with us and disappeared, and once we had coaxed her off the stage the child wouldn't stop crying. She was disturbing everyone else on set. The child after her was trying to sing and it really wasn't fair.

'Simon was kind enough to take her off the studio floor to comfort her in his office. Five minutes later she emerged with a smile on her face and a lollipop in her hand. I remember because the change was so radical. There was no harm done to the child. She was comforted and sent on her way.'

At the television station, Simon had a small office with a desk and a chair, as well as a couch and coffee table. I used to buy giant packets of lollipops for him to put in a glass bowl on his desk. 'Some of them can be very difficult when they don't make the cut,' he told me. 'I like to reassure them that their lives are not over and give them something sweet before I send them on their way.'

'That's nice of you, Simon,' I said, 'but I don't think upset children are your responsibility.'

'Probably not and they can be a little annoying at times but if we're careless with their feelings, they won't want to watch the show. Matthew lectures me all the time on maintaining our audience. Sometimes I let them sit in the office and have a good cry, and then I send them on their way with a quick cuddle and something sweet to eat.'

'Oh, Simon,' I said, 'you're so lovely.'

That's what I thought he was being—lovely and kind and self-deprecating. Despite his high-handedness when it came to dealing with the studio, he still didn't consider himself too important to comfort a child whose heart had been broken. When we were out with friends and he dominated every conversation, irritating me and other people at the table, I would remind myself that he was a man with a soft and generous heart. However bombastic and arrogant he might sometimes be, he was always deeply caring about the plight of those less fortunate—especially children. He served on the boards of at least five children's charities and was always happy to appear for free any time they needed him to.

After the stories began, what I hated most was that everything he ever said or did was called into question. Things that had merely been said in passing or done without thinking now took on a sinister gleam. Was he just comforting children and giving away lollipops? Was he being kind or was he turning the children's distress to his own advantage? Was he evil or did he just push being friendly a little too far?

That's what Matthew told the newspaper. 'He's simply a friendly man. He would hug me goodbye before he went on holiday. He hugged everyone. He liked to touch people. The fact that these girls misinterpreted his actions and that the media have now deemed him a predator speaks more to the changes in our society than to Simon Winslow's character. When did a simple hug become a reason for child protection militants to accuse someone of paedophilia?'

'Do you see?' said Simon as he read out the article to me. 'Do you see that the truth has finally come out?'

I looked at my husband and nodded. In the months since the allegations began he had aged. His eyes were bloodshot and his shoulders more rounded. Each time a new woman came forward he would lock himself in his study for hours. He was drinking too much and I worried about him having a heart attack. Our local doctor was a frequent visitor. I told Simon I was calling Dr Robins for myself, but before he left he always said to Simon, 'Why don't I just have a listen to your ticker, old man?' He had prescribed us both sleeping pills. Sometimes I was afraid that between the pills and the alcohol we would both be found dead in our beds one morning. What would the press say then?

I know that if I had been outside the situation looking in, I would have been absolutely convinced of his guilt. By the time Simon died, twelve women had accused him of touching or groping them. But it was not as simple as all that. Two of the women were instantly discredited when it emerged that on the dates they claimed Simon had assaulted them the show was on hiatus. Our whole family was travelling through Europe at the time. Then the first woman who came forward was offered a book deal that she gratefully signed, and Simon's supporters went into a frenzy on social media, claiming that she had made it all up for financial gain.

'All of the children left the studio happy,' Matthew told the newspaper. 'None of them seemed damaged in any way. Surely if these things were happening they would have said something at the time. Why come forward now? Is it not possible that the news of his induction into the Hall of Fame has led some who have known him, however briefly, to question their own lives? These women who have come forward have since been catapulted into the national and even international spotlight. They did not go to the police privately. They did not even contact Simon Winslow to accuse him. They went to the press. What does that tell you about them? What kind of people are they?'

And those were all reasonable questions. I stood by my husband because I wasn't sure, not until the very end. I stood by him, and Rosalind supported him as well. 'I know him,' she said to me.

I know him too, I thought, but then I wondered.

He lost Portia after the television interview. She couldn't get past what the woman had said. She became suddenly very busy with work, unable to join us for dinner or even a quick cup of tea.

'I feel as though she has died, my dear,' said Simon.

'What rubbish,' I replied. 'She's just taking some time. Give her some space, and when all this is over she will come back to us.'

'Ah yes, possibly, but then will we want her back? How can she stand on the side of my accusers and still call herself my daughter?'

'She is your daughter, Simon. She is our daughter and I will not discuss this any further.' I felt a streak of anger go through my body. Mostly I pitied Simon, was very worried about him, wished it all away, but sometimes I would feel a red-hot rage at what was happening to my life. At those moments I reached for the wine bottle. I couldn't leave the house for a calming walk, so I drank a glass or two and convinced myself that this time in my life would pass. So many years had passed since the alleged incidents, and many of the women couldn't recall exact details. It seemed possible that it was all a huge mistake, that Simon was being targeted by vicious women who were jealous of his success and his renewed fame. I had been married to Simon for decades, there was no way I could have taken the word of someone who knew him for one day at the most. I had to trust my own judgement until the point when he told me the truth. Only then did I understand, and on that day, that day over a year ago now, I did the right thing.

I think it was the right thing. I think he was finally telling me the truth after all the months of lying. I think, I think, and some days I feel I would give anything to know for sure, and on other days I would give anything to never know.

Chapter Nineteen

'So,' says Henrietta, 'have you thought any more about contacting your mother?'

I shake my head. Every week Henrietta asks me the same question. It's annoying. If I wanted to talk to my mother I would tell Henrietta or I would tell Lila. Every Wednesday Lila sends me an email about Isabel, and every Wednesday she puts at the end, *Mum would really love to talk to you*. I don't want to speak to my mother ever again. I'm glad that after I go home I won't have to see Henrietta anymore. She is pushy like a zebra finch.

'You might feel better if you apologised,' says Henrietta.

'Yes,' I say. 'You keep saying that, and Emily said that too. But I'm not going to say sorry to her. She knows I'm sorry for hurting her. I don't want to talk to her.'

'Birdy, you broke her jaw and shattered her cheekbone. I'm hesitant to sign off on your release from here until you take responsibility for what you've done, or at least explain it so I can try to understand.'

'I know what I did. I know it was wrong. People need to be punished when they do the wrong thing. I feel bad for hitting her, but I don't want to talk to her.'

'I know you've been punished, but won't you feel better if you and your mother can be friends again? She's a very important part of your life, and Isabel's life as well.'

'I have to go home to Isabel,' I say. 'I have just over a week left. I have to go home.'

'I know, Birdy, stay calm now. I don't want you to get upset, but you need to try and explain what happened. Please try.'

'There's nothing to explain,' I say. 'I got angry and I hit her. I didn't realise she was so weak. I was so skinny and light when I hit her. I didn't mean to hurt her. I was just angry.'

'You're not skinny now.'

'No, I'm not.'

'Do you feel stronger now that you're bigger?'

'I feel better.'

'Can you explain what you mean by that?'

'Not really.'

'When you get out you may want to lose some of the weight. It's not good for your body to carry so much weight. It's unhealthy.'

'You're a doctor for my mind, Henrietta, not a doctor for my body.'

'You seem angry today.'

I sigh. 'I'm not angry. I'm just tired of always talking about the same thing. I hurt Mum and I'm sorry for it. I won't hurt her again. I won't hurt anyone, but you can't make me be friends with her. I'm too big for that.'

'I have to know that you're not going to let your anger lead you astray when you get out of here. I have to be certain that you know how to control it.'

'I can control it. I've never hit anyone before and I won't ever again,' I say. 'Jess has taught me about the monkeys.'

'The monkeys?'

'See no evil,' I say, and cover my eyes, 'hear no evil,' I stick my fingers in my ears, 'and speak no evil.' I cover my mouth so she almost can't hear the words.

'And do no evil,' says Henrietta.

I put my hands behind my back. 'Do no evil,' I say, and then I laugh, and even Henrietta has to smile.

'I'm not going to hurt anyone again,' I say, and the bubbling in my stomach comes back because I'm lying and I'm not telling Henrietta about my agenda.

'We only have one session left after this. I'm going to give you some exercises that you can use in case you get angry again. I don't want you to hurt anyone else ever again.'

'I won't hurt anyone ever again.' I squeeze my hands together and cross my fingers to keep my agenda from coming out of my mouth.

Henrietta tells me about meditation. 'Just listen to your breathing,' she says. 'Sit quietly and listen to the sound of your breath going in and out.'

I'm not very good at meditation. My hand gets itchy and then my foot gets itchy and then I have to move because I'm uncomfortable.

'Just listen to your breathing and think of a place that makes you feel happy and calm,' says Henrietta. I scratch my chin and then I move my leg again. I try to think about a place that makes me feel happy and calm but I can't think of one. I think about the finches and how I need to clean the whole cage and then I think about Mr Winslow's cage and how clean it always was and then I think about how I hurt my mum.

I don't like to think about what I did to her. When it happened it was a Tuesday afternoon in summer and it was hot, really hot. Maybe it was the heat that made me hit her?

I came home from work and Mum and Isabel were in the backyard, and Isabel was running under the sprinkler in her undies. She was wearing her pink Dora undies. She was like a little puppy, making happy noises. Every time the water touched her she laughed and then Mum laughed as well. Her curls were wet in some places and dry in others and when she ran into the sun her whole head looked like it was covered in gold. I looked at her and I thought that maybe she wasn't real because she was so beautiful.

I got some Diet Coke from the fridge because I liked to drink that when I came home from working at the fruit shop. I used to drink Diet Coke all day long. It made me feel not so hungry but still light and free.

'You need to eat more,' Mum said to me whenever she saw me drinking Diet Coke. She had been saying that to me for years and years and years. After we moved away from the big house I thought I would feel light again, but I still felt heavy and I knew I would always be too heavy to run away. You have to be light to run so fast you are almost flying like a finch. If I didn't eat I was light. I didn't say that to Mum. I knew she wouldn't understand.

That hot summer's day I sat down on the back step with a can of Diet Coke and watched my daughter play in the sunshine. Me and Mum still lived in the shitbox, but it wasn't really a shitbox. After we moved away from the big house, Mum got a job working in a shop selling clothes. 'Who knew I would have such a flair for fashion,' she said every day when she came home. She liked the shop and she liked Mrs Rahal who ran the shop. Mrs Rahal was very nice and she let Mum come in after she had taken me and Lila to school.

Lila was in preschool and I was in primary school but we could see each other through the fence. At lunchtime I would go over to the fence and watch her playing with all her friends. I wanted to be with her, but primary school children weren't allowed in the preschool. I used to sit and watch her and eat my lunch and then I didn't mind that

I was eating lunch alone because it didn't feel like I was alone. I was with Lila.

Mrs Han from next door would fetch us from school and take care of us until Mum came home and told us about her flair for fashion. It took a long time for Mum to stop being angry and crying, but eventually she did. She was a better mum in the shitbox. She didn't talk about my dad anymore and how he had a whole new family. She didn't mention him at all. We all pretended that he wasn't real. Lila and I got bigger and bigger and I stayed light so that I could run fast and fly away if I needed to, but I never needed to. When Lila was fourteen she said to Mum, 'Are you going to get married again?', and Mum said, 'Not a chance. I'm never going to put myself in that place again.' Sometimes Mum went out with her friend Mr Michaels, but we never got to meet him. One day Mum came home and said, 'well that's that—I'm really done with men now,' and after that she didn't go out with Mr Michaels anymore. I don't think she had other boyfriends, but she may have just kept them a secret. It's funny to think about Mum keeping secrets.

After a long time I didn't think about Mr Winslow anymore. He used to come into my dreams at night and tell me about the finches and I would try to run away from him and then I would see that I was locked inside the aviary and I couldn't get away. But after I got bigger and bigger he didn't even come into my dreams.

Sometimes I would think that Mr Winslow was part of my imagination and that he had never tap-tapped on my private place. Mum didn't talk about Mr Winslow at all. It was like we had never lived next door to him. We didn't even watch him on television, because Mum liked the other channel. Mum fixed up the shitbox. Aunty Violet sent us some money from London. Some men came and took away the sticky grey carpet and they fixed the windows and the cupboards. After that Mum fixed the bathroom and the kitchen and I loved the shitbox, only we didn't call it that anymore. We just called it home.

After Isabel was born, Mum stopped working at the shop with Mrs Rahal and she stayed home to take care of Isabel so that I could keep working at the fruit shop. She was a good grandmother to Isabel. I know that.

That hot afternoon I was tired from being a good cashier and concentrating hard so that I didn't make mistakes, but when I looked at Isabel I still felt filled with joy.

'Time to go inside, little girl,' said Mum, and I stood up and got the towel to wrap Isabel in. She didn't like cuddles anymore, and that made me sad, but she let me wrap her in a towel and pick her up.

'I have a little sausage girl,' I said, and Isabel laughed.

'Don't eat me, don't eat me.'

I put my mouth near her ear and blew and she laughed and wriggled. 'Put me down, Mum,' she said as soon as I sat down in the kitchen.

'No,' I said. 'I need to eat another piece of little girl.' I put my lips on her neck and blew raspberries and made eating noises and her giggles filled the air.

'No . . . no,' she said, 'down now.'

I put her down because her voice was strong. I liked that she could say what she wanted. 'Put on your PJs,' I said.

'She hasn't had a bath,' said Mum.

'It's too hot for a bath,' said Isabel. Mum looked unhappy because she didn't like it when Isabel was bossy.

'It's fine, Mum,' I said. 'Off you go, Isabel.'

'Is Lester coming to dinner?' Mum asked me.

I took out my mobile to check, but Lester hadn't sent a text. He always sent a text when he was coming to dinner. He wasn't allowed to stay over, because Mum said that wasn't right, but he was allowed to be in my room until late.

'I don't think he's coming. Let's have macaroni and cheese.' Lester didn't like macaroni and cheese. I didn't mind that he wasn't coming over. I knew that Mum liked him, but sometimes I just wanted it to be me and Isabel and Mum.

'I think he's going to ask you to marry him soon,' said Mum.

I didn't say anything. Lester had already asked me and I said, 'I'll think about it,' because that's what Lila had told me to say. 'Give yourself a few days, Fliss, and really think about what you want. Don't worry about Mum. She just wants to see one of us married. It doesn't mean you have to be with Lester forever.'

Lester had asked and I was thinking about it. Thinking and thinking.

'I don't like Lester's tickles,' said Isabel.

She was standing in the kitchen doorway, dressed in her pyjamas. Her pyjamas also had Dora the Explorer on them. She loved Dora more than anything in the world. She had a Dora lunchbox and a Dora backpack and Dora sheets. Now that she's older she likes ponies. She started to like ponies after I was sent to prison. I'm sad that I missed her liking ponies instead of Dora. Lila has bought her lots of ponies.

'What do you mean?' I asked. I was stirring the macaroni in the water. I wasn't really listening, so I heard what she said but I didn't hear what she said.

'I don't like his tickles,' she said again and she used a loud voice. She was making sure that I heard her. I know that my mum was worried about me being a good mum. I know that she thought I wouldn't be able to take care of a baby because I needed to hear things again and again until I remembered them, but I know I'm a good mum. I know I'm a good mum because when Isabel says something, I really listen. My mum didn't listen even though she is clever like Lila. I heard what Isabel said. I heard it loud and clear. I stopped stirring, because my hands didn't want to work.

'Why don't you like them?' I said. I felt heavy even though I had only had Diet Coke all day long. I thought I was going to sink into the floor. When I think about it now I know that I didn't know what she was going to say but somewhere inside me I knew everything.

'I don't like them and when I say stop he doesn't stop,' she said. 'His fingers hurt and it doesn't feel like tickles.'

I walked over to Isabel and crouched down next to her. She was so little and so pretty. My legs felt heavy, so heavy.

'Isabel,' I said, and my voice felt like it was too loud in the kitchen, 'where does Lester tickle you?'

She shook her head and put her thumb in her mouth.

'You can tell me, sweetie,' I said. 'You can tell me anything.'

'Lester says you'll shout at me,' she said.

'He's wrong about that. You're my little girl. You're my number one. I only shout when you won't go to bed.'

'Or when I don't eat my banana.' She twirled her hair with her finger. She was tired.

'Yep, or when you don't eat your banana, because bananas are good for you.'

'Filled with vitamins,' she said around the thumb in her mouth.

'Yes, that's right. I'm not going to shout if you show me where Lester tickles you.'

Isabel took her thumb out of her mouth and ran her hand across her chest and down her stomach and into her pyjama pants.

I took a deep breath and stood up. 'Thank you for telling me, Isabel. That was very brave of you. I'm very proud of you because you told me the truth. Lester won't tickle you anymore. I'll make sure of that. If you don't like what someone is doing, you tell them and then you tell me. No one is allowed to touch you when you don't want to be touched. Okay? And if someone tells you that I will be angry with you, you say, "Oh no, my mum will only be angry with you!"'

'Lester said you would be really cross because he was being nice to me and he got me an ice cream.'

'Lester is wrong about that. Mummies don't get cross with little girls when they tell the truth. Now, what would you like for fruit?'

'Not banana,' said Isabel.

'No, not banana,' I said. I dragged my body to the fridge and got an apple for Isabel. I was very good at acting like everything was okay. I felt like I was back in the big house and Mr Winslow was waiting for me next door—only he wasn't waiting for me, he was waiting for Isabel.

I cut up Isabel's apple and put it on the kitchen table for her and then I got out the small pot to make the white sauce. I watched my hands pour the milk and put in the butter and I tried to breathe slowly. I was good at making macaroni and cheese because I learned how to do it at school. Mrs Brown was my teacher in food technology and she showed me over and over again how to make it.

Mum looked at me and I looked at her. She shook her head. She had heard what Isabel said, and even though she didn't say anything to me, I knew that she was going to find a way to make the things Isabel said be not said.

'Oh, Isabel,' said Mum, and she used a light voice as if to say that everything was just a joke and there was nothing to be bothered about, 'Lester was just being friendly.

I'm sure he didn't do anything wrong. Maybe you made a mistake. Are you really sure about his tickles? You shouldn't say things you're not sure about. You don't want to cause a fight between Lester and Mummy by saying something silly, do you?'

And that's when I hit her.

My body was heavy but my arm was light and quick and it moved so fast that I didn't know what had happened until it was over. I was still holding the small pot. I didn't just hit Mum with my hand, I hit her with the pot, but she didn't tell that to the policeman and the policewoman when they came to our house. She was quiet about that. It's because I hit her with the pot that there was so much blood, but even though the policeman asked her again and again, she just said, 'No, only with her hand.' Even Lila doesn't know the truth.

After I hit Mum with the small pot there was blood, and Isabel was screaming and crying and Mum was moaning. I feel bad about hurting Mum, and I also feel bad about scaring Isabel. Little girls should not have to be scared of their mums. I never want Isabel to be scared of me again. When she came to visit me at the Farm for the first time, she cried because she didn't know she was going to see me, but she also cried a little even when she did see me because I had scared her when I hit Mum. The first time she came to visit I told her over and over again that I was sorry, and I talked quietly and I was very nice to her so she would know that I was still a good mum. She still asks about it every time she comes, but I don't mind answering her question over and over again about me hitting Mum. Sometimes even smart people need to hear things more than once.

On that bad day Mum was moaning and Isabel was screaming and I could hear my heart going *thump, thump* in my ears and I had to think fast even though I'm not good at thinking fast. I grabbed a dishcloth and gave it to Mum and then I picked up Isabel and put her in her room with her apple.

When I came back, Mum had called the police on the phone.

She had also taken the pot and put it in the dishwasher and she was cleaning up the mess in the kitchen. The milk and butter had gone everywhere. The whole kitchen was covered in splatters of milk and butter and blood. It looked like all my anger had come out and covered the kitchen in red and yellow. I helped Mum clean up. I didn't like seeing what I'd done. Mum was holding the bloody dishcloth over her face and I tried to take it away from her but she wouldn't let me touch her. Her mouth was bleeding and her nose was bleeding. The blood kept coming out of Mum and I cleaned and cleaned but I couldn't clean it all up.

I heard the siren of the police car.

Mum said something but I couldn't understand her because she couldn't talk properly. 'What did you say?' I said.

'I said *oh God*!' she shouted. 'I called the police, Felicity.'

'The police?'

'Yes, yes, the police. Call Lila, call Lila right now.'

'What did you hit your mother with?' asked the police-woman. She talked to me and the policeman talked to Mum.

'Her hand,' shouted Mum, and then she nodded at me. It sounded like mum had a bad cold but I understood her.

'My hand,' I said. 'I didn't mean to. I just got angry.'

'This wasn't caused by just a hand,' said the police-woman. 'This kind of trauma is caused by an object. Your hand couldn't have done this much damage.' The police-woman had small round eyes. I thought she could see the truth. The dishwasher washed everything clean and the policewoman waited for me to tell her the truth.

Then Lila called on the phone. 'I'm on my way,' she said. 'Don't tell them anything.'

'I'm not allowed to talk to you,' I told the policewoman.

The ambulance came and took Mum away, and then Isabel and I waited for Lila. 'You can have a sleepover with Aunty Lila,' I told Isabel, because I knew I would have to go to the police station.

'I just panicked,' Mum told me afterwards when she called me from the hospital. 'I thought you'd gone mad.'

I think that I hadn't gone mad. I think I'd gone sane.

But they sent me to prison anyway.

'Don't tell them about the pot,' Mum told me on the phone before I went to court, and I nodded my head and Lila had to take the phone and tell her that I wasn't speaking to her. I didn't want to speak to her ever again.

'I hate going to see the finches,' I told Mum when I was seven and we lived in the big house.

'Oh, Felicity, no you don't. Mr Winslow says you love them. He lets you help take care of them. Just go next door and play. Lila's having her nap and I need some peace and quiet.'

'I'll be quiet. I don't want to go and see the finches. I hate them and I hate him. I'm too old for his nonsense.'

'Why are you always trying to cause trouble? Mr Winslow has been very nice to us. He even gave me some money so the bloody bank would give us time to sell the house. He likes you to visit, so go next door now!'

Adults like to tell children what they think and what they feel, but that's not right. I was only little but I knew what I thought and I knew what I felt.

Mum heard what I said but she never heard me at all. She could see me but not see me. I wasn't going to be like that with Isabel. I heard her and I saw her, and when Mum tried to make her not heard and not seen, my arm moved by itself. I won't ever tell Henrietta this or anyone else, but I don't wish I hadn't hit Mum. I just wish I hadn't been holding the pot.

'Okay, Birdy, we'll leave it at that,' says Henrietta after a few minutes. 'I really hope you keep going to therapy when you leave here and that you'll try to talk to your mother. You'll need her help with Isabel. She loves you and she misses Isabel and she has no idea what she did wrong.'

'No,' I say, 'she has no idea.'

Henrietta looks at me for a long time and then she says, 'I'll see you next week, and we'll try some more breathing and meditation, okay?'

'Okay.'

I shouldn't have hit Mum. I should have breathed in and out and waited until I was calm and then I should have explained. I'm an adult and adults need to explain why they are angry. But sometimes I think about Mr Winslow and I feel like I am seven again. I can breathe and breathe and breathe and I will still never feel calm.

I think that when I'm done with Rose and she is sorry for not saving me then I will be able to breathe and calm down and explain.

But only then.

Chapter Twenty

My body is used to the work in the garden now. It means I sleep less and dream more. The first few weeks I was here I would sink immediately into a dark dreamless hole only to wake when the alarm went off at six in the morning so we could drag ourselves out of the unit and onto the little veranda, waiting to be ticked off the list. Now when the lights are out I lie in bed and think, and when I do finally fall asleep my dreams are waiting for me. Simon is waiting for me. 'Just leave me alone!' I want to scream. Before I came here I could block him out with pills and alcohol. There are no buffers here, just you and your nightmares.

In the hours before sleep claims me, I think about my last days with Simon, especially the final day. I try to wish it away, to pretend it never happened. I close my eyes and tell myself that when I open them again I will be in my own bed enveloped by the aroma of brewed coffee, listening to his tread on the stairs, waiting for the door to open so I can watch him walk in and place my cup next to me. Even when things were almost unbearable and we could not be in the same room together for too long, he never stopped bringing me my coffee. I miss him. I love him. I hate him.

I am too old to believe in wishes.

It was only twelve months ago, but already it feels like another lifetime. But then it also feels like it was only twelve days ago, only twelve minutes ago.

I was making dinner when he called down to me from his study. Dinner was just about the only thing I could concentrate on by then. Some days, if neither Rosalind nor Portia had been over and I ran out of something, I would have to make do with whatever was left in the fridge. It is unimaginable to think you can be denied the simple pleasure of a quick trip to the shops, but I was unable to go out. I have been sentenced to three years in jail, but I was already serving a kind of sentence in my home. The press were outside, camped on the nature strip, talking and throwing paper coffee cups everywhere. The neighbours were leaving rude messages in the letterbox asking us to move out so they could get back to their peaceful lives. Eric was calling on an hourly basis to check how we were and to update Simon on things that were being said on the internet. There were nuisance phone calls from people saying vile things about how Simon should be locked up or how he should have his penis cut off or simply that he should die.

I felt watched and hunted, but I knew that no matter how terrible I felt, he felt worse. His whole life was in tatters. Everything he had ever done, everything he had achieved meant nothing. As the days went on I noticed that his shoulders hunched more and more. Most days he got around in his pyjamas and robe, and the shuffling sound made by his slipper-clad feet told me where he was. His age was finally apparent, and the gap between us was more obvious than it had ever been.

'For God's sake, get dressed, have a shower, do something!' I wanted to shout, but I could see that even climbing out of bed had become a monumental task for him.

'He should be on antidepressants,' said Rosalind when we discussed his dejected state.

'I've tried, but he refuses to take them,' I told her.

'This will all be over soon, I'm sure,' she said.

'Yes,' I agreed, but neither of us spoke with much conviction.

'They have withdrawn the offer to induct me into the Hall of Fame,' he had told me the day before.

'Oh no, Simon. How could they? They have no proof. You haven't been charged with anything.'

'I haven't been charged with anything yet, my dear, but that, I fear, is coming. They're going to launch an investigation and then they will dissect our lives and hound me until I confess to whatever crime they want.'

I couldn't find the words to comfort him. I couldn't find a way to make it right. If I had been able to believe him with the same unconditional trust that I'd felt when the first woman came forward, I might have found the words to reassure him, but there were too many stories, too many women and I was doubting him, doubting myself, doubting everything.

I was stirring pasta and crying softly when he called me. 'Rose dear, will you come up here for a moment.'

I turned off the stove and wiped my eyes. He did not like to see me cry. Thank God I turned off the stove before I went up to his study. It was directly above the kitchen, so it was easy to hear him when he called. In any case, I had been listening for him. I suppose I had been listening for him my whole life, waiting for him to need me or want me.

He was sitting at his desk and I thought again how old he looked. He was only seventy, but he was as bent and frail as someone near the end of his life. The skin on his hands was covered with liver spots, and the veins were so prominent I could almost see the blood moving through. His hair was snow white, not a trace of gold left, and the deep blue of his eyes had faded to a milky washed-out colour. *Age is so cruel*, I thought when I looked at him, separating myself and my own ageing from the way my husband looked. *How can they have done this to him?*

'I have just received a call from Eric, my dear,' he said.

'And?'

'And it seems that all the little worms are wriggling out from under their rocks.'

'What does that mean?'

'More women are coming forward. More every day. They are saying that I have done things to them, terrible things. They are accusing me of touching them when they were on the show, of molesting them in corners like a common criminal. And Eric says that the police will announce the official launch of an investigation in the next hour.'

'What do you mean there are more women? How can that be possible?' I said.

'Indeed, how can any of this be possible?'

'How many more women?'

'Now there are twelve in total,' he said.

'But how can that be possible?' I said again. I could feel my body turn away from him just a little. One woman was easily discredited, two women could be looking for their own fifteen minutes of fame, three women were a pattern but could still be dismissed—but four, five, six, seven, eight, nine, ten, eleven, twelve women were ... what? Twelve women were a certainty.

'How can it be possible? I will tell you how, because evil exists in the world, Rose. You are isolated from it, cocooned in this house and your blissfully safe domesticity, but I have always known it was there. You have no idea what I have had to face, what I have sacrificed. I have played the clown so that you could have everything your heart desires. I have gone out to work to support my family, knowing that I needed to keep my show on the air lest the three of you lose the lives you have become accustomed to. These latest women who are coming forward have their own agendas. Perhaps they are unhappy that they too have not been the focus of some sordid magazine article. Perhaps they find themselves older and still without fame and that makes them angry.'

'Perhaps,' I agreed, but I felt as though I was hearing, for the first time, something else behind the words Simon was using. Behind the denial was the thin thread of justification that I could almost hear running through his head. I wanted to reassure him that everything would be fine, that these women should be ignored and that we should just get on with our lives, but something stopped me. I could not play the same tape again. I could not repeat the words he wanted to hear.

'Simon, is any of this true?' I said, and I realised as I said it that it was the first time I had asked the question. The first time I had asked it directly, looking straight at him, not comforting, not consoling, not wanting to hear anything but the truth.

He looked up at me. 'Does it matter, Rose?'

'Does it matter? *Does it matter?*' I raised my voice. 'It is the only thing that matters. It is the only thing that has ever mattered. I will support you, I will stand by your side as I have done since this began, as I have done our whole lives, but I need to know if you have done things that were inappropriate. I need to know.'

'I have been a faithful husband.'

'I'm not questioning that. I'm asking you if you've . . . if you've touched a child. Have you done the things the woman in the article accused you of? That all these women are now accusing you of? It's a yes or no question, Simon.'

'Badgering me, always badgering me,' he said, wringing his hands in his lap and directing his words to the wall behind my head as though he were speaking to someone else. 'You're just like them. Just like all the dreadful people saying all those things about me.'

'I am not just like them! I'm the only one making you dinner. I'm the one who will sleep next to you tonight. You need to explain this to me. I need to know if you've done these things.'

I had never, in all our married life, questioned him in this way. Simon had told me when we would get married. He had bought the house without discussing it with me. He'd furnished it without my input. He made the rules for our family. I had been so young when we had met. I hadn't had time to grow fully into myself. His opinions became my opinions. We never fought about anything, except occasionally the children when they were being difficult, and at those times I would try to keep them away from him. I sheltered and protected and loved and adored him.

'I need to know, I need to know now,' I said, and it's a strange thing to say but at the age of fifty-four I felt myself, for the first time, to be an adult.

Simon leaned forward and opened the top drawer of his desk and took out the antique gun I had inherited from my father. It is a Luger P08. It was manufactured in 1944 and was stolen from a dead German officer by my father. He fought with the resistance because, as he said, 'Evil cannot be allowed to triumph in this world.' Since he'd had no sons it had come to me when he died. I wanted to simply get rid of it, but Simon said, 'No, my dear. This will be very valuable one day. It's a collector's item and should be saved.' As always, I gave in, but I insisted that it be kept somewhere secure. 'Lock it away,' I'd said. 'My father took very good care of it and I know it still works. I wouldn't want the children getting hold of it.'

On that evening twelve months ago, I hadn't seen the gun for twenty years. I watched Simon's hands touch the polished metal of the barrel and was suddenly incensed that he should be touching something that had belonged to my father. I felt that his hands were making the gun that had meant so much to my father—a man who had never swayed from his values and morals—dirty.

'What are you doing with that?' I said and he looked up at me and gave me an odd humourless smile. My heartbeat sped up and then a ringing started in my ears. I put my hand to my chest.

'My heart is broken, Rose. The police are coming. They will search our house and my things. They will question me and humiliate me. I cannot let that happen.'

'You're being ridiculous. Anyway, if they search the house they will find nothing. Eric will sort all of this out. You still haven't answered my question.'

'They mean to destroy me.'

'Simon, I cannot keep talking in riddles. Who is "they"?'

'The women, all these vengeful women. They were lovely little girls, sweet and filled with innocence, but they have grown into harpies, dreadful crazed harpies, demanding my blood.'

'Stop being so bloody dramatic. Tell me what happened. Tell me what you did.'

Simon shook his head at me and then he opened another drawer and placed a small Polaroid photograph on the desk. 'The truth, the truth,' he almost sang, 'everyone wants the truth.'

I took a step closer so that I could see it clearly. The girl in the picture looked vaguely familiar, around thirteen years old. In the photo she was wearing a blue dress printed with red cherries. I could see from her hairstyle and the faded print that the photo was more than twenty years old.

'Who's that?' I said, and then I looked at it again. 'Is that the woman from the magazine? It is her, I can see that. She doesn't look that much different to now. Is that her? Where did you get this picture?'

'I took it the day she auditioned. She let me take it. She wanted me to take it. Do you see how happy she was? Does she look hurt or upset?'

'Why have you kept it? Why do you have it?'

He didn't answer me. Instead he reached into the drawer again and brought out another picture of a girl. This one looked older than the first girl, about fifteen or sixteen. She also wore a pretty dress and smiled at the camera. Just like the first picture, this one had been taken in Simon's office at the studio. Behind the girl was the familiar painting of a sailboat out on the ocean that I had helped Simon choose to hang on the wall. That I had agreed would be a good picture. I had accompanied him to buy it. The choice had been all his.

'I don't understand,' I said. My palms were clammy. I said I didn't understand but I was beginning to. I knew what he was saying, but because he wasn't using words I couldn't put my fingers in my ears and silence the truth. The pictures were speaking for him, and as I watched he took another one out of the drawer, and then another and another. Behind each little girl the boat floated on the ocean, riding on the waves, illuminated by sunlight. They kept coming one after the other. All those little girls, so many little girls. All smiling dutifully for the camera, all happy to be in the office of the great Simon Winslow. I looked at them, all of them, so many more than just the twelve who had come forward. I looked at their eyes, studying them for evidence of his crime, but the truth was hidden. They hid behind their prettily cocked heads and wide smiles.

My whole life has been a lie, I thought.

Even now, looking back, I do not know how to process it. I believe I went into a state of shock. I stood there watching him place picture after picture on the desk until the entire surface was covered.

I had always stayed out of his study. He even cleaned it himself. 'In marriage it is a good idea for a husband and wife to each have their own private spaces,' he told me when we first bought the house.

'I don't need to keep anything private from you,' I said.

'Well, I need my space, my darling, and I'm sure that you will not begrudge me this little room.'

It is almost laughable now when I think that I'd imagined he was using the study to attempt to write a book—a dream he'd always had.

'I don't . . . I can't . . . Why, Simon . . . why?'

'It's what they wanted, my dear. I was powerless to resist. But I never cheated on you, Rose. I did nothing wrong. They came to me with their little breasts pushed forward. They wanted to be touched. "Oh, Mr Simon,"' he said in a high-pitched, eerie girlish voice, '"I'm so sad about not coming first, please just give me a little hug. Can you see how pretty I am, Mr Simon? Don't you want to touch me? Please touch me." How could I say no, my dear?'

'Oh, Simon,' I said, because there were no words. 'Oh, Simon.'

'I didn't hurt them, Rose. I didn't hurt any of them. It was just a little touch here and there. Most of them probably can't even remember it.'

He was touching the pictures, running his fingers over them, occasionally picking one up and bringing it close to his face. As he ran his hands over his ghastly mementos, a smile played on his lips. He was speaking to me but he was lost in the memory of those girls, lost and happy to be there.

'Oh God. I think I'm going to be sick,' I said, and I turned to go.

'Wait!' he commanded. 'You must help me. You cannot leave me to face this. I will not be held up to ridicule. I would rather die, but you must help me.' He picked up the gun and handed it to me. I took it, intending to fling it out of the window, but he grabbed my hand and made me hold on tight.

'Let me go,' I said, and I was astonished at the strength in him. He looked weak and frail but I could not pull myself away. I glanced over at the desk again and my eyes swept across the pictures. I felt my body grow limp as I recognised one that hadn't been taken in the office at the studio. It was taken in front of the aviary. 'Isn't that the little girl from next door?' I said. And then her name came back to me. 'Is that Felicity?'

He held me fast and nodded his head. 'She was such an angel. Such an angel. She was so open to being loved by me, to being touched by me. When we were together she gave me such joy . . . such joy. It was almost as though God himself had sanctioned us. How can that have been wrong, Rose? How could it have been wrong?'

'But she was just a child, she was so little. Only six or seven. Oh God, let me go. Let me go right now! How could you have done such a thing? How could you?' I was fighting him again. I summoned all my energy. I needed to get away from him. All I could think about was being out of his study and far away from him.

'I wanted you to know, Rose. I have wanted you to know for such a long time. I have kept part of myself from you, my darling, and I never wanted to. I have loved you always, and I know you love me. Help me now, Rose. Don't let them take me away.'

'Let go!' I shouted. 'Let go right now!'

But he didn't let go. As I struggled to back away, he pulled me closer. He wrapped my hand tighter around the gun and I felt my finger touch the trigger. As I tried to pull away from him I worried that the gun would simply explode, killing us both, and at the same time I was sure that the gun was too old and it would no longer work and Simon would have a heart attack. His face was flushed red and we were both panting as we continued our struggle. If I had been watching elderly white-haired Simon grapple with his middle-aged wife I'm sure I would have found it almost comical.

I tried to kick out at him but I couldn't lift my leg high enough. 'I mean it, Simon, let go.'

He took one hand away from me but the other held me fast, and then he reached into the drawer again and pulled out one more picture.

'I fear my own desires, Rose. I fight against them every day, but I fear them.'

He turned over the picture.

It was Lottie. My granddaughter. Our granddaughter. It was Lottie.

She was standing in front of the aviary. Her long brown hair hung in a braid over her shoulder, and her smile showed the gap where she had lost her two front teeth.

'Help me, Rose,' he said, 'help me.'

And the gun went off.

Chapter Twenty-one

Rose is in the hospital unit. She sprained her ankle running to Allison's office. She fell over and hurt herself.

She will only stay there for one night. If she was very sick, Allison would call an ambulance and she would be taken to the big hospital, but only her ankle is sore so she is not very sick. Jess told me about Rose. She was there when Rose fell and she helped her.

I need to go to the hospital unit. I have been thinking and thinking about how to make sure she understands that what she did was wrong, but as soon as I heard about her hurting her ankle I knew what to do. In the hospital unit I will be close to Rose, and I need to be close to her.

I have to go to the unit and I know how to do that. I can make myself vomit. Vomit and vomit and vomit.

I will make sure that Jess knows I'm feeling sick and then I will keep vomiting until they take me to the hospital unit for the night. I will be put into a bed right next to Rose, because there are only two beds in the hospital unit. It's not really a hospital at all.

Two months ago I cut my hand on some metal in the shed. I was trying to get to the seed so I could fill up the trays and I didn't see the metal and my hand got cut. Monica sewed it up for me, but because she said it was a bad cut she made me stay in the hospital unit for the night. 'Just so I can check on you every couple of hours,' she said. Monica runs the hospital unit but she sleeps next door and comes in to check up on her patients. She checks every couple of hours. I only need a few minutes.

I will lie next to her and I will wait until she is asleep. I will think about Mr Winslow and about how he stood next to me at the finch cage and turned into the raggedy man. I will let myself hear his raggedy, raggedy breathing and I will let all the bubbling anger inside of me come out.

I know what I'm going to do and I don't even need to 'get directions', because Rose is right here.

Right here where I am.

Chapter Twenty-two

The hospital unit is really just a room with a couple of beds in it. It's for prisoners who aren't sick enough to go to hospital but are injured or sick enough to have to be watched. I only have a sprained ankle but they're a little concerned that I may have hit my head when I fell over. I told Allison that I did no such thing but she isn't taking any chances.

Earlier today when I got back from the garden for lunch there was a note on my bed telling me to call into Allison's office. I knew that it must be news from Eric. He told me last night that he would hear today about my appeal, and I felt the same stomach-churning anxiety as I had just before the judge read out the verdict.

On the way to Allison's office, I tripped over my own feet. I was hurrying and I tripped over my own feet. I feel so silly. It's very quiet in here, but the nurse, Monica, has just told me that Birdy will be coming in as well. 'We think she has a bit of food poisoning,' she said. 'We just want to get her on a drip overnight so she doesn't become dehydrated.' I'm quite glad that she's coming. I won't mind the company.

The appeal has been granted.

I would like to share my news with someone, with anyone, really. Because I'm stuck in here I can't email the girls, but I'm sure they're as excited as I am. At least, I hope Rosalind will manage to be happy for me. I will never tell her about the picture of Lottie in Simon's study. I have to believe, I absolutely have to believe that he didn't touch her. Showing me her picture was a cry for help. He wanted to be stopped. He wanted me to stop him, but I cannot share that with Rosalind, even if she remains angry with me forever. I am her mother, and as her mother I would rather never speak to her again and protect her from this knowledge than tell her what I know. The truth will always be lost.

Eric left a message with Allison saying that he should have me out on bail in the next two or three days, and she was kind enough to let me call him while I sat in her office with a bag of frozen peas on my ankle.

My time here is almost over, for now anyway. Of course I'm worried that a new trial will go the wrong way. There's always a chance of that, but Eric and Robert will do their best, I'm sure. At the moment I have nothing to do but lie here and think about what it will be like. I hate the idea of being thrown back into the spotlight, but apparently it will be a judge-only trial. Perhaps the press will be kept out of court as well.

I find myself going back and forth over the idea of telling Eric about the pictures. They may not convince a judge entirely as to Simon's state of mind, but they may help. They would also allow the ugly allegations to rear up from the depths and take hold again and I don't know if I can put my girls through that. If telling the world about the pictures meant an absolute guarantee that this time I would be found not guilty then I would do it, but it is not necessarily the case.

'She was trying to prevent him from shooting himself,' Robert told the jury. 'They struggled and the gun went off. It was an accident.'

'Both Mr and Mrs Winslow's prints were on the gun,' said Ms Kirk. She was very good at her job. She would begin a sentence and then pause halfway through, leaving the jury hanging. She would wait until they had literally moved forward in their seats before continuing. 'But,' she went on when she was sure she had everyone's attention, 'only Mrs Winslow's fingerprint was on the trigger. And, ladies and gentlemen of the jury, let us not forget that Simon Winslow's life was insured for ten million dollars. Rose Winslow had become tired of her husband. He was an inconvenient old man dogged by scandal. She took the gun to him so that she could end his life, and that's when the struggle happened. He was trying to stop her.'

I lost the jury the first time the prosecutor uttered the words, 'ten million dollars.' *What would she know about ordinary life?* I could see them thinking, and just like that they were gone. My hair was too neat, my suit too expensive, and the millions I would make from his death sealed my fate. Of course they thought I killed him.

'She never knew about the policy,' Robert told them again and again in his summation, but by then it was too late.

Would the pictures have made a difference? Will they make a difference in a new trial?

'Look who's here,' says Monica, helpfully breaking me out of my thoughts as she guides Birdy onto the bed next to mine.

'Oh, Birdy,' I say, 'how are you feeling?'

'I'll be better soon,' says Birdy.

Chapter Twenty-three

I keep my eyes closed and breathe in and out slowly the way Henrietta taught me. I hear Monica's footsteps and feel her hand on my wrist. I listen as she goes over to Rose's bed, and then she slips quietly out of the room. We are alone again. I am very, very quiet. I sit up and touch the needle going into my hand. It hurts to pull it out but I don't care. I push myself up on my elbows and look at Rose in her bed.

Rose isn't pretending to be asleep. She really is asleep. It isn't that dark inside the room because Monica leaves a light on all the time so that she can see to check on her patients. I slide my legs quietly out from under my covers and stand up. Now I am right next to Rose.

I watch Rose and I am quiet and then I lean forward.

My fingers go around her throat. At first I don't even touch her, I just form a cage with my hands and I watch her breathe. She is a quiet sleeper. The only way you know she's not dead is by the small rise and fall of her chest.

I can't look away. Her life is right there, in my hands. I am right next to her and she doesn't even know I'm there.

I stand there for five minutes or five hours. I have no idea how long. I think about the way Rose used to cut the toasted cheese into triangles and put a straw in a glass of Coke for me and how she used to talk to me. I think about her telling me that I could come over whenever I wanted to and then I hear her voice, almost as if she is really speaking to me. 'Go and help Mr Winslow down at the finch cage, quickly before he finishes feeding them. Off you go.' And off I went.

It won't take very long. She's such a little woman. She has lines around her mouth and a small face. I could strangle her with just one hand. Up and down goes her chest. Her warm minty breath fills my nose.

I wait until I feel my legs begin to cramp. *Now*, I think, and I take a deep breath, and that's when she wakes up.

'What?' she says, struggling to sit up.

'Don't move,' I say, and my hands touch her throat.

'God no, who . . . Birdy?'

'No, not Birdy, not Birdy,' I say, and I take one hand off her throat to switch on the lamp next to her bed. The other hand holds her down by her neck. There isn't enough light for her to see me clearly even though I can see her. She needs to see me clearly. When the lamp is on I can see that she is scared. I can see in her eyes that she is very scared. It feels good to see that. She is scared, scared and trapped. She cannot get away no matter how small and no matter how light she is.

'Please, Birdy, what's wrong? Tell me what you want.'

Both hands go back to her throat and I begin to squeeze. I don't like the way her throat feels, all ridges and swallowing. But I like that she is finding it hard to breathe.

'Birdy,' she chokes, 'please . . . please, Birdy.'

'Not Birdy,' I whisper fiercely. 'Not Birdy. See me, Rose. See me.' I squeeze harder and I hear a gurgle in her throat. I can feel it begin to crush. I let go a little. She can't die, not yet. She has to see me first.

'See me, Rose,' I whisper again as she takes in gulps of air. I start to squeeze again and she looks at me, really looks at me for the first time. Oh,' she gurgles, 'oh God. Felicity,' and then her eyes roll back a little. 'Felicity, I'm . . . I'm sor . . .' she gurgles, and then she is quiet.

I snatch back my hands. 'Rose,' I say. 'Rose, what were you going to say? Tell me, Rose.' I lean over her and give her a little shake and then I give her a big shake. Her head bounces against her pillow. Her body is loose and her chest does not rise and fall.

'Rose!' I scream. I scream again with all the bubbling anger and fear I have inside me. I scream loud enough to wake the dead.

And then lights go on everywhere and Monica is there and she's shouting and I'm screaming for Rose, who has finally seen me.

Chapter Twenty-four

They didn't want to let me see her, but I insisted, and then Eric got involved and he talked to Robert and of course Robert can talk his way into anywhere. A maximum-security psychiatric facility presents no problem.

Robert and Portia are walking around with silly 'parent-to-be' grins on their faces. Rosalind is finding them both insufferable, but I'm completely delighted that Portia didn't miss her chance to have a child. I'm quite happy to listen to her endless lectures on proper nutrition during pregnancy. I don't believe I will mention the occasional glass of wine I drank and the few cigarettes I smoked when I was pregnant with her.

I'm buzzed in through three different doors and my purse is taken away before they allow me in to see Felicity.

'She's been moved to a minimum-security part of the building now,' said Robert when he told me where I would be going. I don't want to think about what the other areas of this place are like. She's been in the facility for nearly six months now. I can't imagine how terrible those first few weeks must have been after the relaxed environment of the Farm.

I have spent a lot of time thinking about her in the last few months. Her face is almost constantly on my mind. Those around me do not understand why I don't feel even a trace of anger towards her. She lashed out and nearly killed me, but I don't think a grown woman tried to hurt me. I think the person who put her hands around my neck was only seven or eight years old and in terrible pain.

'I don't understand how you can feel that way,' said Rosalind.

'I don't understand how to feel any other way,' I replied.

She's lying on a single bed in a small room. She's facing the wall. At first I think they must have made a mistake, because the slight woman barely denting the mattress below her cannot be Birdy. 'This is Felicity Adams?' I say to the nurse who led me to the room, and she nods impatiently.

It's possible that I would have recognised her when we first met at the Farm if she hadn't been covered in her layers.

'Please keep the door open,' says the nurse.

'I will,' I say.

'She's still medicated, but we're weaning her off slowly. Please don't upset her.'

I turn around to face the nurse, taking in her unlined face and her obvious youth. 'I wouldn't do that,' I say in my raspy, slightly threatening voice. 'I'm just here to visit for a little while.'

The nurse nods and backs out of the room as though afraid that I might attack her on her way out.

'Bir- . . . Felicity,' I say quietly. There is no movement from the bed. I step a little closer, feeling anxious and wary.

'Felicity,' I say again.

She still does not move and I think that she may be asleep. I want to go over to touch her on the shoulder but I know that would be unwise. I have no idea how she would react. I stroke my throat absentmindedly—something I have taken to doing lately.

'Your voice may never be the same,' said the doctor at the hospital.

'That doesn't matter,' said Rosalind for me. 'She's alive.'

Rosalind and Portia sat next to my bed in the hospital until I begged them to go home. 'I'll be fine,' I croaked. I needed some space and time to think about what had happened, about why it happened.

Just as I am about to leave, Felicity turns over and looks at me. Her eyes widen.

'Why are you here?' she says.

'Oh, I was just about to go. I thought you were asleep.'

Her brown eyes are dull and flat. I stroke my neck

as I see the face of the child I knew, the desperately sad little face.

'I just wanted to visit,' I say.

'Why?'

'Do you mind if I sit down?'

Felicity shrugs. I drag a chair from its position against the wall and pull it closer to the bed.

'Your voice sounds funny,' she says.

'Yes, it will for some time. Maybe forever. But I can speak and I can breathe. I wanted you to see that I'm all right.'

'Well, I've seen. You can go now.'

'I also wanted to tell you that I'm sorry.'

'You're sorry?' she says, as though she doesn't under-stand the word.

'Yes, I am.' And then I say the words I have been rehears-ing in my head for the last few months. I say the words that I would like to say to every little girl Simon put his hands on. Eric has advised me against doing this—not wanting me to leave myself open to being sued—but he was not there that night. He did not see the broken child who put her hands around my throat. I cannot go back, I cannot undo the damage but I am hoping that if she knows that I am sorry it may help her recover and move on with her life.

'I should have protected you from him,' I say. I didn't know what he was doing, but even so I should never have let him take you off to the aviary all the time. I should have known something wasn't right. You tried to tell me that you didn't want to go. You wanted to stay with me and I didn't let you. I should have done better.'

'You didn't hear me,' she says and she sits up on the bed and leans towards me as if to make sure that I understand where I went wrong. 'You didn't hear me,' she says again.

'No, and I should have heard you.'

'My mother didn't hear me either.'

'I'm sorry about that too, Felicity. We should have kept you safe. It's the job of all the mothers to protect all the children.'

'Not my mother,' says Felicity.

'I can't speak for her,' I say.

'No, I guess not.'

'I brought something to show you.' I fish in my bag for the photograph, pull it out and hand it to her. Birdy takes the photo from me and looks at it and then she runs her fingers over the smile on the child's face.

'That's me,' she says.

'Yes. Simon had it in his study. I thought you might want it. I don't know why.' I had thought about simply throwing the photo away, but that would have been wrong. I give it back to Felicity because I cannot give her back any other part of her childhood.

'I look happy.'

'Yes, yes, you do, but you were sad, I think. He made you sad.'

'He made lots of girls sad.'

'He did,' I say, and the simple acknowledgement almost

takes my breath away. I don't know if I will ever be able to think of what he did without being profoundly and completely shocked. I don't know if I will ever be able to stop questioning everything he said and did and everything we were together.

'Is that why you shot him?'

'I didn't . . . It's complicated. I know it's hard to understand, but I can't explain it all.'

'Are you going back to jail?'

'No, no. The judge overturned my conviction. He said that it was an accident, which means I don't have to go back to jail.'

Eric and Robert had pushed ahead with the appeal despite my condition. 'Let's just get it over with,' Eric said to me when he came to visit me at home.

'She needs time to recover,' said Rosalind.

'No,' I whispered. 'No, it needs to be over.'

'I'm so sorry, Rose,' said Eric. 'I can't bear to think of you being in that place. I'm so sorry that Robert and I failed you. We will not fail you again.'

'It wasn't you,' I whispered to Eric. 'You did your best.'

Eric stood up to leave and I got off the bed to show him out. Lottie and Sam were downstairs watching television. 'Stop that!' I heard Lottie shout at her brother. 'Don't you dare touch me!' Lottie's indignation made me smile. She is terribly sure of her rights. Her voice has not been silenced by anyone.

'I can't keep those two from trying to kill each other,'

muttered Rosalind, and she went downstairs to separate her warring children.

'Eric, before you go,' I said, and he turned back to me. 'I have something to show you.'

'You do?' he said.

I nodded my head, affirming my decision to myself. 'Yes, I do.'

Before Eric took the photos away to be placed into evidence, Rosalind and Portia shuffled through them for almost an hour, studying each face, communing with each child. I didn't show them all of the pictures. The picture of Lottie was in my bedside drawer. I wanted to throw it away but I couldn't bring myself to let go of it. She looks so happy. She is just a little girl enjoying an afternoon with her grandfather.

The overturning of my conviction and revelation of Simon's collection of photographs made international headlines. The circus came back to town but I coped better this time. I had nearly lost my life. Aggressive journalists felt like the least of my worries. Rosalind is still struggling with the truth. Her father was her hero and it's terrible to lose your hero. Now she's doing what I've been doing for such a long time—questioning, rethinking and wondering about her father. She has not wanted to leave my side since the night Felicity put her hands around my throat.

Felicity stares at me as I stroke my throat, soothing the dryness there. 'I didn't really want to hurt you,' she says quietly.

'I didn't want to hurt you,' I say.

'It wasn't you. It was him, and he's gone now.'

There isn't much for me to say after that.

'You need to get better so that you can go home to Isabel.'

'I'm getting better,' she says. 'I'm getting better so I can go home to Isabel and Lila.'

'I hope you'll be with them again soon,' I say, but she doesn't reply. She just nods and smiles as I'm sure images of her young daughter dance before her eyes. I leave her sitting up quietly on her bed. When I am at the door she says, 'Why did he do it?'

It is a simple enough question and I know she is looking for a simple answer. I could tell her about all the reading I've been doing. I can be on the internet for hours, reading stories and papers about paedophiles. I can tell her about how some people think it's genetic and others think it comes from abuse in childhood and then there are those who think it is all about control and power but that's not what she wants to hear. She wants to know why and so in the end I give her the only answer I can.

'Because we let him,' I say.

And then I leave.

Benjamin is waiting for me outside the hospital. He is the bodyguard my children have insisted upon. No one can get near me. Ben holds out a huge hand and clears a path through journalists and interested people alike. Next week I shall go to Greece for an extended period of time. I will return when I'm no longer of any interest to anyone in this country. I have bought a house there and my girls will bring their children to visit.

I cannot remember who we were and what our lives were like before all this began. My therapist, Donald, has told me that the only solution is to move forward, to always move forward.

Once I had recovered enough to speak I made sure that I explained everything to the police because I understood immediately. The moment I recognised Felicity I understood. They have taken it into account and according to her sister it is also connected with her original crime of assault against her mother. She has been so angry with the women who were supposed to keep her safe. It is, I think, entirely justified.

I didn't tell her that Eric has set up a trust fund for her and her daughter. I have spoken to her sister Lila about it. I'm sure she will explain it all to her.

'You don't need to do that,' said Portia. 'It wasn't you, it was him, and the money won't bring back her childhood.'

'You're right about that. It is perhaps the smallest gesture I can make, but I must make it.'

Eric has set up a fund to award all the other women small payouts as well. There have been some rumblings on the internet about me buying their silence, but I cannot listen to all that. I do not want them silenced.

I just want them to know that they have been heard.

Chapter Twenty-five

I am writing a letter to Isabel when the nurse comes in and tells me that I have a visitor.

'Who is it?' I ask, but she just waves her hand at me and walks out. The nurses here are less friendly than the guards in prison were. Maybe they get tired of crazy.

Only Lila comes to visit me here so I think it will be Lila and I hope that she has brought Isabel with her even though I've asked her not to. I don't want Isabel to see me in here, but I miss her so much my chest hurts. Rose came to visit me once but I don't think she will come again. Rose's voice is strange now. She is different. I have made her different. I thought I would feel happy about that but I don't.

Dr Lin told me today that I'm going home soon. He is very pleased with me. I am a good patient. I'm not like

I was with Emily and Henrietta. I haven't hidden anything from Dr Lin. He knows all my secrets and he is still pleased with me. I talk to Dr Lin all the time about the bubbling anger, but now when I talk about it I don't feel it. The Felicity who had all the bubbling anger inside her feels like someone else, not me.

'You have every right to feel angry and betrayed,' said Dr Lin when I told him about Mr Winslow and the finches.

'Emily said that I have to forgive my mum and forgive my dad. She wanted me to forgive everyone.'

'That may be what you eventually have to do, Felicity, but first you need to know that you have a right to feel angry. Anyone in your situation would feel angry.'

'Even a clever person?'

'Especially a clever person.'

I try not to think about Mr Winslow turning into the raggedy man, but sometimes the thoughts come into my head and I can feel his hands all over me and I feel heavy and sad. Then Dr Lin says that I must think about something that makes me feel better. I think about Isabel and Jess and Lila. He also made me write about the raggedy man. 'This will help,' he said when he gave me a notebook and a bendy pencil that can't hurt anyone. 'I don't have to read it unless you want me to, but it will help.'

I didn't want to write about Mr Winslow turning into the raggedy man, but one night when I couldn't sleep I started to write about the finches, because I worry about them and I miss them. I wrote and wrote and wrote. I don't think I have spelled all the words the right way but Dr Lin says that doesn't matter. I wrote about the finches at the Farm and then I wrote about the finches in Mr Winslow's cage and then I wrote about the raggedy man. My hand got sore but I kept writing until my eyes wanted to close. Now if the bubbling anger starts to come back I know I can write it all down. Dr Lin is very pleased with my writing.

Jess is home with her girls now and she has a job at a nursery. She writes me letters and when I go home me and Isabel will go and visit her and her girls.

I walk into the common room and look around for Lila but she is not there. I turn around to leave and then I realise that someone is there to visit me.

My mother is sitting in a chair by the window. I want to turn around and walk right back out, but Dr Lin is there too, talking to the parents of one of the other patients, and I know that he's seen me. I don't want anything to get in the way of my release. I also don't want to have to discuss again what I did to my mother.

I sit down opposite her.

She is wearing one of those parachute tracksuits that old people like and I can see that she's lost a lot of weight. She's never been fat but now even her bones look small. I have also lost weight and now Mum and I look a lot like each other. Her face is also lopsided. I did a lot of damage.

When I see her all I feel is ashamed. She looks broken. I broke her. I don't know what to say and all that comes out of my mouth is, 'Oh, Mum, I'm so sorry.'

I put my head in my hands because there is no way I can stop myself from crying. 'I'm so sorry,' I say over and over again so that she will understand.

'Oh, Felicity—oh, sweetheart, please stop crying. Please stop or I'll start and then everyone will think we're crazy.'

That makes us both laugh.

'I am crazy, Mum.'

'Rubbish. You've just had a bad time, and you're getting better. Lila says that you're coming home soon.'

I nod.

'Before you do I wanted to . . . I wanted to make things right. I know it's been a long time since we've seen each other. I wish you would have let me visit you. There was so much I wanted to say.'

I nod my head to let her know that I am ready to listen.

'You're my child, Felicity. No matter how old you get, you will always be my child. I know you didn't mean to hurt me—'

'I didn't,' I say. 'I really didn't, I just got so angry.'

'Listen, love, you need to let me finish.'

I want to keep talking but I bite my lip instead.

'I wanted to tell you that I'm sorry, Felicity. I'm sorry for saying that to Isabel. I know that nothing is more important than she is and I know that if she said Lester was . . . was touching her, then he was. You believed her and I tried to make light of it, and I've had a lot of time to think about that, and I wanted to tell you that I'm sorry that I didn't protect you the way you protected your child. I shouldn't have let you go anywhere near him.'

After I told Dr Lin about Mr Winslow and the finches, I told Lila. She was sad and angry and she cried. 'It's good he's dead,' she said, 'or I would have to kill him.'

'I should have told Mum,' I said to Lila.

'Maybe you tried. I don't know. I don't remember much about that time.'

'We have to tell about Lester,' I said. 'Even if Isabel is scared I have to make her tell. Lester mustn't be allowed to hurt any more children.'

'Oh, Fliss, you've got so much stuff to deal with.'

'I know, but I didn't want Isabel to be hurt by Lester. I don't think any other mother wants their child hurt by Lester.'

'I'll see what I can do. I'll make sure that someone finds out. I'll take care of it and you concentrate on getting better. That's all you need to do now.'

I knew Lila would tell Mum about Mr Winslow.

'You couldn't have known, Mum,' I say. 'At first I even liked going there and you were—'

'I was a stupid woman more concerned with myself than my own child. You told me you didn't like the finches. You told me that you didn't want to go to his finch cage anymore, and instead of questioning you further, instead of investigating, I ignored you. I didn't want to know and I didn't want to listen. I'm sorry I let you down.'

'I'm sorry I hit you.'

'Let's leave that now, let's just leave it behind us. I want you and Isabel to come back and live with me. I want to take care of her again. I know I didn't do a good job with you and Lila, and I want to do better with Isabel. I want to be a good grandmother. I want to be as good a grandmother as you are a mother. You're a good mother, Felicity.'

'Yes,' I say. 'I am a good mother. I love Isabel and I can see her and I can hear her, and whatever happens I can help her. You didn't see me.'

'I let you down. You were so little and I let you down, but you didn't let Isabel down. You listened and you believed and you didn't let her down.'

'I didn't, did I? She didn't have to eat the bear alone.'

'She what?' says my mother, and then she smiles because she remembers. 'No, she didn't have to eat the bear alone, because you were there—and if you let me I will be there too and together we can all eat the bear.'

'And drink the witch,' I say.

'And cut the giant's head off.'

'And cure the doctor.'

Mum laughs. 'Yes, we'll do all that, and we'll make sure that Isabel never has to worry and that she never has to scream or scurry.'

'Say it, Mum,' I say. 'Say it all.'

Mum takes a deep breath and I can see her thinking about the words. I want to help her but I don't because I know she knows them. She knows them all. She pats my hand and smiles.

'Isabel met an enormous bear . . .' begins Mum.

Other titles by Nicole Trope

Acknowledgements

Thanks, as always to Jane and the team at Allen & Unwin
To my lovely editors Clara Finlay and Belinda Lee
To Gaby Naher for her continuous support
To Jake Marusich for his help on the law questions
My mother for her beta reading
And as always to David and the cherubs

And finally to all the children, past and present,
who have been hurt:
Do not be silenced, do not be hushed
Sing little birds. Sing.